BACHELOR DUKE

Mary Nichols

D0333101

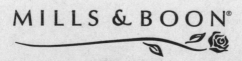

All the characters in this book have no existence outside the imagination of the author, and have no relation whatsoever to anyone bearing the same name or names. They are not even distantly inspired by any individual known or unknown to the author, and all the incidents are pure invention.

First published in Great Britain 2005
Paperback edition 2006
Harlequin Mills & Boon Limited,
Eton House, 18-24 Paradise Road, Richmond, Surrey TW9 1SR

© Mary Nichols 2005

ISBN 0 263 84629 6

Set in Times Roman 10½ on 12 pt.
04-0106-89762

Printed and bound in Spain
by Litografia Rosés S.A., Barcelona

'Good heavens, a blue stocking!'

'That, sir, is better than being a milksop, dependent on the generosity or otherwise of a man who can give it or withhold it at his pleasure.'

James had a sudden vision of what it might be like to be a young lady alone in the world. He was used to the ladies of the *ton*, or demi-reps who flouted convention. But the woman who faced him now was neither. He wished he had not been so sharp with her, but he did not know how to retrieve the situation.

Born in Singapore, **Mary Nichols** came to England when she was three, and has spent most of her life in different parts of East Anglia. She has been a radiographer, school secretary, information officer and industrial editor, as well as a writer. She has three grown-up children, and four grandchildren.

Recent titles by the same author:

THE HONOURABLE EARL
THE INCOMPARABLE COUNTESS
LADY LAVINIA'S MATCH
THE HEMINGFORD SCANDAL
MARRYING MISS HEMINGFORD

BACHELOR DUKE

Chapter One

April 1814

The slight breeze that played along the shaded balcony took the heat from the afternoon sun and allowed the scent of bougainvillaea and orange flowers to drift past Sophie and mask the less pleasant aromas from the street below. But she was unaware of odours, either pleasant or unpleasant, as she gazed over the pink tiled roofs to the glittering blue sea of the Bay of Naples. There were more things on her mind than pleasing views and contrasting scents. She was in a dilemma of such magnitude, she did not know how she was going to come about. Her father had died, having ruined his health with wine and spirits, and followed her darling hard-used mother to the grave; now she was alone in a foreign country. Twenty-one years old, unmarried, with no close friends and no relatives who were prepared to acknowledge her, and, to top it all, the rent of this tiny villa was due at the end of the week.

The knock at the door had to be repeated before she heard it; by that time the lady doing the knocking had opened it and was tripping into the room. 'Sophie, my dear, such news, such wonderful news!' The middle-aged Lady Myers was short and plump, dressed in a light muslin gown more fitting to someone of Sophie's years. Her hair, under an enormous bonnet intended to protect her complexion from the sun, was dyed black as a raven's wing. But she had kind hazel eyes and a warm smile. Seeing her, Sophie realised she had been wrong about having no friends; she did have one. 'The war is over. Napoleon Bonaparte has capitulated. The allies are in Paris. We can all go home.'

'Home,' Sophie repeated. Where was home? In the last ten years, she had lived for a time in France, a strange place of contrasts since the revolution; in Spa in Belgium; in Chamonix in Switzerland, where the sweet mountain air and wonderful landscape had served to raise her mother's spirits for a short time until they were forced to flee again. Oh, Papa never admitted they were running away, but that is what it was; a vain bid to escape his creditors. Living abroad was cheaper than in England and they might have managed tolerably well but for her father's vice, which pursued them wherever they went.

After Switzerland there was Vienna, where she and her mother spent hours exploring and her father filled his time with gambling among other expatriates, convinced he was on the verge of the 'big win' and they would once more be in funds and able to look their friends in the eye, not to mention hoteliers, landladies and mantua makers. The coup never came and Papa was the only one surprised at that, but it meant that they could no longer pay their hotel bill and had to make a hurried exit in the middle of the night, which the fifteen-year-old Sophie had found exciting, but which did her mother's nerves no good at all. They went to Venice, then Milan, Turin, Florence and Rome in turn, always one jump ahead of the dunners, until two years ago they had arrived in Naples. By then her mother was seriously ill, but she had been cheered to discover Lady Myers living close by. 'She came to live near us when she married Lord Myers and we became friends,' Mama had told her. 'Lord Myers was in the diplomatic service and they were always on the move, and later so were we and we lost touch. Now we can renew our acquaintance.'

Their small entourage of valet, footman and maid had already gone in order to save paying wages. Now they were forced to stay in one place. The coachman had gone too, and the sale of the coach and horses and most of her mother's jewellery had kept them going for a time, particularly as Papa, overcome by guilt, swore he had turned over a new leaf. But it was too little too late. As far as Mama was concerned, they were stranded in a foreign country in the middle of a war with no hope of returning to England; though Papa continued to maintain he would soon set all to rights, Mama gave up believing it and soon gave up on life.

Lord Langford's grief at his wife's death had been astonishing to behold. He wept for days, wallowing in remorse and self-loathing, asking Sophie for her forgiveness and drinking copious amounts of wine and cognac to deaden his pain. Sophie had been numb with grief herself and had no comfort to offer him. She went about in a daze, knowing it was no good relying on him to provide for them and she would have to do something herself if they were not to starve.

A month before her twentieth birthday she had become the breadwinner, teaching Italian children English and conducting foreign tourists about the city. Few of them were English because the war had put a stop to sending

young men on the Grand Tour, but as Sophie had a keen
ear for languages she was able to act as guide in French,
German or Italian. Now Papa had died, and violently too,
making his drunken way home one night, and Lady Myers
talked of going home!

'Yes,' her ladyship said, concerned by Sophie's long silence, but then the poor girl had only recently lost her papa
so it was not to be wondered at that she was a little distracted. She was sitting there in a dowdy black dress, her
dark hair tied roughly back with a ribbon, but in spite of
that the chit had a natural grace. Her complexion was a
little more tanned than fashion dictated, but she had good
bones and her brown eyes were uncommonly lustrous.
'Home to England.'

'It is good news, of course, but I cannot go.'

'Why ever not? You cannot possibly stay here alone.
Surely you have relatives in England who will give you a
home? Lord Langford…'

Sophie gave a bitter laugh and bent to pick up a crumpled ball of paper from the floor where she had flung it a
few minutes before. 'You mean my father's brother? I
wrote out of courtesy to tell him of Papa's demise, though
I have no doubt the lawyers will have told him immediately he had inherited the title.'

'And?'

She smoothed out the paper. 'This is his reply. He re-
pudiates me.'

'But that is wicked! You were only a child when you
left England and none of your father's troubles was your
fault. Are you sure?'

'Oh, he leaves me in no doubt. He says if my father had
not been trapped into a disastrous marriage he would never
have been a gambler. My uncle says if I think to throw myself upon his generosity, I may think again, and as for

stooping so far as to work among foreigners, it has undoubtedly coarsened me and made me unfit for polite
company.' It was said in a flat tone that did not disguise
the bitterness she felt. 'He requests me not to write to him
again.'

'My dear child, that is appalling. I never heard the like.
I have a good mind to write to him myself.'

'Oh, please do not do that. It would mortify me. I have
never begged and I will not do so now. I shall carry on
doing the work I have been doing. Now the war is over,
English people will be travelling again.'

'No doubt they will, but you can be sure the *beau
monde* will not ask you to show them the sights. It might
have served while your papa was alive, but a young lady
living alone would be frowned upon as outside the bounds
of decent society. No, Sophie, that is not to be counte-
nanced.'

Sophie had not thought of that, but her ladyship's words
had the ring of truth, so what was she to do? Teaching English alone brought in no more than a pittance. 'I'll take
up writing,' she said after a moment's thought. 'I will
write a book about my travels. Mama and I spent hours
and hours exploring everywhere we went and she encouraged me to make notes, not only about the places and
buildings we visited, but the customs and the people. I
could write about those.'

'I have no doubt of it, but how will you live while your
book is in the writing?' She paused, but, when Sophie did
not vouchsafe an answer, went on. 'Come back to England
with us. Surely there is someone you can approach. What
about your mother's relatives?'

'Mama was a Dersingham, niece of the third Duke of
Belfont, but he was quite old when we left England and I
am sure Mama said he had died. He had no son, and, as

Mama's father, the next in line had predeceased him, their younger brother, Henry, became the heir. That would be my great-uncle, would it not?'

'Yes, but surely he would give you a home?'

'I never met him and the connection is so distant…'

'Sophie,' her ladyship said firmly. 'You have no choice but to appeal to him. I cannot believe you will be turned away…'

'The Dersinghams did not approve of the marriage either. I suppose they knew what Papa was like. But he could be very charming when he chose and Mama loved him…'

'None of which has anything to do with you.' Her ladyship paused. 'I'll tell you what we will do. You shall come and stay with me and Lord Myers until we can arrange to go home, then you shall come with us and we will take you to his Grace. And if that gentleman is so insensitive as to turn you away, then I will undertake to launch you into Society myself and find you a husband.'

'I never thought of marriage, my lady…' How could she have done so? She had been too busy nursing her mother, then taking care of her father. In any case, who would marry the penniless daughter of a compulsive gambler who could not rustle up a penny piece for a dowry?

'Well, it is about time you did. I shall not take no for an answer. Whatever would people think of me if I were to go home to England and leave the daughter of my dear friend to fend for herself?'

'Oh, Lady Myers, you are so good to me, I cannot think how I shall repay you.' She laughed suddenly, the first time she had laughed with genuine amusement in the month since her father's death. 'I will become rich and famous from my book and then I will see you are rewarded.'

'If that comes to pass, then I shall accept payment in

the spirit it is given, but we will not think of that now. I shall go home and send my carriage back for you, so begin packing at once. The sooner you are safely under my wing, the better.'

She rushed off, leaving Sophie smiling. Her ladyship was indeed like a plump mother hen, but Sophie was not at all sure she would like being under her wing. She was, after all, an independent woman used to going out and about on her own, not a naïve schoolgirl, but on the other hand, with Lady Myers she would not feel so bereft and lonely, even if the price of that was to suffer her ladyship's clucking.

Packing did not take long; she had so few possessions. Her mother's gowns had been sold long ago, and after Papa's funeral she had disposed of his belongings in order to pay the rent; there was just enough left to cover what was still owing. The only thing of value she had refused to part with was a pearl necklace, given to her mother by her own father on her come-out and in its turn given to Sophie. She would starve before she sold that.

She had half a dozen serviceable gowns in lightweight materials, which was all she needed in the heat of Naples; a few petticoats, chemises and hose; two pairs of shoes and a pair of boots. She had two bonnets, one velvet and one straw; a light pelisse and a warm cloak with a hood. Heaped on her bed, waiting to be packed into her trunk, the collection looked pitifully inadequate. If her memory served her correctly, England was a cold place, even in summer. And the gown she was presently wearing was the only one she had in black. She had bought it to go into mourning for her mother nearly two years before and had brought it out again on her father's demise. But if she were honest with herself, she could not mourn him as she ought and it seemed hypocritical to invest what little money she had in black clothes.

Taking a deep breath, she folded everything and put it into the trunk, added the jewel case containing the pearls, some toiletries, a brush and comb, a tiny miniature of her mother and her travel notes, and slammed down the lid. The whole process had taken less than half an hour. When she thought of the mountains of luggage they had brought with them when they first came out to the continent, luggage that needed a second coach to transport, it made her shrivel up with shame. She sat on the trunk and looked about the bare room. She was sitting on the sum total of her life. The only baggage she had was her memories. And the future? What did that hold?

Suddenly she straightened her back and lifted her chin. She had nothing to be ashamed of and would not go about looking cowed. She had had an excellent education, one that many a young man might envy, thanks to her mother, who had been something of a blue stocking, and she would put it to good use. If her great-uncle was good enough to offer her a roof over her head, that was all she would ask of him. She would use her brain to earn a living. And if he did not? Then there was nothing else for it, she must accept the help offered by Lady Myers and hope to be able to repay her. As for finding a husband, that idea was laughable. She did not want a husband, if husbands were all like her father.

Lord Langford had been an inveterate gambler and a dissolute soak, as well as a charmer. He would tell the most outrageous lies about how his fortune had been delayed in reaching him; or he had had his money bags stolen; or the lawyers were holding up his inheritance over a technicality, which would soon be resolved; or he had been cheated by a scoundrel, none of which was true, but it was said with a charming smile, an air of apology, even a false tear or two, and somehow he would find someone to believe him and lend him money. Sophie had made up her mind she would never put her trust in a man, though she had once loved her father. He had been fun when she was a small child, giving her little treats when he was in funds, taking her out riding on her little pony, talking to her of things way above the heads of most children of her age, which she soaked up like a sponge. Surely an education such as she had enjoyed must stand her in good stead?

Before she left she meant to say goodbye to her parents and so she put on her straw bonnet, tied with black ribbons in deference to her state of mourning, and set off for the nearby church where so many British people were buried: soldiers, sailors, diplomats who had died while on a tour of duty, tourists who had succumbed to the climate or to sickness, exiles like her parents. She knelt a little while by their graves, murmuring tearful goodbyes, then stood up and consciously straightened her shoulders, ready to meet her future with courage.

They should not miss the opportunity to go to Paris, Lord Myers maintained over supper the evening Sophie arrived, when they were discussing the best way to reach England. 'The Comte de Provence has been declared King Louis XVIII and has arrived in Paris to take up his throne; according to my informant, the whole world is flocking there in his wake, all eagerly awaiting the arrival of the Duke of Wellington.' The British commander had won the last great battle of the campaign by taking Toulouse and had been honoured with a dukedom for it. He was expected to stop in Paris to pay his respects to the new king and greet his ally Marshal Blücher before returning home. 'We could be there, when he is there. What do you say, Alicia, my dear?'

He was only slightly taller than his wife, a little more rotund than she was, with a round red face and pale whiskers. Sophie was unsure who wore the breeches, him or his wife, but they seemed to jolly each other along, being excessively polite to each other. 'Why, I should like that very much,' her ladyship said. 'You know how I dislike the sea, especially in the Bay of Biscay.' She gave a little shudder and turned to Sophie. 'I shall never forget the voyage coming out. The ship nearly overturned and I was so unwell I thought my end had come.'

'I am happy to do whatever you say,' Sophie said.

'Then I think we should set out as soon as possible, or we shall miss him,' his lordship decided. 'Lady wife, when can you be ready?'

'Goodness, my lord, you should know me by now. I can be ready tomorrow if you so wish.' She turned, laughing, to Sophie. 'We moved so often when Lord Myers was in the diplomatic service I had it down to a fine art. Everything is labelled to match the chests and trunks, so that it is only a question of organising the servants while Lord Myers deals with the transport.'

'I've done that,' he said. 'The bulk of the stuff will go by sea, we shall take only what is needed for our personal comfort. I noticed Miss Langford likes to travel light, which is very sensible of her.'

Sophie smiled. He was as kind as his wife to make excuses for her lack of baggage. 'I need not unpack then. My only hesitation is because there has been no time to receive a reply to my letter to the Duke of Belfont.'

'That is of no consequence, my dear,' Lady Myers put in. 'We have already agreed that you shall come to England with us, so it makes no difference what his reply is. We will deal with the Duke when we arrive.'

How did one deal with a duke? Sophie asked herself.

Lady Myers was evidently not daunted by the prospect, but Sophie herself could not help wondering about him. He was obviously younger than his brother from whom he had inherited the title, but, even so, he must be in his sixties. Was he a crabby old man, or had age made him tolerant? She hoped the latter if he was to overcome the family's antagonism towards the Langfords, of which she was one. If the reaction of her father's brother was a yardstick of what she might expect, then she had a mountain to climb. Going home overland would delay the moment of truth and for that reason alone she was willing to fall in with Lord Myers's plans. Besides, seeing Paris again and being able to compare it with the Paris of ten years before, and talking to the people, would provide more material for her book. She was beginning to set great store by the book.

Two days later they set out in his lordship's coach, followed by another bearing his valet, a footman and her ladyship's maid and their luggage. They were all hardened travellers so the discomfort of the journey, bad roads, unsavoury inns, baking sun and torrential rain were endured with fortitude. It took a week to cross into France and then the hazards were not so much natural as man-made. Napoleon might have abdicated and been exiled to the island of Elba, but he was far from discredited with his people. Bands of marauding soldiers with no one to lead them attacked travellers, shouting '*Vive L'Empereur*' and 'He will be back!' It was only Sophie's skill as a linguist that convinced them they were not the enemy, but friends who would rejoice at Bonaparte's triumphant return. It was quite frightening at times, worse than being an alien in Italy, which was itself a conquered nation, and she was relieved when their carriage drew up outside the Hôtel de Luxembourg in Paris.

The city was so full it was almost impossible to move and if Lord Myers had not sent ahead to bespeak rooms, they would never have found a pillow on which to lay their heads. Their rooms were comfortable, but they were so tired it would not have mattered what they were like and Sophie slept soundly.

After breakfast the following day the two ladies, accompanied by her ladyship's maid and the footman, set out on foot to explore the city while Lord Myers went off to call on the Duke of Wellington and to pay his respects to the new monarch, though how long the latter could hold on to his crown, Sophie was doubtful. He was no more popular with his subjects than the Regent was in England.

Although the city had been spared a battle it looked shabby and dirty, a state that was not improved by the mass of common soldiery, mostly Austrian and Prussian, who roamed the streets and lived in tented quarters in the parks, behaving like turkey cocks, mixing with the tourists who came in the thousands. The ladies were agog to see the fashions, rakes and dandies come to chance their arms either with the ladies or at cards; some had come to view the art treasures Napoleon had looted from the cities he occupied, some even to sample the food and wine, though how they expected that to be as good as before the war Sophie did not know.

Strolling down the wide boulevards and busy side streets, Sophie was startled by the contrast between the rich tourists and well-stocked shops and the abject poverty of the inhabitants who importuned them for alms or offered items for sale that Sophie, even in her own pocket-pinched state, would have consigned to the midden heap. 'I do not feel at all comfortable,' her ladyship said, as they were roughly pushed aside by an officer trying to control a mob bent on raiding a baker's shop. 'Let us go back to our hotel.'

It took them half an hour to battle their way through the throng and by that time both had had more than their fill of Paris. 'Henry, I think we should set off for England at once,' Lady Myers told her husband when he joined them for supper. 'I have seen enough of France; besides, if we stay here, Sophie will miss half the Season…'

'Oh, please do not take that into account,' Sophie said. 'I shall be content simply to have a roof over my head.'

'Fustian! I undertook to bring you out and bring you out I shall. That is if Dersingham is so ungracious as to refuse you, which I am persuaded he will not. After all, he is a duke and duty-bound to look to his family. Lord Myers, are you set on staying?'

'Not at all, my love. We will set off for Calais tomorrow. The King is going to England himself and we can follow his retinue, it will be safer.' Why the King, who had only just returned to Paris after years of exile, should decide to leave it again so soon was a mystery to Sophie.

Trailing behind the new king was an exhausting business. Sometimes they travelled at breakneck speed because his aides feared ambush, sometimes they crawled because his Majesty was tired and wished to sleep, so that his coach crawled along. In Calais they had to wait about while the packet carrying the royal party set sail and then negotiate a passage on the next one. It was not until they were halfway across the Channel on *The Sea Maid* that Sophie began to wonder what lay ahead of her in England.

Would the Duke acknowledge her? Would his wife

welcome her? There would be children and grandchildren, other cousins surely? Lying on her bunk while the ship tossed about on the rough sea of the Channel, she wondered what he would be like. Fat or thin? Proud or jovial? And his home? Her mother, in one of her rare moments of nostalgia, had said Dersingham Park in Suffolk was a huge palace with hundreds of rooms and extensive grounds, but in late April the Duke would no doubt be at his London mansion in South Audley Street. Unless, of course, he was too old to indulge in the Season's amusements and preferred to remain in the country all the year round. Then perhaps his sons and daughters would have come to London for the Season and what would they make of her, the poor relation?

All this conjecture only served to show her how little she knew of the family and how foolish she was to expect anything from them. She was beginning to regret the letter she had sent introducing herself. She had not exactly thrown herself on his Grace's mercy, but had told him she was alone and returning to England and would like to call on him. Had it sounded like begging? Or too proud? Tossing and turning, as the vessel tossed and turned, she could find no rest and wished herself at the bottom of the sea, a wish she expected to be granted at any moment. But she slept at last; when she woke, the sea was calm and so was she. Whatever lay ahead she would meet head-on. Her pride would sustain her.

'Harri, do I know anyone called Sophia Langford?' James asked his sister.

'My dear man, you surely do not expect me to remember the names of all your little bits of muslin? They change almost daily. Why do you ask? Is some young lady importuning you? Oh, you haven't landed yourself in a coil, have you?'

'No, certainly not. Credit me with a little discretion, I beg you. And do you suppose I would forget the name of any lady with whom I choose to spend my time?'

James Dersingham, fifth Duke of Belfont, was neither old nor married. Yet. But when a Duke is single and very wealthy, he is bound to attract the attention of mamas with marriageable daughters; if he is also young and handsome, those same mamas will eagerly fall over themselves to make sure their daughters are noticed. He would have to be made of stone not to be flattered. This particular Duke had a string of hopeful would-be brides hanging on his every word and gesture, and it mattered not one jot that he had the reputation of being something of a rake. Money and an elevated position in society would more than compensate for that. But he was becoming very bored with it all.

'Then why did you ask?'

'This Sophia Langford claims to be kin. And you may be right about her importuning. I have a letter here in which she says her mother died two years ago and now her father has died too and left her without support. She is lodging with a friend of her mother's in Naples, but she cannot continue to impose on her good will. I gather she thinks I should make myself responsible for her.'

'Langford,' Harriet said thoughtfully. 'Didn't Papa have a niece who married a Langford?'

'Did he?'

'Yes, now I come to think of it, he did. Do you remember Uncle Robert? He was Papa's older brother and would have inherited if he had not died so young. He had a daughter, Louise—I think it was Louise—who married Lord Langford. He was a gambler and a wastrel and the family refused to acknowledge him. I think he ruined them and they went to live abroad.'

Lady Harriet Harley, at thirty-six, was two years older than her brother and, since the death of their mother when they were both young, had been his mentor and confidante, which continued even after her marriage to Sir Granville Harley. Their father, the fourth Duke, had died the year before and James had inherited a vast fortune, several properties and the responsibility that went with them, much sooner than he had expected to; he was finding it hard work. It was doubly so at this time because he was on the Regent's staff, one of those responsible for his security, and, what with the celebrations attached to the victory over Napoleon and his Highness's unpopularity, he was expected to be everywhere at once. The last thing he wanted was the added responsibility of a child. 'That accounts for the letter coming from Italy. But what can I do about it? I am a bachelor. I don't know anything about children…'

Harriet tilted her head on one side and smiled half-mockingly at her brother. 'If you found yourself a wife, you might soon learn…'

He gave a bark of a laugh. Harriet was always urging him to settle down and marry, but he had never yet met a woman who came anywhere near his exacting standards. Either they were too young and foolish, too serious and stiff-rumped or too old and ugly. Besides, he was too busy and, when he wasn't busy, was amusing himself with young ladybirds who had no ambition to be duchesses, which relieved him of the problem of having to think about it. 'That has nothing to do with this.' He tapped the letter in his hand. 'I can't have her here. And how can I be sure she is who she says she is? She might be an impostor.'

'I have no doubt we could soon establish her credentials with a few pertinent questions.'

'We?'

'Of course we. As you so correctly pointed out, you are a bachelor. I could not leave the matter to you, could I? You would frighten the poor thing to death. And, I confess, I am curious. When is she arriving?'

Her referred again to the letter. 'She doesn't say, which only goes to prove how empty-headed she is. Does she suppose I will sit at home and wait for her arrival?'

'No doubt she is waiting for you to reply and invite her to stay.'

'And you think I should?'

'James, she has lost her parents. She is alone and probably very frightened. You would give a stray puppy a home under such circumstances, so why not a child? Why, Dersingham Park is so big, you would not even notice she was there.'

This was true, but he was still reluctant. He could foresee all manner of problems. What did a girl brought up in Italy know of English life? Was he expected to provide her with a maid, a companion, a school mistress and a school room to put her in? Would he have to entertain her? Did she know how to behave in polite society? And, in the fullness of time, would he have to give her a come-out and a dowry? It was all beyond him. It was not the cost—he could bear that and not even notice it—it was the responsibility. Oh, he knew he would have to put his mind to such things when he married and had children of his own, but other people's? Besides, he had no intention of marrying until he was good and ready, and a little waif was not going to make him change his mind about that, whatever Harriet said.

On the other hand, if she really was a relation and in dire straits... James Dersingham, fifth Duke of Belfont, man of the world, reputed rake and steadfastly single, had a compassionate heart and could readily imagine what it must be like to be alone and unprotected. He smiled at his sister; it was a smile that transformed his rather austere countenance. His grey-blue eyes twinkled and his firm mouth curved into a smile, so that his whole face lightened. 'Very well, but you write to her. It would be much better coming from you.' Which was a statement with which she heartily agreed. 'Besides, I must go. His Highness has taken it into his head to meet the King of France at Dover and I have been given the task of organising the coaches and outriders. He is not content but that we must have a triumphal procession.'

Having left the problem of Sophia Langford in the capable hands of his sister, he went on his way, prepared to forget all about the little waif. It would take weeks for the exchange of letters and even more before the child arrived; by then, perhaps the frenzy that had seized the populace over winning the war might have died down and he could give her the attention she deserved. By the time he arrived at Carlton House, the Regent's residence, he was once more the urbane and efficient equerry, who appeared to have no other life than pleasing his sovereign.

In spite of being several hours behind the royal vessel, *The Sea Maid* was obliged to ride at anchor outside Dover harbour while the King and his retinue disembarked, which did nothing to calm Sophie's mounting nervousness. The first sight of the cliffs of her homeland had had a strange effect on her, which was totally unexpected. It was almost twelve years since she had left it, a nine-year-old child, looking forward to the adventure, unafraid because she had two loving parents to take care of her. She had no idea she would not set foot on English soil again for so many long years in which she would live through a savage war, lose both her parents and grow up all too quickly. Deep inside her, she felt a stirring of a strange emotion, a feeling of coming home, as though the place, if not the people, welcomed her. It made her impatient and she paced the deck, unable to stand still.

'Ah, we are on the way again,' Lord Myers said as the rattle of the anchor being wound up came to their ears. 'It should not be long now and we will be on terra firma again.'

'Lady Myers will be much relieved,' Sophie said, for her friend had been confined below decks with *mal de mer* for the whole of the eight-hour crossing.

Sailors swarmed along the spars and the sails filled and gradually they inched their way into the quayside beside the royal vessel and came to a stop. Sophie went below to help Lady Myers on deck, while his Lordship spoke briefly to the captain about the unloading of their baggage. Half an hour later they were standing on the quay looking about them. The area was thronged with people, far more than any of them had foreseen. Besides seafaring men and the populace of the town, there was a company of Horse Guards in magnificent uniforms and civilian gentlemen on horseback dressed lavishly, their riding hats decorated with white cockades. 'In honour of the Bourbons,' Lord Myers said.

It seemed to be organised chaos, for in the middle of it all were several carriages, one of which bore the arms of the Regent. Of that gentleman there was no sign, nor of the King of France, but there was a man standing by the last coach, directing affairs. Sophie found herself surreptitiously watching him. In the face of all the confusion, he seemed calm. He was not in uniform, but in a magnificent riding coat of blue cloth that fitted his figure so closely she was able to make out the bulging muscles of his shoulders and arms beneath it. He wore soft doeskin breeches and boots that would have done duty for mirrors, a pale blue waistcoat and a pristine white cravat. His hair, beneath his tall riding hat, was fair and curled into his neck. Her heart gave a wild leap as he looked towards her, but the glance was only momentary before he turned away to speak to one of the uniformed officers, almost as if she were invisible. Perhaps she was. She felt suddenly forlorn and dowdy in her brown cloak and straw bonnet with its black ribbons.

'I suppose they have come to meet the King,' Lady Myers said. 'And we shall be left to lag behind as we were before.'

'It certainly looks like it, ' her husband agreed. 'I am come to think that it was not a good idea to attach ourselves to his entourage. I am very sorry to have suggested it, my love.'

'Let us go into the hotel and have some refreshment,' she said. 'Perhaps by the time we are rested the crowd will have dispersed and we can continue our journey in peace.'

Lord Myers led the way, but they were stopped from entering by the same gentleman Sophie had noticed earlier, who had evidently seen their intent and hurried to intercept them. 'I am sorry, sir, ladies,' he said politely but firmly. 'But you cannot enter, not until his Royal Highness and the King leave.'

'Why not?' Sophie demanded. 'It is an inn, is it not, and bound by law to provide refreshment?'

He turned towards her. The brown cloak and the plain bonnet did not indicate a young lady of substance; she was probably the older lady's companion, someone who was supposed to melt into the background, a shadow of her employer, but the sharp rejoinder and the bright eyes told him she did not enjoy her role. Those eyes were blazing defiance, but at the same time there was in their brown depths a hint of doubt. She was sure of her facts, but not of her position. It made her seem vulnerable. On the other hand, he could not allow her to dictate to him. His job was to protect his royal employer and he would be failing in his duty to allow anyone to cross the threshold. Assassins—those who wished the Regent ill, and there were many—could be female as well as male.

'Indeed, miss, but the needs of his Highness must be met first.'

'Then where are we to go?' Lady Myers put in before Sophie could make matters worse by insisting on entering. 'We have come off the packet and need refreshment before continuing our journey.'

'Then let me direct you to the garden at the rear. There are tables and chairs there. I will ask Captain Summers to request the landlord to bring you cushions and refreshments. I am sorry I must deny myself the pleasure of conducting you myself, but my duties do not allow me to leave the escort.' He turned and beckoned to a young officer and spoke briefly to him before bowing and returning to the carriage, just as two very fat gentlemen waddled out of the inn and made for the Prince's coach.

'My, is that the Regent?' Sophie whispered, recognising the other as the one-time Comte de Provence, now King of France.

'Yes, it is,' Captain Summers, who was young and cheerful, answered her as the coach creaked ominously when the pair were helped into it. 'I am afraid you are bound to be delayed if London is your destination. There is quite a procession and it will not be travelling very quickly.'

'Oh, we are becoming used to it,' Sophie told him.

They watched the procession set off: the Horse Guards,

outriders, carriages containing the royal retinue and, last of all, the state carriage drawn by eight cream horses, its occupants smiling and waving to the crowds who seemed singularly disinterested. Behind and a little to one side rode the handsome aide who had so taken Sophie's attention, riding a magnificent black stallion. He looked about him as he rode as if expecting trouble.

'You may enter the inn now,' Captain Summers said, conducting them inside. 'Regretfully I must leave you and take up my position in the cavalcade.' He touched his tall hat in salute and strode away to where his horse was tethered.

'What a fuss!' Lady Myers said as they found their way to the dining room. 'My Lord, let us stay here until they are well on their way, for I should be mortified to be too close behind those two pretentious coxcombs. We might be mistaken for one of the party.'

His lordship agreed and, in a way, so did Sophie, who had been less than impressed by the two rulers. On the other hand, the gentleman on the black stallion and the young captain of the Horse Guards were much more interesting, especially the taller one; she would not mind following on behind him. If only she was not dressed so shabbily, if only she had a little more aplomb, she might have smiled at him and then, instead of looking straight through her, which he had done, even when addressing her, he might have smiled back... She shocked herself to think she could have such improper thoughts and quickly turned her attention to her host, who was reciting the bill of fare in a swift gabble as if he could not wait to be rid of all his guests and have a little peace and quiet. She must remember she was in England now and must behave with the decorum Lady Myers expected of her. And that meant not challenging authority. If she wanted the Duke to give her a roof over her head—she could not call it a home, having no idea if it could ever be that—she must curb her tongue and be meek and docile. Any rebellious or un-ladylike thoughts and opinions must be kept for her book.

Chapter Two

Sophie woke up the next morning, wondering where she was. It was much more sumptuous than her room in Naples. She sat up and looked about her. The sun was shining through lightweight curtains and she could make out solid furniture; besides the big bed there was a washstand, a wardrobe, a dressing table, another small table in the window flanked by two chairs and a couple of cupboards in the fireplace recess. A clock on the mantel told her it was half past ten. She had not slept so late in years! She scrambled from the bed, padded across the thick carpet and drew back the curtains to find herself looking out on a busy street. Not Naples, not Paris, but London.

It all came back to her then: the long, exhausting journey by land and sea, the slow progress behind the Regent's procession, which they had come up with only an hour after leaving Dover. The Regent was either very vain or very stubborn because he had insisted on stopping to greet his people, even when they were only a half a dozen on a street corner who looked to Sophie as if they had only been waiting to cross the road. Whenever they stopped the tall equerry was in evidence, shepherding people away from the royal carriages, looking about for trouble, trying his best to keep the cavalcade moving. Sophie wondered what his name was and if he had a title and decided he must be a lord at the very least. In her imagination she dubbed him Lord Ubiquitous because he seemed to be everywhere. No doubt if anything bad befell his charges, he would have to answer for it.

He had controlled his horse with consummate skill, was polite if a little frosty to the people around him and smiled when speaking to the Regent and his guest. Not for a moment had he shown any sign of impatience, but somehow Sophie sensed it was there, carefully hidden. It revealed itself in the way he carried himself, in small gestures, in the lifted eyebrows to Captain Summers when his Highness insisted on stopping. On one occasion the Regent had beckoned to a little urchin playing in the dirt and given him some small token, though the child seemed to have no idea what to do with it. Lord Ubiquitous had leaned down from his mount and whispered something, which made the boy laugh and he had run off, clutching his prize.

There had been no possibility of overtaking the royal carriages, so Lord Myers had instructed the coachman, hired at Dover, to stay well back, and Sophie was able to look about her. The countryside was verdant, the sun had a gentle warmth, not the uncomfortable heat of Naples. There were people working in the fields, plodding behind working horses. In the meadows cattle grazed and young lambs trotted behind their mothers, bleating for attention. This was the England she remembered, the England her mother had yearned for all the years of her exile. Was that why it felt so much like coming home?

London, when they reached it, was packed, just as Paris had been. Rich and poor jostled each other, carriages vied for space with carts, and the noise of it all assailed her ears: grinding wheels, ringing hooves, neighing horses and voices, some high-pitched, some raucous. When the crowd saw who sat in the grand carriages smiling and waving fat beringed hands at them, they were openly hostile. Sophie heard one wag shout, 'Where's your wife?' And this was echoed by others until it became a chorus.

'What do they mean?' she asked Lord Myers.

'Oh, they are referring to the Princess of Wales,' he said. 'She is far more popular than her husband, who tries very hard to pretend she does not exist. The people like to remind him of her now and again.'

Their ways diverged after they crossed the river and the Myers's coach went on to Holles Street, where the servants had been expecting them hours before. It was extremely late, the dinner spoiled and they had to make do with a cold collation before tumbling into their beds.

And now it was morning, the first day of her new life and whatever was in store for her, she would have to make the best of it. Until she had made her call on the Duke, she could make no plans, and meeting the Duke was something that filled her with trepidation. She dressed hurriedly and went down to the breakfast parlour where she found Lady Myers immersed in the morning paper, which reported the arrival of the French King and a great deal of other news, some of it political, some of it mere gossip. She laid it aside on Sophie's entrance. 'How did you sleep, dear?' she asked.

'Like the dead,' Sophie said. 'I was worn out.'

'That is hardly to be wondered at. Shall we stay at home and rest today? Tomorrow will be time enough for paying calls if you are too fatigued.'

Sophie was very tempted. It would be so easy to presume upon her ladyship's generosity and do nothing, but her circumstances and sense of fair play would not allow it. 'Unless you have other plans, I think I should make my call at Belfont House first,' she said. 'It has been playing on my mind. If the Duke is from home, I can ascertain if he is at Dersingham Park.'

'Do you not think you should purchase a new gown before presenting yourself?' her ladyship suggested.

Sophie looked down at the lilac muslin she had fetched out of her trunk. It was so simple as to be childlike, with its mauve ribbons under the bosom and round the puffed sleeves. Its only decoration was a little ruching round the hem, which had been mended more than once. 'You think I should be in mourning?'

'Do you?' Lady Myers countered.

'No. I mourned Mama and I mourned the man my father once was, but that was three years ago and, strangely enough, Papa's last words to me were, "Do not mourn me, I am unworthy of it."'

'Then lilac is perfectly fitting, except that gown is very simple.'

'Simple things do not become outdated so quickly and I cannot afford to buy something just because the fashion changes.'

'Hmm, no doubt you are right,' her ladyship said. It was sympathy and help the girl needed and strutting about in the height of fashion would not further that end, though she was wise enough not to utter her thoughts. 'I will order the carriage for noon.'

Sophie was shaking with nerves by the time the barouche drew up outside the house in South Audley Street and only Lady Myers's hand under her elbow prevented her from taking flight. She was being a ninny, she told herself sternly. There was nothing to be afraid of; she was her mother's daughter and Mama had always told her to be proud, hold up her head and look the world in the eye, and that is what she would do. If the Duke of Belfont refused to recognise her, then so be it.

'Lady Myers and Miss Sophia Langford,' her ladyship said, handing the liveried footman her card. 'We wish to speak to the Duke on a personal matter.'

'I will ascertain if his Grace is receiving, my lady,' he said pompously. 'Please be seated.' He waved them to a row of chairs ranged against the wall of the vestibule and disappeared down a marble tiled hall, his back stiff, his white-wigged head held high.

Lady Myers sat down, but Sophie could not sit still and began looking about her. There was an ornate cantilever staircase that set off at the centre of the hall and divided on a half-landing before climbing again to a gallery lined with pictures. On each side of the stairs the hall was lined with doors, all of which were closed. The footman had gone through one of them and shut it behind him.

'Oh, I wish I had never come,' Sophie whispered. The grandeur of the place was overwhelming.

'Take heart, dear. I am right beside you and I will make the introductions.'

The footman returned, leaving the door ajar. 'This way, ladies, if you please.'

They followed him and waited while he announced them. 'Your Grace, Lady Myers and Miss Langford.' Then he stood aside for them to enter the room.

A second later Sophie found her jaw dropping open because the man she faced was not the sixty-year-old duke she had expected, but the handsome equerry she had dubbed Lord Ubiquitous, elegant in dark green superfine coat and cream pantaloons, his fair curls brushed into attractive disorder. And he was looking just as astonished as she was.

'Good God!' he murmured loud enough for her to hear.

Before she could open her mouth to retort, Lady Myers spoke. 'Your Grace?' It was a question, not a greeting.

He recovered himself quickly and bowed. 'At your service, my lady.'

Her ladyship curtsied. 'Your Grace, may I present Miss Sophia Langford? You have been expecting her, I think.' She gave Sophie a prod with her elbow because the girl seemed to have forgotten the basic courtesies.

Sophie, jolted from her contemplation of the man who had occupied so much of her thinking in the last twenty-four hours, dropped a curtsy. 'Your Grace.'

James, who had expected a child, a schoolgirl at the most, found himself looking at a grown woman, a woman he had seen before, though for the life of him he could not remember where or when. It was hardly surprising; she was not particularly memorable. Her lilac dress was so plain, it could have been worn by one of his chambermaids and not been considered too grand. She had a hideous bonnet that hid most of her face and almost all her hair, but her figure was good. 'I am afraid you have me at a disadvantage,' he said.

'How so?' Sophie asked. 'Did you not receive my letter?' If he had not, then she would have to explain who she was and why she was standing in this magnificent drawing room and wishing herself anywhere but there. He was not welcoming and certainly not smiling.

'I received a letter from Italy, yes, but I had not expected its writer to turn up on my doorstep the very next day.'

'You may blame me for that, your Grace,' Lady Myers said. 'Lord Myers and I were returning to England; as poor

Sophie had no one else to escort her, I undertook to bring her to you. I am afraid it was not possible to wait for your reply.'

That was where he had seen them, in Dover, trying to enter the hotel where the Regent and the King of France were taking refreshment and he had noticed them later, following the procession. Being anxious about security, he had been concerned they might be jeopardising that and had kept an eye on the carriage, until it had turned off north of the river. He had laughed at himself for his suspicions.

'And now you are here,' he said, wishing Harriet were on hand to relieve him, 'what do you expect me to do?'

'Nothing, your Grace,' Sophie snapped. 'I was mistaken in coming here…'

Again that defiance; it was almost a defensiveness, as if she expected to be turned away as she had been from the hotel in Dover. And so she should be, turning up at his door as if he should take in every waif and stray who claimed kinship! It was all very well for Harriet to say his father's niece had married a Langford, but he had never met this cousin and there might have been a very good reason for the family not to acknowledge her. His uncle could have been a reprehensible reprobate who had disgraced the family name; his daughter might have been a demirep of uncertain reputation and her husband an unmitigated rogue, which was more than likely if they had to live abroad. Until he knew the truth he could not risk taking her daughter in. 'If you expected me to fall over myself to offer you a home, then I am sorry to disappoint you…'

'My disappointment is not on that account,' Sophie said. 'It was in thinking that I was dealing with a gentleman.' She had no idea what made her say that. Perhaps it was the dismay which had been evident on his handsome countenance when they arrived, or the lack of a welcome. Why, he had not even offered them refreshment!

He had never met anyone, certainly not a chit of a girl, who was prepared to answer him back in that fashion and for a moment he was taken aback, and then it amused him. Beneath that muslin-covered bosom there beat a heart of fire. She was beginning to intrigue him. 'Be thankful that I am gentleman enough not to entertain such a ridiculous idea…'

Lady Myers put her hand on Sophie's arm to stop her answering. 'Your Grace,' she said placatingly, 'we had no idea… We assumed… Sophie thought…'

'What did Miss Langford think?'

'That you were old,' Sophie burst out.

'Old!' He gave a bark of laughter. 'I am but four and thirty.'

'I can see that,' she countered. 'But Mama told me that the third Duke had died and his younger brother had inherited and so I assumed…' Her voice faded away to nothing.

'It is a mistake to assume anything,' he said, remembering how he had assumed she was a child. If he had stopped to think, he would have realised it was unlikely. His uncle, her grandfather, had been the second eldest of the third Duke's brothers and would have inherited if he had not died first. It would have made all the difference to the young woman who faced him now; her mother would have been a duke's daughter and she would not be sitting there in that hideous gown, appealing to his softer nature. Perhaps it was as well he had, over the years, managed to stifle that. 'The brother you mentioned was my father, the fourth Duke. He died last year and I came into my inheritance.'

'And does that make a difference? Would he have been more welcoming?'

He suddenly realised how vulnerable she was, that she had the most lustrous eyes and they were bright with unshed tears. His conscience stabbed him. His problems were not the fault of Miss Langford and he could not expect her to understand them. 'I am sorry,' he said. 'We have not made a good beginning, have we? Let us start again. Please be seated. I will have refreshments brought in. Tea, perhaps, or ratafia? ' He turned and tugged at the bell pull by the mantel. The footman arrived almost immediately and, on the ladies saying they would prefer tea, was instructed to bring the tea tray and some cakes. 'If I had known you were coming today,' he said, after the man had gone to obey, 'I would have asked my sister, Lady Harley, to be present to act as hostess.'

'You have no wife?' Lady Myers had availed herself of one of the sofas, a pale green brocaded affair, and Sophie perched herself beside her, every sense alert, wanting to run, but conversely determined not to be driven away, simply because the man had taken a dislike to her. Why he should, she did not know. He was not completely unfeeling; she had seen evidence of his kindness on the way from Dover, but that was to other people, not herself.

'No, I am single,' he said, smiling at Sophie to try to mitigate his earlier brusqueness. It wasn't like him to be impolite, but this pair had taken him so much by surprise, and, at a time when he had so much on his mind, he had been less than welcoming. Not that he meant to alter his decision, but he could have put it more kindly.

'Oh, I see,' Lady Myers said. 'Then as you are a bachelor, we understand that taking in a young unmarried lady would be out of the question.' She paused, unwilling to abandon her quest. 'But you mentioned your sister. Does she reside here?'

'No, her home is in Suffolk, but when she is in town for

the Season, she stays here. She undertook to reply to your letter on my behalf, but of course that is of no significance now.'

'And what would her reply have been?' Sophie asked. 'Would she have repudiated me on the grounds that the family did not approve of my parents' marriage and, because I have been brought up abroad, I am not fit to be seen in society?'

'Has someone said that?'

'The present Lord Langford,' Lady Myers said. 'Miss Langford's uncle.'

'Oh.' He had been going to suggest she appeal to her father's family, but it seemed she had already done that and been turned away. He found himself thinking, 'Poor child!' and then smiled at his foolishness. She was not a child and he suspected had not been one for a long time. He had no idea how old she was, but she had a maturity that had nothing to do with years.

'Miss Langford may count on me, of course,' Lady Myers went on. 'But how long Lord Myers will remain in London, I do not know. He travels a great deal and I always accompany him…'

'I see.' He did see, very clearly. Lady Myers's offer was made out of duty, out of the charity Miss Langford so much denigrated, and she would be glad to have someone take the girl off her hands. And Miss Langford was intelligent enough to realise that.

'Lady Myers,' Sophie implored her, 'please do not go on. I am not incapable of earning a living and would rather do so than be the object of charity, especially charity so reluctantly given.'

'Earn a living,' he repeated, ignoring her accusation. 'How?'

'I have an education, I can teach—I have done it before. I could offer myself to a girls' school or find a position as a governess or companion.'

'And what will you teach?' He did not know why he was quizzing her in this way—to see how resolute she was? Or simply to tease? There was a faint blush to her cheeks that could have been embarrassment, or anger—he suspected the latter.

'Whatever is asked of me,' she said. 'The basics of reading and writing, literature, languages. I speak French well, German a little and Italian fluently—'

'Good heavens, a blue stocking!'

'That, sir, is better than being a milksop, dependent on the generosity or otherwise of a man who can give it or withhold it at his pleasure.'

He had a sudden vision of what it might be like to be a young lady alone in the world. She must either work or beg, scrimp to eat and to buy the clothes for her back, unable to go into society, unable to enjoy the sort of social occasions most young ladies of his acquaintance took for granted, unable to marry well. He was used to the ladies of the *ton*, aristocrats who peopled the Regent's court, simpering helpless females who did nothing without the permission of fathers, husbands or guardians, or demi-reps who flouted convention and were therefore not received in respectable drawing rooms. But the woman who faced him now was neither. He wished he had not been so sharp with her, but he did not know how to retrieve the situation.

The footman reappeared with the tea tray. 'Lady Harley has just returned, your Grace,' he said, as he set it down. 'She asked me to say that as soon as she has taken off her hat, she will join you.'

'Thank you, Collins.'

The footman began pouring the tea into thin china cups

and, while he did so, Sophie was able to look about her for the first time. The room was dominantly pale green and cream, light and restful to the eye and furnished in the French style; it seemed the war with France did not inhibit people from wanting beautiful things no matter where they came from. There was no fire, but the hearth contained a huge bowl of cream roses whose scent filled the room. A Turner hung over the mantelpiece and a cabinet displayed porcelain figurines, which she recognised as Italian and very valuable. The windows were deep and long and looked out into a narrow garden with clipped lawns and beds of those same cream roses; a blackbird flew down to worry a pair of thrushes, squawking its annoyance until they left what he considered his domain. She wished she was out there, walking in the fresh air and not sitting on this elegant sofa being watched by the master of the house, who stood facing them with his back to the fireplace, a picture of studied elegance.

She risked a glance at him, but his expression was bland. He would be difficult to get to know, she decided, a self-contained man who did not let his feelings show. Was that because he belonged to the English aristocracy or was there a deeper reason? As Lord Ubiquitous who could make a small child laugh, she had been drawn towards him; as the Duke of Belfont, she found him top lofty and unsympathetic. It was almost as if he were two people. But wasn't everyone like that? Did she not have two sides to her? The sad, lost child, in spite of her twenty-one years, and the independent, prickly woman of the world vied with each other according to the situation in which she found herself.

She looked up as a newcomer entered who could only have been Lady Harriet Harley. Dressed becomingly in amber silk, she was slightly older than the Duke; her features, though like her brother's, were softer, more rounded, and her eyes were not the steely blue of his, but a soft aquamarine. Her hair was a shade darker and piled up on her head and fastened with two jewelled combs. She came forward, smiling.

'Harriet, may I present Lady Myers and Miss Langford,' James said, vastly relieved to see her. 'Ladies, my sister, Lady Harley.'

Sophie rose along with Lady Myers to greet the newcomer, but before she could curtsy, she found both her hands grasped and Lady Harley holding her at arm's length to look at her. 'Oh, my dear, how pleased I am to make your acquaintance. If I had known you were arriving today, I would have been at home to greet you. But never mind, I am here now and you shall tell me all about yourself. I see Collins has brought in the tea.' She turned to the footman who was standing by the tea urn, a cup in his hand. 'You can leave that, Collins, I will see to it.' Then to Sophie, 'Come and sit by me and we shall get to know each other.' She drew the girl to another of the three sofas that furnished the room, leaving Lady Myers to sink back into her original seat opposite them. 'When did you arrive in London? Where are you staying?' She stopped suddenly and looked up at her brother. 'Oh, do sit down, James, you look so forbidding hovering there.'

He folded his long form into a winged back chair on the other side of the hearth and waited. Harriet could take over now; he need say no more, which was a great relief. He was a man of the world, used to dealing with all sorts of people and situations, known to be cool in a crisis, not easily shaken, but this child-woman had set him at a stand. He had no idea what to do with her.

'Lady Myers, you will forgive me, I know,' Harriet said. 'But I want to hear all about Sophia from her own lips.' To Sophie she added, 'You do not mind me calling you Sophia, do you?'

'Mama and Papa called me Sophie,' she said with a smile, which made James, watching her, realise she was not plain after all, nor overweening, simply shy. No, definitely not shy, he corrected himself, reserved perhaps, a private sort of person and proud with it. 'I was Sophia only when they were displeased with me.'

'And we are certainly not displeased with you, are we?' She appealed to her brother, who nodded agreement, his mouth twitching slightly. 'So Sophie it shall be.' She rose and busied herself with the teacups and handing round a plate of little cakes before resuming her seat. 'Now, my dear, do begin. Tell us first about your mama and papa. You see, we never knew them. I remember Papa had an older brother called Robert. That would be your grandfather, would it not?'

'I believe so. But I can tell you very little about him. I believe he disapproved of Papa and so Mama did not correspond with him.'

'Oh, how sad it is when families fall out,' Harriet said. 'It leads to so much conflict and it is not right to visit that on the next generation.'

'Just what I hoped you would say,' Lady Myers put in suddenly. 'It wasn't Sophie's fault. Lord Langford was a—'

'Lady Myers, please,' Sophie begged her, hating to hear anyone condemn her father, however justified that might be. She had loved him once and her mother had never ceased to be held in thrall by him even when their fortunes were at their lowest.

'Very well, I will say no more. Lady Harley may draw her own conclusions. I have told his Grace and will not repeat it.'

Harriet looked at her brother, who shrugged his elegant shoulders and smiled. 'It seems Miss Langford had already appealed to the present Lord Langford and been rejected.'

'Oh, how mortifying. Sophie, why did you not come to us first? My goodness, how anyone could turn away a relation in need is beyond me. Never mind, you are here now and we will do our best to help you.'

Sophie looked from one to the other, wondering why one should have been so dismissive and the other so welcoming. Even now, his Grace was frowning as if he were afraid his sister might offer something he could not agree to, although Harriet seemed unaware of it. 'I only need somewhere to lodge until I can find my feet,' she said. 'I can and will earn my keep.'

'Miss Langford has expressed the intention of becoming a companion or a governess,' James told his sister.

Harriet turned to Sophie; there was a smile and a hint of friendly teasing in her eyes, which made Sophie warm to her. 'Is that really what you wish to do, or was it said in a spirit of independence?'

Sophie found herself smiling back in spite of her discomfort. 'Independence, I think, but that doesn't mean I was not serious.'

'No, of course not. I admire you for it.'

'What I really want to do is write a book,' she said.

'A novel?'

'No. The story of our travels on the continent, the places we went to and the people we met. You see, Mama instructed me, showed me how to look at buildings and monuments with a fresh eye, how to observe characters, and she encouraged me to write about them.'

'How very clever of you!'

'Mama was the clever one.' She did not add that her

mother's cleverness irritated her father. Sometimes when he was disguised in drink he would call her a blue stocking—it was not meant as praise, but in the same derogatory way the Duke had meant it. Mama had told her that men did not like clever women, because it diminished them and shattered their illusions that women were not only physically inferior but mentally too. It was best not to flaunt one's cleverness; though Sophie did not hold with boasting, she did not see why she should hide what talents she had. After all, she was not beautiful; no one would fall at her feet on that account. 'But until it is written and I have interested a publisher in it, I must live and being a companion will serve…'

'I doubt that,' James put in. 'I believe ladies' companions are on call twenty-four hours a day—you will have no time to yourself.'

'Then I will make time.'

'That is very commendable,' Harriet said. 'But we will not talk of companions or governesses. There is no need.'

'Miss Langford is lodging with Lady Myers,' James told his sister in a warning voice, which she ignored.

'It is very good of Lady Myers,' Harriet said, smiling at the lady to mitigate what she was about to say. 'But what would everyone think of us if we were to allow Sophie to lodge anywhere but with us…?'

'Harriet,' he warned her, 'you know my feelings on the matter.'

She laughed. 'Indeed I do. You are as sensible of your duty as any man I know and I am persuaded you are determined to take Sophie into the bosom of the family and do your very best to make her happy. To do anything else would be quite scandalous…'

Sophie was well aware, as was everyone else, that Lady Harley had manoeuvred him into a corner. Though she

longed to tell them she would not stay if she were not welcome, she also knew that living permanently with Lady
Myers was also out of the question; the lady herself had
made that clear. She waited, unspeaking, pinning her
hopes on Lady Harley.

'Of course,' he said, giving his sister a grin that told
her she had won. 'But you must make yourself responsible for her.'

'Oh, I shall. I am quite looking forward to taking our
cousin out and about.' She turned to Sophie. 'Take no notice of his gruffness. What with all the fuss over King
Louis's visit and more state visits to come later in the year,
he has a great deal on his mind at the moment. But we can
manage quite well without him.'

'Thank you, my lady, I am grateful, but there is no
need to take me out and about. I shall be quite content to
have a room and board until I can earn enough to repay
you.'

'Repay us! What nonsense. You are kin and it is our
privilege to give you a home for as long as you want it.
Now, off you go with Lady Myers and fetch your belongings. By the time you return, your room will be ready.'

Sophie heard the Duke give a low groan. He had been
bested and she was not sure whether to feel satisfaction
or mortification, but beggars could not be choosers, she
told herself. He had come to his feet and she rose too and
faced him. 'I do not expect to be given a come-out, your
Grace. I am determined never to marry. I accept your offer
of a home only because I have no choice, but rest assured
I shall be as little trouble to you as possible.' She turned
to Lady Harley. 'My lady, I am grateful for your interven-
tion and with your permission will return tomorrow, if you
tell me a time that will be convenient.'

'Any time will do. I have no pressing engagements.'

'Then I shall bring Sophie at three,' Lady Myers said. 'Good day, Lady Harley. Good day, your Grace. Come, Sophie.'

Sophie curtsied and followed Lady Myers to the door. An imp of mischief made her turn as she reached it. 'My lord, what was it the Regent gave the little boy yesterday?'

'Little boy?' he queried, then smiled as he remembered. 'A silver button from his waistcoat. His Highness's coats are so tight the buttons are always popping off.'

'The child seemed bemused. What did you say to him?'

'I told him it was real silver and he should sell it and buy his family a good dinner before someone stole it from him. Why do you ask?'

'Oh, I rather envied the little one that he had managed to elicit a kind word from you.' And with that, she sailed out on the heels of Lady Myers.

His initial annoyance gave way to a wry grin as he turned and saw his sister laughing.

'You deserved that,' she said.

'No doubt I did. But I wonder if you know what you have taken on. It will not be easy. She is too proud and outspoken for her own good.'

'Of course I know, but that is due to her strange upbringing. She is a delightful girl and when I have done something about her clothes and shown her how to go on, she will take beautifully, you'll see.'

'Perhaps. She certainly needs someone to look to her wardrobe. Why, that yellow gown Lady Myers was wearing would have suited her better than that colourless lilac. I had begun to wonder if they had exchanged wardrobes or perhaps their maid was half-cut and confused the two.'

Harriet smiled. 'James it is not kind to make fun of her. She was in desperate straits...'

'She could have stayed with Lady Myers.'

'And been an unpaid companion because that is what she would have become and, although the woman did say she would bring her out, I doubt she would have made a very good fist at it. And think how badly that would reflect on us.'

'I know, which is why I agreed, but I warn you if she does or says anything to embarrass us or our friends, she will be packed off to Dersingham Park and I do not care what social occasions you have planned for her. Is that understood?'

'Yes, but I don't know why you are so gloomy about it.'

He did not know either, he admitted to himself, as he left her to meet Richard Summers at White's. How could a slip of a girl make him feel so old, so weighed down with cares? She meant nothing to him and he would not need to see anything of her; Harriet would look after her. It must be a family trait, this stubbornness, he decided, for his sister had taken the girl's future on herself, dismissing his misgivings with a wave of the hand as if they were no more important than dandelion seed. She was right of course, he could not have turned the chit away without bringing down the censure of the *haut monde*, but, having done his duty, he could forget her.

Richard was sitting in the library of the club reading a newspaper, a glass of cognac at his side. He looked up as James flung himself into a chair opposite him. 'You look as though you need a drink.' He reached for the bottle and filled the empty glass beside it. 'Ellen playing up again, is she?'

'Ellen?' His mind had been so much on Sophie he had forgotten his erstwhile mistress, who seemed unable to understand their affair was at an end. She had done her best to embarrass him in public, hoping to wriggle back in his favour, but he had never shared his mistresses with anyone, except their husbands, naturally, and he did not propose to make an exception now, especially as the man she had been seeing was Alfred Jessop, his cousin and heir. 'No, nothing to do with her.'

'Then what has given you that air of distraction? It can't be his Highness, can it? You usually take his whims and tantrums into your stride…'

James gave a grunt. 'He is behaving as if he had won the war single-handed and accepting the adulation of his subjects as his due. I cannot make up my mind if he is deluding himself or trying to persuade those around him that he is not the most unpopular ruling prince the country ever had. It makes my job doubly difficult.' He drank his brandy in one swallow, holding out his glass for a refill. 'Yesterday was a case in point. Why was it necessary to go to Dover to meet Louis and, when he did, to keep stopping and making a fool of himself and laying himself open to an assassin?'

'Nothing happened, did it? No one took a shot at him, no one attempted to pull him out of the coach and tear him to shreds. The abuse is only verbal and he seems to be able to ignore that.'

'He can, but I can't. Not that Louis is any better. We had no sooner delivered him to Grillon's, than he sent for a chair and insisted on sitting in the vestibule holding court like some fat potentate. Good God, it's a hotel where anyone can come and go. His Highness was with him some of the time and they were sitting targets. It is making me very on edge and I find myself suspecting everyone…'

'Even two dumpy travellers and a mousy companion in

that hired coach, which followed us all the way to London. But perhaps you were right; they could have been in disguise.'

'Those! That was no disguise. It was Lord Myers, one-time ambassador to somewhere or other, his lady wife and Miss Sophia Langford, or Sophie as she prefers to be known.'

'You are acquainted with them?'

'Until today I was not. Miss Langford is a cousin of mine, though I don't know how many times removed, but the number of removes seems not to weigh with her. She has turned up from Italy, having just buried her father, and expects me to welcome her with open arms…'

'And her mother?'

'Died some time ago. She was my Uncle Robert's granddaughter.'

'Then the relationship is not so distant. It is not like you to be uncharitable, James.'

'Oh, I have taken her in—had no choice since Harriet has taken a liking to the girl, and I felt sorry for her. Not that she invited sympathy; she has the Dersingham pride and obstinacy, no doubt of that. Said if I didn't take her in, she would become a governess. Couldn't let that happen, could I?'

'No, you could not. So, what is the problem? Lady Harley will do the necessary.'

'I have no doubt Harriet will expect me to give her a come-out and that means escorting her to whatever occasions my sister deems necessary.'

'And from what I remember when I met her at Dover, she is too plain for you. You were always known for having the most beautiful women on your arm.'

'Her plainness or otherwise has nothing to do with it. Nor will she be "on my arm", as you put it; I shall be her sponsor only. It is simply that I do not know how I will find the time. His Highness expects me to be everywhere at once. Goodness knows what he will think of doing when the Tsar and the King of Prussia pay a state visit later in the year. London will be crawling with foreign royalty and all of it expecting protection, not to mention the return of Wellington, which will be a far more popular event. It will need a whole regiment and more to keep order and since I no longer have a command, I will have to liaise with the military and give way to them on the grounds that I am a mere equerry.'

'You are far more than that and everyone who matters knows it. Why, if it hadn't been for you, Boney might never have found himself with no choice but to abdicate.'

James had once been a soldier, and a very good one, but Wellington had soon realised his potential as a spy and he had found himself out of the army and wandering about Europe under a false name, pretending to have a grudge against his own people in order to gather intelligence. It had been dangerous and secret work. It was still a secret except from those who had worked with him at the time and that included Richard, who had been his contact with their commander. When his father died and he had been recalled to become the next Duke of Belfont, he had thought to see an end of it, except that the Regent, on being told of his exploits, insisted on having him in his entourage.

'And if you think that is the end of the man, you are mistaken, Dick, my friend,' he said grimly. 'He will not take his defeat as final. I have already heard rumours…'

'Oh, that old chant, "I will be back." Wishful thinking.'

'We shall see and before another year is out.'

'Twenty guineas says he stays comfortably on Elba writing his memoirs.'

'Done.' James beckoned to one of the waiters to fetch the book of wagers, and, when it was brought, carefully wrote in it, 'The Duke of Belfont bets Captain Richard Summers the sum of twenty guineas that Napoleon Bonaparte will leave Elba and attempt to regain his throne before a year is out.' They both signed and dated it.

'That will put the cat among the pigeons,' James said. 'It might even bring the worms out of the woodwork.'

'Oh, I see, you engineered the wager. I might have known. You are not one to make foolish wagers. But watch your back, my friend.'

'Oh, I leave that to you, I shall be far too busy.'

Richard grinned. 'Taking a young lady out and about, I collect.'

'It is my duty as head of the family,' he said, so pompously that Richard, who knew him well, laughed.

'You never know, you might end up leg shackled yourself and it won't be before time. You should have set up your nursery ten years ago.'

'How could I? I was in no position to offer for anyone, and, since returning to England, I have met no one with whom I would want to spend the rest of my life.'

'You will.' Richard paused, then, deciding he had teased his friend enough, added, 'Are you dining here tonight?'

'No, I am expected at Carlton House, some banquet or other. I will be glad when the season is over and I can retire to Dersingham Park and look after my estate. In the meantime, duty calls. Keep your eyes and ears open, Richard. Contrary to the Regent's belief, I cannot be everywhere at once.'

The two men parted and James strolled back to Belfont House, but strangely it was not his problems at court that occupied his mind, but a pair of lustrous brown eyes. How could anyone be described as plain who had eyes like that?

Chapter Three

Sophie's arrival at Belfont House with all her belongings the following day did not go as she expected and planned. She had hoped only for a garret room, where she could sit and write, not the sumptuous bedchamber she was given. It was furnished in mahogany and walnut; its thick carpet, in shades of blue, reflected the pattern in the curtains at the windows and those about the large four-poster bed. Adjoining it was a small sitting room. 'I have had a desk and some shelves brought in,' Harriet told her when she conducted her there after Lady Myers had been entertained with tea, been bidden goodbye and left, promising to call in a day or two to see how Sophie did. 'Then you can write if you feel the inspiration. But I do not want you to think that you must do it. Look on it as a pastime when you have nothing better to do.'

'I do not see it as a pastime, my lady.'

'No, of course not. How foolish of me. What I meant was that I want you to make this your home. Write if you wish, but I should like it very much if you would accompany me on outings. There is so much going on in London this Season, it is beyond anything the capital has seen before, and it is not much fun if you have no one to share it with. The Duke is too busy.'

'Is your husband not able to accompany you?'

For a moment her bright smile vanished. 'He was killed at Oporto in '09.'

'Oh, I am so sorry. I did not know…'

'No reason why you should. It was a comfort to know that James was with him when he died. He stayed abroad until last year when our father died and he became the next Duke. It was a relief to have him safe home again.'

'I am sure it was,' Sophie murmured.

'I have two darling daughters, Beth and Olivia, but I left them at home in Suffolk. I cannot imagine they would find London in summer to their liking. They are more interested in ponies and country walks. When the Season is at an end, you must visit us and meet them.'

'I should like that very much.'

'Now, here I am prattling on about myself when what I really want to know is all about you. What was it like to be in Europe when Napoleon was Emperor? Did you ever meet him? Some people here say he was an ogre and others that he was a hero. I cannot find that very patriotic, can you?'

'No, and I never met him. I saw him in the distance when we were in Paris, and we were in Austria when his son was born and there were tremendous celebrations. But I did meet some other interesting characters. Papa seemed to attract them. He was such an affable man and was always bringing people home for dinner.' She did not add that it had stretched their housekeeping money to breaking point to entertain them.

'And is that what is going into your book?'

She had not consciously thought of doing that, but she did know a simple travel book would not interest a publisher; there were dozens of those already. She must make it different, and interesting characters might do that. People lived abroad for many reasons; some, like her father, to escape their creditors; others to get over an unhappy love affair or to run away with someone else's spouse. Some eloped when parents refused to countenance their marriage and some moved to a warmer climate for the sake of their health. Whatever the reason, there was always a nucleus of expatriates in the major cities of the continent, even during the war. 'Yes, but I shall have to be very careful not to name names, I do not want to antagonise people. And they will only be part of the descriptions of how we travelled and the interesting places we saw.'

'It must have been very exciting for a young girl to see so much of the world, almost like a Grand Tour.'

Sophie laughed. 'It was never like that. And when Mama died—' She stopped, unable to go on.

'I feel for you, Sophie. Lady Myers told me a little of it, when we had a few minutes alone together, but you must put all those difficulties behind you now. I am going to enjoy dressing you up and taking you out.'

'Really, my lady, there is no need...'

'I want to, and please call me Harriet. Your mama was our cousin and that makes you a cousin too and families should not be formal with one another.'

Sophie laughed suddenly. 'But when one of them is a duke...'

'Oh, James is nothing like as top lofty as he pretends. He stands on his dignity to keep the doting mamas and their simpering daughters at bay. Being a bachelor and a duke, he is the target of every ambitious mother of an unmarried daughter.' She chuckled suddenly. 'I have told him he will have to marry soon and he ought to be looking for a wife, but he remains stubbornly unwed.'

'No doubt he is particular. His wife will be a duchess and he must be sure she is up to it.'

'True.' She rose and shook out her blue taffeta skirt. 'Now, I shall leave you to settle in. Dinner is at five and afterwards I have an evening engagement that I cannot cancel, but tomorrow we will go shopping. Shall I send a maid to help you unpack?'

'No, thank you. I can manage.'

She left and Sophie sat on the bed and regarded her trunk, sitting in the middle of the floor, where the footmen had left it. It was scuffed and scratched, its straps wearing thin, proclaiming her poverty. In it was everything she possessed. She could not bear for a servant to see that. Sighing, she unpacked it, putting the gowns in the wardrobe, her other clothes in a drawer and her writing things on the desk with the miniature of her mother. She had just finished when a maid arrived with hot water and an offer to help her dress and to do her hair. 'My name is Janet, miss,' she said. 'Lady Harley says I am to look after you until a maid can be found for you.'

Dinner would be an ordeal, she knew that. It was not that she did not know how to behave; she had dined with some very aristocratic people when her father was in funds, but this evening she expected the Duke to be present and he would quiz her, or perhaps ignore her; either would be mortifying. She found a spotted muslin that was not too creased, draped a silk shawl that had been her mother's over her upper arms and followed the maid down to the first-floor drawing room, where she had been received the day before. The Duke and Lady Harley were waiting for dinner to be announced.

'Miss Langford, good evening.' He rose politely. 'I trust you have settled in.'

He was dressed formally in a blue long-tailed coat, an

embroidered waistcoat, over which a froth of ruffles tumbled, powder blue silk breeches and white stockings. She noticed how well cut his coat was and how it showed off his broad shoulders and that his fair hair, though in the latest short style, curled over the high collar. He was the most handsome man she had ever met and she could understand his popularity with mothers of marriageable daughters. She wondered why he had not married before now; after all, he had admitted to being four and thirty, long past the age when men in his station of life married and set up their nursery. He would naturally be particular, but surely there were dozens of young ladies with beautiful faces and trim figures who would make elegant duchesses?

This reflection made her acutely aware of her own poor garments and she felt like turning tail, but then her pride came to her rescue and she bent her knee. 'Yes, thank you, your Grace.'

'And are you satisfied with your accommodation?'

'Entirely,' she said, unwilling to admit she had expected much less considering his lack of a welcome.

'I have given Sophie the blue room,' Harriet said. 'The little boudoir next door to it is ideal for a writing room.'

Sophie turned from her secret contemplation of the Duke to face her hostess, whose gown was of forest green silk with deep lace ruffles round the hem. It had a very low *décolletage* and huge puffed sleeves. Her hair was piled up in a complicated knot and threaded with gems and there were more studded into a pendant around her neck. She patted the sofa next her. 'Come and sit down, Sophie. I wish I were not going out this evening, I would much rather have stayed at home to talk to you, but I am promised and cannot disappoint my friends.'

'Oh, please do not think of if,' Sophie said. 'I shall be quite content. I think I might do some writing.'

'Ah, the book,' James said in a tone that made her hackles rise. He might treat it as a matter for jest now, but one day she would make him take her seriously. 'You must tell us all about that.'

'I do not think it would interest you, your Grace.'

'Why not?'

'It is but a little thing and you must have been to all the places I have and seen it all.'

'When?' he asked sharply. Did she know something he would rather not have made public? He had never met her before, had he? She was never in any of the places he had been operating in, was she? Always alert to danger, from whatever direction, he suddenly felt threatened.

'When?' she repeated, puzzled. 'I assumed you went on the Grand Tour before the Continent was closed to travellers.'

'Oh, yes, a rather curtailed Grand Tour, as I remember. It was 1799, Napoleon was on the march and Europe was in turmoil.' He was being foolish, he told himself. What could a chit like her know of espionage and those engaged in it? She would have still been in the schoolroom when he was sent to Austria. Or was it something else altogether making him feel he ought to take more interest in her? Her vulnerability in spite of her efforts to hide it?

A footman arrived and announced that dinner was served and James moved forward and offered his arm to Sophie. She got up and laid her fingers on his sleeve and even that slight contact made her catch her breath. She was shaking with nerves and had no idea why. He was only a little above average height, but he had an overpowering presence, as if he was used to having his own way and would brook no argument, but she had no intention of arguing with him. He was her host, her provider, and, however much it irked her to admit it, she could not afford to alienate him.

'We are eating in the small dining room,' Harriet told her, as she took her brother's other arm. 'It is much less formal than the large room we use when we entertain, and we can talk comfortably without having to raise our voices.'

And talk they did. While eating their way through a delicious fish dish, roast beef, boiled potatoes and mushrooms in a cream sauce, they spoke about the celebrations, the visits of foreign royalty, the plight of the soldiers coming home to unemployment and hardship, about Wellington and Napoleon and the latest *on dit*, which meant nothing to Sophie, though Harriet did her best to explain who was who. The Duke was an affable host and seemed to forget his earlier antagonism. Sophie found herself relaxing a little, though not completely. She was only too aware that she was the poor relation, there under sufferance, though she meant to remedy that situation as soon as she could afford it.

'Is it true that the Regent hates his wife?' she asked, when everything had been removed in favour of fruit tartlets, jelly and honey cakes. She had been too nervous to eat heartily; in any case, she had become so used to frugality, her stomach would not take rich food.

'I am afraid so,' he said. 'His father badgered him so much to marry, he agreed to marry her without ever seeing her and he disliked her on sight. How he is going to keep her from the celebrations, I do not know. She is related to half the crowned heads of Europe who are coming and expecting to meet her.'

'I am sorry for her. How dreadful it must be to be despised and unloved in a strange country.'

'She is hardly unloved,' Harriet put in. 'She is very popular with the people.'

'It isn't the same though, is it? The public face and the private one. I think it is very important to have a fondness for the person one marries and it doesn't matter if you are a prince or a duke or the man who clears the middens.'

'Love,' he murmured, making Sophie turn to look at him, thinking he was laughing at her, but though he was not laughing, there was a slight twist to his mouth that might have been humour directed against himself. 'Are princes and dukes allowed to fall in love?'

'Of course they are,' Harriet said bracingly. 'The world would be a very poor place without it.'

'Mama loved Papa,' Sophie said. 'And he loved her. He was brought so low when she died, he never properly recovered.' It was said with a kind of defiance, which was meant to offset whatever tale Lady Myers had told Harriet, who would undoubtedly have passed it on to the Duke. She did not want him to blame Papa, or feel sorry for her. Or perhaps just a little, she amended, just enough to give her a roof over her head and food to keep her from starving until she could prove to him and the world that she was an author to be reckoned with.

It was as if her listeners understood her point, for neither commented and a minute later the footman came to tell her ladyship the carriage was at the door. Harriet rose to go. 'I must be off. I will see you tomorrow, Sophie, and we will make plans.' She bent to kiss Sophie's cheek. 'Sleep well. You are very welcome.'

Then she was gone in a rustle of silk, leaving Sophie to face the Duke. 'Am I?' she asked in the silence that followed.

'I beg your pardon?'

'Am I welcome? Or am I an encumbrance you would rather do without?'

'You are certainly forthright,' he said, laughing. 'But I assure you, you are not an encumbrance. This house is large enough for two dozen guests; one little cousin who is determined not to be noticed is not going to upset my routine.'

'Then I am glad of it.' She spoke with a certain amount of asperity; it was so very difficult being beholden.

He knew he seemed cold and heartless, but that was his way. He had taught himself to be self-contained, not by word or gesture to reveal what he was really thinking. It was all very well for people like the Regent to weep copious tears over nothing at all, but if he had been emotional when he was living with the enemy, when he had to pretend to be at one with them, a show of feeling, even the twitch of an eyelid, could have meant death. It had become a habit hard to break. 'Do not be so prickly, Sophie,' he said, trying to unbend a little. 'Naturally you are welcome, you do not need to question it. And Harriet will love having you for company. Since her husband died, she has not been out and about so much as she was used to and I have not been able to accompany her as I would like.'

Did that mean she was to be an unpaid companion? Perhaps, though Harriet had given no indication that was what she expected. She had taken a liking to Harriet and bearing her company would be no hardship. 'Thank you, your Grace.'

'Now, I, too, must leave you,' he said, rising. 'I am afraid duty calls.'

'I understand,' she said, then laughed. 'I must not disrupt your routine.'

'*Touché!*' He took her hand to raise her to her feet, then solemnly kissed the back of it. 'Goodnight, cousin.' And then he was gone.

She stood for a moment, looking at the back of her hand where his lips had briefly touched, wondering why the mark of it did not show; it had made her feel so hot, almost melting. Sighing, she made her way up to her room, where she went through to the boudoir and sat down at the desk. Drawing a sheet of paper towards her, she picked up a quill, dipped it in ink and then stopped. The flowing phrases she had rehearsed in her head refused to come. Her mind was blank. No, not blank, for it was filled with what had happened that day, from getting up that morning; breakfasting with Lady Myers, who chatted about the Duke as if she had known him for years; to the carriage ride and her arrival at Belfont House; the welcome of Lady Harley, who pretended not to notice the paucity of her luggage; and then the sumptuous dinner and her conversation with the Duke. The Duke more than anything filled her mind.

He intrigued her. One minute he was arrogant and overbearing, the next trying to put her at her ease. He obviously did not think a great deal of her ambition to be a writer; he was probably one of those men who decried educated women. He had called her a blue stocking which was palpably not true; she was not learned. She could not converse in Latin or Greek, though she could chatter to her heart's content in French, German and Italian. She knew only a smattering of mathematics and architecture, but she prided herself on getting on well with people. But the Duke wasn't 'people', was he? He was different. He made her heart thump and her hands shake and yet she would not admit she was afraid of him.

Why had he never married? The romantic in her began to weave stories of unrequited love or unfaithful lovers. He had murmured about dukes falling in love as though he wished it were possible and knew it was not. Must he marry to oblige the family with an heir and nothing more? Did he enjoy the work he did for the Regent? Did he have to do it? Was his wealth and prestige dependent on it? Why did she think that was unlikely? Because he was proud, she answered herself, too proud to demean himself to anyone, not even a future king. Would that pride make a broken love affair harder to bear? She laughed softly at her own foolishness; why did she imagine he had been thwarted in love? He had been born and bred an aristocrat, one of the top one hundred, and ever since her mother's father died, he had known he would be the next duke; it was his manner to be distant, nothing more.

It was no good sitting there being fanciful, nor to try to write; she was too tired to work. She put down her pen and moved into the bedroom to prepare for bed. Perhaps tomorrow she would feel more like it. Tomorrow she would go through her notes and that would start her off. Climbing between the sheets, she turned down the lamp and shut her eyes. Tomorrow…

The Regent was having one of his interminable receptions, showing off his opulence, being the jovial host, making jokes, flirting with the ladies, and James, keeping watch in the background, wished himself anywhere but where he was. He would rather be talking to that dowdy cousin at home than standing here, pretending to enjoy himself. It was strange he had never heard of her before now, yet he had little doubt, and Harriet none at all, that she was who she said she was. From what she had told them, his uncle had not approved of her mother's choice of husband and Lady Myers had hinted that Lord Langford was a wastrel and a gambler and that, after his wife's death, Sophie had been forced to work to keep them both. What father worth his salt would allow such a thing? Not that Sophie had complained, had not said a word about it, pretending it was the demise of her father that had forced her to seek sanctuary with her mother's family. It could not have been easy for her to do that, being proud and wanting very much to be independent. As if writing a book, even if it found a publisher, would achieve that for her!

'What, all alone?' a female voice said at his elbow.

He did not need to turn to know who had spoken. Not only did he know every nuance of her voice, every seductive drawl, but, being observant, he had seen her crossing the room towards him, though he had given no indication of it. Ellen Colway had a tall, shapely figure made taller by the huge trio of feathers that adorned her pink satin turban. It matched her gown, which was draped so close to her figure it left little to the imagination, though he did not need imagination when memory served him better. She had firm rosy flesh and she knew how to seduce a man, even one as tightly in control as he had imagined himself to be. He had enjoyed her for a time, but her charms had already begun to pall when she deceived him with his cousin. That he could not condone.

It was not so much her perfidy that hurt but the fact that Alfred was a jackstraw, still attached to his mother's apron strings, who spent his time gambling, tolerated by the *ton* because he was heir presumptive to the Belfont dukedom. What Ellen would want with the fellow, he could not think. She surely did not expect him to become the next duke in the foreseeable future, if ever. He did not intend to remain a bachelor all his life. He would marry when he found a suitable bride and in the fullness of time would beget his own heir. Alfred could not prevent that.

He turned towards her, a sardonic smile on his face. 'Lady Colway, good evening.'

She smiled back, not at all put out. 'So formal we are, your Grace. Can it be the company you keep? I hear the Regent is a stickler for protocol.'

'Perhaps it is the company *you* keep, my lady.'

'Oh, you are not going to prose on about that, are you? I have told you it was nothing. I was miffed with you and wanted my revenge. I did not expect you to make such a mountain of it.'

'Then you do not know me very well.'

'Oh, my dear,' she said, sidling close to him, 'I know you very well indeed, every inch of you…' The voice was seductive and at one time might have had him running with her for the nearest bed, but all it did now was make him laugh.

'And I, Ellen my dear, know you very well too, not just your beautiful body, but your ugly mind.'

She sprang from him, eyes flashing angrily. 'How dare you! If Clarence were to hear of your insults, he would call you out.'

'Would he? He had his chance a year ago and did nothing and from that I deduced he did not care. I have never cuckolded a man in love with his wife, and as you were known for your affairs…' He shrugged and left the sentence unfinished.

She returned close to his side and took his arm. 'Oh, James, do not let us quarrel. Clarence is not worth it and Alfred certainly is not. I came to invite you to a little soirée tomorrow evening. Clarence is still in the country and there will only be a handful of guests. After they have gone home we could be alone…'

'I am afraid I am promised elsewhere.'

'Then you will be the loser,' she said, her vanity stung by his rejection. 'I bid you goodnight.'

'What is it they say about a woman scorned?' Richard

murmured, coming up behind him as he watched her cross the floor towards Alfred. 'You have made an enemy there, my friend.'

'What can she do? I am not the first, nor will I be the last, and if she makes a public brouhaha of it, her husband will no longer be able to ignore it and will have to do something to stop her excesses. I do not think she will want that.'

'You may be right.' He paused. 'Does that mean you have found a new light o' love?'

'Not at all. A man does not have to be on with the new the instant he is off with the old, does he?'

'Then where are you promised tomorrow evening? I know the Regent does not want you, I heard him tell you so.'

'I have a mind to escort my sister and cousin to Lady Carstairs's soirée.'

'The dowdy little mouse? Good Lord, James, I had not thought to see you brought so low.'

'Leave off your quizzing, Dick, I have agreed to sponsor the girl for the Season and it behoves me to act the father figure…'

It was a statement that had his friend in gales of laughter. He was so convulsed it was a full minute before he could speak. 'Father figure! You!'

'Why not? I am head of the family, am I not?'

'True.'

'Then I thank you to keep your mirth to yourself. Harriet has undertaken to dress her so she will not disgrace us and, my duty done, I can forget her.'

Except, of course, she was not easy to forget. Was it her worn and unfashionable garments, the very opposite of the modishly dressed ladies of his acquaintance, that made her stand out, or her composure and belief in herself, which made him think there was more to her than met the eye? Or was it her hair, dark as a raven's wing, or those amber eyes that could be cold as the charity she disdained, or warm as treacle depending on her mood, which were so memorable?

Even now, with the noise of drunken laughter surrounding him, he could hear her. 'How dreadful it must be to be despised and unloved in a strange country.' She had been talking about the Princess of Wales, but it could equally have applied to her. It had unsettled him, made him feel unworthy. Was that what she had intended? And then she had bluntly asked, 'Am I an encumbrance you would rather do without?' So clever of her. Oh, how he disliked clever women. But, for all that, he must do his best for her, make her feel part of the family; nothing less would do, not only for his reputation but his self-respect.

Sophie looked at herself in the long mirror and smiled. Being a single girl not yet out, she should have been wearing white, but Lady Harley had said it did not suit her and her life before returning to England had been so unconventional it was not in the least necessary to follow custom slavishly. Nor would she countenance black. Another colour was called for, one to make her stand out in the crowd. Sophie wasn't sure that she wanted to stand out in the crowd, but when Harriet had taken her to the mantua maker and insisted she try on a gown in a grey-green silk that reminded her of the lakes in Switzerland palely reflecting the green of the trees on their banks, she knew her mentor was right.

The fabric slid over her hips and swirled about her ankles in soft flowing lines and made her feel—oh, she did not know how she felt. Womanly, sensuous, consequential came to mind. She knew she was not beautiful, could never be that, but she found herself wondering if clothes could make a plain person attractive, or was it simply that the excitement of her first public outing was giving her a heightened colour, making her eyes sparkle.

She and Harriet had spent the morning and half the afternoon shopping for clothes. They were looking for something ready made, Harriet had explained, so that she could wear them straight away, but later she could choose some material and have gowns made up for her. In vain did she protest she could manage with the clothes she had, she did not intend to be seen out and about and that it was not right that Harriet should spend money on her.

'It isn't my money,' Harriet had replied, nodding at the assistant who had been serving them to wrap the two day gowns they had chosen, one an azure blue, the other a warm apricot. 'It is James's.'

'Oh, no! What will he say when the bills arrive? I can't accept them. I really can't.'

'He will be insulted if you do not. He told me to buy whatever was necessary.'

'But is all this necessary?' She waved her hand at the pile of parcels waiting to be taken out to the coach.

'Of course it is. You have promised to come out and about with me and you must be properly dressed for each occasion. It would not look well for us if you were not.'

'But—'

'I will hear no buts. You shall have a come-out and I will eat my best hat if you do not make a hit.'

Sophie was not sure she wanted to make a hit, especially if it meant being ogled by all the single young men with questioning eyes. How much was she worth? How big a dowry had been settled on her? Was it worth offering for her, even though she was so plain? Perhaps if she could make herself even more unattractive, they would give up. But when she had slipped into the beautiful gown for her first sortie into society, she knew she didn't want to. It would be lovely, just once, to be admired, to flirt a little, and then retire into the life she had mapped out for herself.

What would his Grace make of her transformation? she wondered. Would he realise there was more to the waif he so disdained than he had at first thought? Would she elicit a smile from him, a genuine smile, not that condescending twitch of the lips that had characterised his exchanges with her until now? But then she stopped herself. He had handed her over to his sister and been relieved to do so, which was hardly flattering, but Lady Harley had been so welcoming and friendly that she more than made up for the shortcomings of her brother. After all, he had far more important things to do than put in an appearance at a musical evening being given by one of Lady Harley's friends. It was a simple affair, she had told Sophie, a suitable occasion in which to introduce her to society.

Rose, one of the chambermaids who had been promoted to look after her, sat Sophie down at the dressing table and arranged her hair in a soft Grecian style, which went well with the classical lines of the gown, and then fastened her mother's pearls about her throat. They lay against her skin, picking up the colours of her dress. 'There, miss, you look lovely,' Rose said.

'Thank you.' She stood up, slipped her feet into her matching slippers and, picking up her fan, drifted out of the room and down the stairs in a kind of waking dream. If only her mother could see her now. She had always talked to her about the grand occasions she had enjoyed as a girl, how she wished she could give them to her, and, if Papa's ship came in, she would. It was an idle dream and they had both known it, but here she was, her eyes

misted with tears at the memory, walking sedately down
the grand staircase of Belfont House to be introduced to
the *beau monde*. She was halfway down when she realised someone was in the hall looking up at her, and it
wasn't Harriet.

If she had not had her hand on the banister, she would
have stumbled, but she quickly regained her balance, pausing a moment before continuing her stately progress down
the stairs. Had she detected a tiny show of appreciation in
his blue eyes as he watched her descend? If she had, it was
gone so quickly she thought she had imagined it. She
must have. He saw beautiful and elegant women every day
of his life, was used to the opulence at court, the rich materials, the flashing jewels, the grandeur. In spite of her
new clothes, she would be an antidote beside them.

She paused on the bottom stair because he had not
moved. She would have to let go of the banister and step
to one side to go round him and she did not think she
could. Her knees felt as if they would not support her. On
this step she was the same height as he was and could see
the dark flecks in his blue eyes, his firm mouth and the
tiny curls of hair about his ears. He had a tiny scar on his
chin, too, which she had not noticed before. It made him
slightly less than perfect, more human.

He had been so taken aback by the vision of her coming slowly down the stairs, one gloved hand on the banister, her head held high, her gown fitting so perfectly to
a figure just the slim side of the curves fashion dictated
that he had been mesmerised. Whatever had made him
think she was plain? She was a vision of loveliness; he
found his heart beating faster than its usual sedate pace
and, for a moment, was deprived of speech. He suddenly
realised she was waiting for him to move aside.

'Miss Langford.' He bowed slightly and stood to one

side, so that as she passed him he caught the scent of violets. He would never be able to smell those tiny flowers again without bringing to mind the picture of Sophie Langford drifting down his staircase like a woodland nymph. Good heavens! He was becoming sentimental. He smiled wryly, more himself. 'Good evening.'

'Good evening, your Grace.' He was dressed in an evening suit of black superfine with velvet facings, a white figured-brocade waistcoat, and an intricately tied white cravat in which nestled a glittering diamond pin. She wondered where he was going; wherever it was, it was not to be as formal an occasion as the evening before when, according to Harriet, he had attended the Regent's reception.

Her question was answered almost immediately by Harriet who had followed her down the stairs, mature in dove grey taffeta with blue lace trimmings. 'There you both are! Is the carriage outside?'

'It is,' he answered. 'And has been these last ten minutes.'

'Good,' she replied, ignoring his slight tone of impatience. 'Sophie, James has been so good as to escort us this evening, is that not wonderful?'

Sophie was taken aback. All her self-confidence evaporated at the thought that she would have to be on her very best behaviour. Instead of being able to blend into the background unnoticed, she would be the focus of attention simply because he was escorting her. No wonder he had looked so critically at her; he had been sizing her up to see if he cared to be seen with her in public. She supposed she had passed muster because he had made no comment either complimentary or otherwise. He was looking at her now, evidently expecting her to reply. 'I am honoured, your Grace,' she said.

'It is my pleasure,' he said, smiling easily now and

sounding as if he might mean it. 'Shall we go?' He offered both arms and the ladies took one each. The footman sprang to open the door and they went down the three steps to where the carriage waited.

'Lady Carstairs is a very good friend of mine,' Harriet explained as they rode. 'She is also known for a society hostess of the first water. If you are invited to one of her soirées, then you know you will be accepted by the *ton* and more invitations will follow.'

'Has she invited me?' Sophie asked, meaning, had she been foisted on Lady Carstairs by Harriet; it would be difficult to refuse the sister of the Duke of Belfont.

'Naturally she has. As soon as I told her about you, she wanted to meet you.'

According to Harriet, the party was not to be a large one and she would soon get to know everyone, but when they were ushered into her ladyship's salon, she found herself wondering what a large party might be like. The room was packed to suffocation, everyone talking and laughing at once; the clamour was unbelievable until the stentorian tones of the footman announced, 'His Grace, the Duke of Belfont, Lady Harley, Miss Langford.' The silence that followed was just as overwhelming as the noise had been as everyone stopped in mid-sentence to turn and look towards the entrance where the Duke stood, surveying the scene, his hand lightly under Sophie's elbow.

He exerted no particular pressure, but she could feel the warmth of his hand through the thin material of her sleeve and was grateful for it; such a light touch and yet so reassuring. He guided her into the room, followed by Harriet, and slowly the broken conversations were resumed, as Lady Carstairs came forward to greet them, her old-fash-

ioned wide skirts billowing around her, a smile of gratifi-
cation on her face.

'Your Grace, you honour us. I had no idea—' She
stopped, suddenly aware of Sophie.

'My lady, may I present my cousin, Miss Langford,'
he said.

'Miss Langford, I am pleased to meet you. Lady Harley
tells me you have recently come home from a protracted
stay abroad.'

'Yes, we could not come home because of the war,' Sophie answered.

'And now you are alone in the world.'

'Not at all,' James put in before she could answer. 'Miss
Langford has returned to live with her family.'

'Of course.' Aware of the set-down, she turned to Sophie. 'One day you must tell us all about your adventures.
But now, do enjoy this evening. We plan to have a little
music on the pianoforte and a string quartet is to play for
us. Later there will be a few country dances for the young
people.' She paused and addressed the Duke. 'You will
stay for those, will you not? I am sure your cousin will
enjoy a measure or two.'

He looked about him. There were dozens of young ladies whose mamas were giving them nudges and whispering. It was always the same whenever he appeared at a
gathering like this, which was why he tried to avoid them.
He could not, for the life of him, think why he had decided
to come tonight. The sooner he escaped, the better. On the
other hand, having offered to escort Sophie and his sister,
he could hardly drag them away too soon. He bowed an
acknowledgement.

'Do you know everyone?' She waved a hand in the direction of the throng. 'If there is anyone…'

He smiled, knowing she would love to be able to say

she had introduced the Duke of Belfont to his future wife and that it was in her salon they had met and fallen in love. 'Not at present,' he said. 'But I am sure my cousin would like to meet some of the company.'

'Of course. Come, Miss Langford, I will make the introductions.'

Sophie followed her into the throng and was soon trying to remember names and faces and the potted histories her hostess was giving her, as they moved from one group to the next. When her ladyship was called away, she found herself the centre of a group of young people, all wanting to know about Europe under Napoleon Bonaparte. 'Were you imprisoned?' one young man asked. His name was Theodore Buskin, the son of an admiral, she had been told when he was presented to her.

'No, we were allowed to live at home and move about freely, but we could not leave. No doubt they were afraid we might pass on intelligence.'

'And did you?' It was asked eagerly.

She laughed, suddenly enjoying their attention. 'Now, that would be telling.'

'You did!' This from a young lady whose name escaped Sophie. She was dressed in bright pink with matching silk roses sewn all over her gown. Sophie thought she looked like an animated rose bush. 'Oh, how exciting. And dangerous.'

Sophie realised her error at once. She should have denied it instead of hinting like that. Now they were sure she had been involved in secret dealings, which was so far from the truth it was laughable. 'We lived very ordinary lives,' she went on, trying to retract, but by now they were determined she was being modest and that her life had been full of excitement.

'Do tell us.'

'There is nothing to tell.'

'Gammon!' another cried. 'You surely do not expect us to believe you spent years living among the enemy and learned nothing at all. Unless, of course, you were on their side all along.'

'We never were!' She was angry, so angry her tongue ran away with her. 'Papa was as patriotic an Englishman as any you could name. He would do anything, give his life, to help his country. It is uncivil of you to quiz me about it.'

'I see, you are sworn to secrecy.' Young Buskin tapped the side of his nose and smiled. 'But the war has ended, it does not matter now.'

'No?' she queried, still incensed. 'What about Napoleon's promise to return? Do you think that was an idle boast?'

They were divided on that issue and her question engendered a lively debate in which she took no part. Glad they seemed to have forgotten her, she tried to slip away, only to find herself confronted by a man who had been standing on the edge of the group, listening but saying nothing. He was older than the others, older even than the Duke, shorter than he was, dressed in a dark green coat and buff-coloured pantaloons. He bowed to her. 'I collect, Miss Langford, that you wish to escape. Let me escort you back to Lady Harley.'

He offered his arm, which she ignored. 'Sir, I do not know you.'

'That is only because James has forgot his manners. He should have made me known to you from the start.' He sighed. 'Like you, I am for ever condemned to be the poor relation.'

'We are related?' she queried.

'Indeed we are.' He bowed again. 'Alfred Jessop,

cousin to his Grace and therefore second cousin to you, and your obedient servant.'

'Mr Jessop.' She curtsied. 'I would like to return to Lady Harley, but I am not sure where she is.'

'In the music room, I think, waiting for the entertainment to begin.'

'Then let us go there at once.' She laid her fingers on his sleeve and together they walked out of the stuffy room and into the hall. 'I am surprised Lady Harley did not mention you, Mr Jessop,' she said.

'Oh, she is always loyal to her brother and would stand buff for him whatever the circumstances.'

'That is commendable, surely?'

'Of course. But, Miss Langford, a word of warning. For all his charm, James Dersingham has a black heart. Do not become embroiled with him or you will surely regret it.'

'Mr Jessop, how can you speak to me so? You do not know me—'

'No, but I know the Duke of Belfont. He is an incorrigible rake who gambles with people's lives. The path behind him is littered with broken hearts. Make sure yours is not one of them.'

'Mr Jessop, please do not say any more. His Grace has shown me nothing but kindness and I will not listen.'

He smiled. 'No, you are right. I should not have spoken. Better to let you find out for yourself.' He pushed open the door of the music room where rows of seats had been arranged around the instruments. 'Ah, there is Harriet.' He led the way to where Harriet sat. 'I have returned our little cousin safely to you,' he told her. 'I am afraid she was being pestered by that bantling Buskin and his friends.'

'Alfred, how do you do?' Her ladyship's greeting was cold.

'I do well enough, though I could do better. I see the Duke is in fine form.' He nodded to where James stood surrounded by eager young ladies, his smile a little stiff as he parried their questions. 'Living up to his reputation.'

'As a gentleman,' Harriet said. 'It is a pity you cannot take a leaf from his book.'

He laughed harshly. 'Oh, I shall, my dear cousin, when the time comes, I shall. Now, if you will excuse me, the music is about to begin and I do not care to stay for it.' He bowed and strolled away, leaving Sophie to sink on to a chair beside Harriet with a sigh of relief.

'He said he was your cousin,' Sophie said when he was out of earshot.

'So he is. He is the son of our Aunt Amelia and unfortunately James's heir.'

'You do not like him?'

Harriet laughed. 'He is a toad.'

Sophie turned to look at his retreating back and chuckled. 'Yes, he does remind one of a toad, all green and slimy. But that cannot be the reason you do not like him.'

'No. He and James have never got on, not since childhood, but that doesn't stop him from holding out his hand for largesse, especially when he loses at cards. Unfortunately James's sense of family honour will not allow him to ignore the pleas, though he threatens to do so every time Alfred comes to him to pay his gambling debts.' She paused. 'Enough of him. Have you enjoyed meeting the other young people?'

'Yes, thank you.' She said nothing of her *faux pas*. The young people were only having a little fun and would soon forget what was said. They were, she had realised, the same age as she was, perhaps a year or two younger in years, but infinitely younger in maturity. She need not bother her head about them.

The musicians began tuning their instruments and James excused himself from his admirers and returned to sit beside Sophie. He did not look pleased; in fact, his face was black as thunder. She was tempted to ask what had angered him, but the music began before she could form the words. It was not until they were on their way home in the carriage that she learned the reason for his annoyance.

Chapter Four

The crowds in the streets prevented their coachman from making any speed and they were going at walking pace. 'Fools!' James said, referring to the press of bystanders. The crowds were made up of people from all walks of life, high and low mingling together, standing about to catch a glimpse of someone important, it did not matter who it was. 'Haven't they got homes to go to?'

'James, what has put you into such a bad humour?' Harriet asked. 'You knew when you offered to escort us what the evening would be like.'

'Yes, listening to a crowd of fribbles with nothing better to do than gossip and speculate and Alfred there, drinking it all in.'

She laughed. 'What else did you expect?'

'I expected Miss Langford to have a little more sense.'

'Me?' queried Sophie in surprise. 'What have I done?'

He turned towards her and, though she could not see his expression in the gloom of the coach, she did not need light to tell he was angry; his voice was full of it. 'What in heaven's name possessed you to boast about intelligence gathering?'

'I did not. They assumed—'

'You must have given them good reason. Miss Langford's father was a spy, I heard. He gathered intelligence about Napoleon's intentions and died because of it—'

'I never said that!' she protested.

'You didn't need to, one hint, that's all it takes.'

'You are making something of nothing, your Grace. It was only a little fun. No one took it seriously.'

'No? They took it seriously enough to repeat it. And then you had to imply you knew something of Napoleon's intention to return.'

'I was only repeating hearsay.' She could not understand why a little harmless tattle could make him so annoyed. 'All the way through France we heard it and I cannot believe it has not reached London.'

'Oh, it has, but when someone comes from the source of it, so to speak, and hints they know something others do not, then who can blame the listeners for wondering and perhaps actively trying to find out the truth. It is a dangerous game you are playing, Miss Langford.'

'Oh, that is ridiculous—' She felt Harriet's hand on her arm and stopped in full flow. Growing up as she had, surrounded by adults, and allowed to speak her mind, she had forgotten for a moment her debt to the Duke. And one simply did not argue with him.

'James, do make allowances, please,' Harriet begged him. 'Sophie meant no harm. The war has ended in victory. There is no need to fly into the boughs.'

He allowed the tension to drain from him and sat back in his seat. Perhaps he was being unreasonable. She was simply a foolish girl wanting to make an impression. It was unfortunate that it was the wrong impression. The image he had wanted for her, what he had hoped for, was that she would be accepted as a demure young lady, ready for marriage. He would have found her a husband and settled a dowry on her and thereby discharged his duty to her. He chuckled to himself. There was nothing demure about Miss Sophia Langford. It was only three days since she had turned up on his doorstep in that childlike faded gown, looking as though butter would not melt in her mouth, and already she was disrupting his life.

He had found himself thinking about her in odd moments when he should have been concentrating on something else, trying to imagine what her life must have been like with her dissolute father and feeling sorry for her. No, he corrected himself, not sorry exactly because she did not invite that—in fact, she positively rejected it—but sympathetic, admiring. Yes, it was admiration for her courage in working for a living, not only her own but her father's too, when the man should have been taking care of her, making sure she was brought out and groomed for marriage.

According to Lady Myers, whom he had quizzed about it, Sophie's future was the last thing Lord Langford thought about. She had been allowed to go out alone to conduct tourists round places of interest for money, to see whom she pleased, argue and debate with her father's cronies. 'It amused them to provoke her,' Lady Myers had said. 'And Langford said nothing against it. When I saw what was happening, I was glad her mama was not there to witness it, she would have been mortified.' She had sighed heavily. 'I did try to make him see, I even offered to take the gel under my wing, but that would have meant he had no one to lean on, and I am afraid I was given the right about for my pains.'

Sophie did not know he had learned all this and he would not wound her pride by telling her, but she must be made to see that such behaviour would not do in London, certainly not in polite society. 'I will say no more about it,' he said, conscious he sounded condescending, but how else could he behave? He was head of the family and as such must keep a firm hand on the reins and a cool head. 'But, Sophie, please think carefully before you allow yourself to be drawn into conversations like that again. The war may be over, but we are not out of the woods and, with London full of strangers, I surely do not need to explain that some of them are not friendly towards us.'

'I am sorry to have displeased you,' she said, noticing that he had dropped the formal 'Miss Langford' and was using her given name again. 'But surely the chatter of a group of young people, who are for the most part ignorant, can have no significance?'

'Probably not,' he said, agreeing with her opinion of her listeners. 'I am afraid my position makes me extra careful.'

'I will try to remember that,' she said solemnly. She still did not understand what she had done that was so wrong, but she was learning not to question him too closely. Her instinct told her he was hiding something, something he knew that no one else did, a state secret perhaps. The idea intrigued her. She smiled to herself in the gloom of the carriage; there she was, fantasising about him again. If she kept on like this, she would finish with a complete fictional history for him. It might make a good novel, after she had written her book on her travels in war-torn Europe: the battle-weary hero saving the heroine from a terrible fate at the hands of the villains and declaring his undying love. No, that was going too far; she could not imagine him doing that—it would mean swallowing that stiff-necked pride of his.

What was she smiling about? he asked himself as the carriage passed close to a street lamp and for a brief moment lit the interior. Did she take him for a doddering fool?

If he had any sense he would pack her off to Dersingham Park where she would not embarrass him. But even as he thought it, he began to imagine Belfont House without her in it and realised he would miss her, miss her lively presence, the way she had of making him see the world from her point of view, bringing him down off his high horse. How could that have happened in the space of three days?

His conjecture was brought to a halt when the carriage drew up at Belfont House and the coachman jumped down to open the door and let down the step. James alighted and turned to help his sister down and then turned back to Sophie, offering her his hand. 'Home again, Sophie,' he said, giving her a genuine smile. Her smile in return warmed his heart. She bore no grudge. But was she child or woman?

Home, he had said, Sophie mused, as she went up to her bedroom and closed the door behind her. Home. How good that sounded. Did he really mean she could call it home? But if she did, then she must also subjugate herself to his will, his way of doing things, his idea of correct behaviour. It might be dreadfully boring after the life she had been used to. And had she not made up her mind she would be independent? The sooner that book was written, the better.

Harriet was 'at home' the following afternoon and the drawing room at Belfont House, though large, was full of callers, matrons in silk turbans, wide skirts swishing; young ladies in thin muslins; and dandified young men with starched cravats and collars so high they could hardly turn their heads. They had been coming and going all afternoon, which Harriet assured her young friend was not out of the ordinary.

'They come in the hope that James will put in an appearance and notice them,' Harriet said. 'But you can be sure he will find something to keep him from home. I have asked him how he proposes to find a wife when he refuses to meet prospective brides, but he simply smiles and says, when he decides to marry, he will have no difficulty. That is true, of course; the mamas will fall over themselves to push their daughters in his path, though I am not at all sure the daughters are as keen.'

'They are a little in awe of him, I think.'

'Perhaps, though I could tell them that the last thing he wants is a simpering schoolgirl who dare not say boo to a goose, let alone express an opinion in his presence. They had been brought up to believe young ladies are not supposed to have opinions.' She smiled suddenly. 'You are not in awe of him, are you?'

'Me?' Sophie asked in surprise, then added, 'No, I do not think I am. His bark is worse than his bite, I think. And sometimes I imagine he is lonely. No, not lonely, because he must have many friends, but solitary perhaps. His responsibilities weigh heavy with him. And I have added to them, even though he denies it.'

'Does he? Deny it, I mean.'

'Oh, yes. He said he would not let my presence in the house disrupt his routine.'

Harriet laughed. 'Oh, Sophie, you are a blessing, you really are. I am so glad you came to live with us.'

'Thank you. But I have already annoyed him.'

'Oh, you mean last night. Do not distress yourself over that. I think he was a little jealous that you had so quickly made new friends.'

'Jealous!' Sophie's laughter pealed out. 'Oh, that is beyond everything. It is more likely that he likes to be in control and it was his way of controlling me. I am the poor relation and must fall in line, like a soldier on parade.'

'Oh, no, Sophie—' She stopped in mid-sentence when she noticed the footman ushering in yet more visitors. 'Oh, no,' she repeated, but this time it was not to answer Sophie, but to express dismay.

'Mrs Jessop and Mr Jessop, my lady,' the footman announced.

Sophie recognised the cousin she had met the evening before as he came in and made his bow. Beside him was a white-haired roly-poly figure in widow's weeds, who could only have been his mother.

'Aunt Amelia, how do you do,' Harriet said. 'May I present Miss Sophia Langford?' To Sophie she said. 'Miss Langford, my aunt, Mrs Jessop.'

'So this is the gel, is it?' Mrs Jessop lifted her quizzing glass from where it hung on her ample chest and subjected Sophie to a prolonged inspection. 'Had to come to see for myself, couldn't believe James could be such a ninnyhammer as to give her house room.' It was evident she did not intend addressing Sophie directly.

'Why should he not?' Harriet demanded, a flush of anger spreading across her cheeks, while Sophie stood beside her, too taken aback to ask the question herself. 'He may invite whom he chooses. Sophie is the daughter of Cousin Louise and that makes her one of the family.'

'She is also a Langford. You should know Dersinghams and Langfords never meet, never acknowledge each other's existence.'

'Why not?' This time it was Sophie who spoke and very loudly so that all conversation in the room ceased and everyone turned to look at her. She was too angry to care.

Mrs Jessop turned and looked her up and down and then sniffed loudly before turning back to Harriet. 'Pushing herself forward, making herself the subject of gossip.

I know what she is up to, don't think I don't. Where is my nephew? I need to make my feelings plain.'

'He is not at home,' Harriet said, looking round at the assembled company, knowing that news of the altercation would be on everyone's lips before the day was out. 'If you wish to see him, then you must come another time. Or, better still, write and ask for an appointment. He is a very busy man.' She picked up the bell from the mantel and gave it a vigorous shake, though there was no need to be so energetic, the silence in the room was profound. Everyone was staring, some with mouths open, others smirking, others trying to pretend they had not heard. Sophie was quaking in her shoes. The Duke had said she would not be allowed to disrupt his household and here she was doing it again. It was all her fault, though she did not understand the reason. She would have to leave.

The footman appeared so quickly that everyone knew he had been listening at the door. 'Mrs Jessop and Mr Jessop are leaving, Collins,' Harriet said. 'Please show them out.'

The lady, her black bonnet askew, her face the colour of a squashed raspberry, turned to her son. 'Alfred, are you going to allow me to be spoken to in that manner?'

'Mama, I think you have said enough,' he said, giving Sophie a look she could not interpret. Was it meant to be apologetic, conspiratorial or simply feebleness? 'Let us leave.' He turned to Harriet. 'My apologies, cousin.' He ushered his mother out without speaking to Sophie.

It signalled the end of Harriet's at home. Everyone began making excuses to leave, though many had already been there longer than the customary fifteen minutes; the entertainment had been too good to abandon and now they must be off to the next call to relay what had happened. Harriet knew it and Sophie knew it and she wished herself anywhere but where she was.

* * *

'I am so sorry you had to suffer that,' Sophie said, when they were alone again and enjoying a fresh cup of tea. 'But I know nothing of a feud between the Dersinghams and the Langfords. I knew Mama's grandfather did not approve of my father, but surely that was not enough to cause such a rift that Mrs Jessop could not even speak to me.'

'I think it goes deeper than that, Sophie. I seem to remember when I was a child my governess talking about them being on opposite sides in the Civil War. The Langfords were for the king and the Dersinghams for parliament…'

'But that was over—' she stopped to calculate '—a hundred and seventy years ago! How can anyone hold a grudge for that long?'

'I don't know. I don't remember the details, if I ever knew them. I expect whatever it was had died down until Louise decided she wanted to marry Hugh Langford. Her father was dead and she was brought up by her grandfather, the second Duke. He had been born at the beginning of the 1700s, I do not know the exact year, but his father, the first Duke, would have been in the thick of it.' She paused. 'But it is of no consequence. I am sure it has nothing to do with Aunt Amelia's antagonism towards you. That was simply an excuse because she would not voice her real reason.'

'And what is that?'

'Can you not guess?'

'No.'

'Alfred is James's heir, but if James were to marry and have a son, then Alfred would be bypassed. There is nothing he wants more than to be the next Duke of Belfont and I am persuaded he and his mother will do anything, short of murder, to make sure that doesn't happen. They see you as a threat.'

'Me?' Sophie was astonished and then remembered Mrs Jessop's words: *I know what she is up to, don't think I don't.* Did she think… 'Oh, Harriet, that is ridiculous.'

'They do not think so.'

'But you told me yourself, his Grace could have the pick of every marriageable lady in London, so why should your aunt single me out for her attention?'

Harriet smiled, but decided not to voice what was in her mind, had been in her mind almost from the day Sophie arrived. She was so exactly right for her brother, but it would never do to say so. They would both be embarrassed, deny such a thing was possible, even pretend to dislike each other. James would treat Sophie like a child and she would rebel, because that was her nature. 'Who knows what goes on inside that lady's head?' she said, dismissively.

'Do you think others might have the same notion?' Sophie was worried. Harriet, and even the Duke in the end, had made her welcome, intimated that Belfont House was home, but it could not be, could it? His Grace tolerated her out of a sense of duty, it was no more than that, and to have his name linked with hers by the tattlers was the outside of enough. He would be furious when it reached his ears.

'Who knows? But everyone is used to Aunt Amelia's ambitions for her son. She pushes him forward wherever she can. I could almost feel sorry for him, but I don't because he is a mopstraw.'

'He was firm with her just now.'

'Even he knew she had gone too far and in front of other people too.'

'I think I had better find somewhere else to live. I am

bringing disrepute on you and his Grace, making you the subject of gossip.'

'There is always gossip; James seems to attract it. No doubt it is because of who he is and the fact that he is unmarried. I will not hear of you moving and neither will my brother. Goodness, what sort of people do you think we are to abandon you at the first hurdle? Think no more of it, Sophie, for I shall not.'

Sophie was not at all sure the Duke would agree with his sister, but she subsided into silence. It was all very well to say she must move, but where could she go? The only other people she knew in London were Lord and Lady Myers and she could not throw herself upon them again. There was always her uncle, Lord Langford, but he had made his feelings very clear and she supposed he also knew about the feud between the Langfords and the Dersinghams and that might have been his true reason for rejecting her. If she had not been so worried, she might have been more curious about it. As it was she excused herself and went to her room to make a determined effort to start on her book.

She sat at the desk and spread out her notes, checking one or two details, then she drew forward a clean sheet of paper and picked up her pen. It was a moment or two before the words began to flow, but once started they carried her along with them.

Three hours later, when Janet came to tell her it was time to dress for supper, she found her neck was stiff and her fingers curled up with holding the pen; it was a minute or so before she could massage them into moving properly. Janet helped her to change into a simple blue gown and arranged her hair, then she went downstairs, shaking in her shoes at the prospect of meeting the Duke again. But he was not there; she and Harriet were to dine alone.

'James often stays at Carlton House overnight if the Regent keeps him late,' Harriet said as they took their places at the table in the small dining room. 'And in the last few weeks that has happened more and more often. Next month the Tsar is paying a state visit and his Highness is determined to entertain his guest lavishly, which means James must become involved in the arrangements. No matter, we shall have a comfortable coze on our own and make plans for the rest of the Season. There are routs and picnics and several balls we could go to. In fact, I am determined to give a ball myself. It will be your come-out—'

'Oh, please do not go to the trouble,' Sophie said, worried about the cost. 'I do not need to be brought out.' She gave a cracked laugh. 'I feel as though I have been out for years already.'

'That is not the same. Sophie, dear, you missed out on so much when you had to take over the housekeeping for your papa and I want to make it up to you.'

'You are very kind and I am truly grateful for your friendship and for being allowed to stay here. It is enough.'

'You may think so, but you may be sure the *ton* won't see it like that. The Duke of Belfont is known to have very deep pockets and if he cannot give a cousin who has no other kin a good home and all the advantages she would have had if—' She stopped suddenly, realising she was about to criticise Sophie's father.

Sophie laughed. 'If the Dersinghams and the Langfords had not been on opposite sides in the war between king and parliament.'

'Yes,' Harriet agreed, though that was not what she had been thinking. Her mind had been on Hugh Langford's gambling. That had been the reason the family had gone abroad, why Sophie had missed having a Season, why she had been forced to grow up too quickly. Sophie knew that as well as she did. 'So, for James's sake, let me have my way on this.'

'He might not agree.'

'I promise you he will.'

As soon as the meal was finished they retired to Harriet's sitting room where she fetched out a pile of invitations. 'Now, let us make up our minds which of these to accept.'

James had been working very late at Carlton House. The Regent was having a suite of rooms made ready for the state visit of the Tsar, whom he particularly wished to impress, and James had been made responsible for his security, which meant overseeing the workmen and delivery men and checking every new item brought into the house and everything leaving it. And then he had to attend the unending receptions. He hated it. The Regent could be charming when he chose, but he could also be difficult. He would quarrel with his friends, flirt with their wives, behave abominably towards his own wife and play the heavy-handed father with his daughter, while at the same time pretending great affability to those currently in favour. Unfortunately James was one of those. If he could find an acceptable excuse for resigning, he would do so, but so far every reason he had put forward had been dismissed as of no account.

It was three in the morning before he was allowed to go and normally he would have sought out the bed he had not far from the Regent's own apartments, but tonight he felt he had to get away from the stifling atmosphere, the false *bonhomie*, the fawning sycophants, among whom

Alfred and Ellen were prominent, and so he decided to walk home and sleep in his own bed and breakfast with Harriet and Sophie. At least they were sane!

Sophie. She was unique, an intelligent young lady who did not simper and giggle, who did not agree with every word he said simply because he had said it. Not that he would agree she was right, but it was a refreshing change to have an argument. He smiled as he let himself in the front door, waking the night footman who slept in his chair beside it. The man scrambled to his feet in a fluster at not being alert to the need to open the door, but James merely smiled and bade him goodnight as he passed him. It was unreasonable to expect a man to sit and do nothing and not fall asleep and he would not censure him for it, but if he were to catch him asleep when there were guests or strangers in the house, woe betide him.

He paused at the top of the stairs, before turning towards his own suite of rooms. The house was silent, but he could see a slit of light under Sophie's door. Surely she was not still awake? He moved towards it and stood outside. Not a sound. He should have gone on, but instead he turned the handle and gently pushed the door ajar, looking towards the bed. He knew it was a shameful thing to do, but he did not seem able to walk away. He was only making sure she was all right, he told himself, that she hadn't fallen asleep and left the candle burning because that could be dangerous and he would enjoy telling her so.

The candle on the chest beside the bed was down almost to a stub, but she was not in bed. He pushed the door open a little further and looked round the room. She was not there. He crossed to the open door of the connecting room. She was sitting at the desk, her head on her arms, her hair spread about her, fast asleep. A quill had dropped from her right hand and splashed ink over the sheet of paper she had been writing on. A lamp burned at her elbow. He trod softly over the carpet to stand beside her. She did not wake. 'Come, little one,' he murmured, gently picking her up. 'Time for bed.'

She was light as thistledown. He looked down at her, cradled against his chest, her hair falling loose, her lips slightly parted as if she were about to say something, but she was still asleep, did not know who held her. If she was dreaming, it was a pleasant dream, for a half-smile played about her mouth. She was wearing a nightgown and a thin robe that did little to disguise her figure. He should not have been looking at it, but he could not help himself and a wry grin spread across his features. To think that he had thought she was a child at first, and, even when he realised she was not, had still imagined her as a chit not long out of the schoolroom. How wrong he had been. He had a woman in his arms, a very beautiful and desirable woman. He felt his loins stirring. He had to get out of there before he disgraced himself.

He put her on the bed and covered her before bending down and lightly touching his lips to her forehead. She smiled, her eyes flickered, but she did not wake. He blew out the candle, turned and crossed the room to put out the lamp, then he left, closely the door gently behind him.

Sophie was having such a pleasant dream she did not want to wake up. She was being held in someone's arms, someone strong, someone who made her feel safe and loved. She had not felt like that since she was a little girl, before Papa had ruined them with his gambling, before Mama had died, before she had assumed the mantle of breadwinner. But that was in the past; she did not need to struggle now, because whoever held her would protect her. She dreamed on, savouring the feeling of being warm and comfortable.

* * *

She woke only when Janet came in with hot chocolate and warm water to wash. The euphoria lasted while she sipped her drink and dressed herself. Who had been the man in her dream? After saying goodnight to Harriet, she had prepared for bed, but then, thinking of something she wanted to add to her notes, had returned to the desk. How long had she worked? She could not remember stopping and getting into bed. She must have been so tired, she had done it half-asleep. But her dream was so vivid. Of being cradled in someone's arms, of a gentle masculine voice. She was being foolish, she told herself. No one had come into her room in the night—she would have been awake in an instant.

She went downstairs to find Harriet and James already seated. He was dressed in a brown riding coat of Bath cloth, a yellow-and-white-striped waistcoat and a plain neckcloth. He rose politely as she entered and she noticed well-fitting buckskin breeches and highly polished boots. Harriet was in an undress robe of green silk. Sophie bade them good morning and went to the sideboard to help herself to bread and butter. She rarely ate more than that before midday.

'Did you sleep well?' Harriet asked her, pouring her a cup of coffee from the pot at her elbow.

'Very well,' she said. 'I had such a strange dream…'

'A nightmare? Something frightened you?'

'No, nothing like that. I felt so easy, comfortable and protected. Someone was holding me. It must have been my father. I know I felt safe.' She stopped suddenly when she heard the Duke gave a quick grunt, as if he did not believe her. 'There is no call for you to be so disparaging,' she said hotly. 'He was a very kind papa until his affliction got the better of him.'

Affliction! James longed to tell her the truth, to denounce her father as a wastrel and toadeater, who cared little for his daughter, but he could neither destroy her illusions about her father, nor admit that he had been in her bedchamber in the middle of the night and carried her in his arms. It had been a despicable thing to do. 'Of course,' he said. 'If I sounded disparaging, then I beg your pardon.'

'I have been talking to James about our ball,' Harriet said, quick to intervene. 'And he agrees you should have a come-out.'

'Do you?' she asked him. 'Or have you been bullocked into it?'

He laughed. 'Do you think me so weak that I let a woman bullock me into anything?'

'I think you are very fond of your sister and would do anything to please her.'

'So I would, but I would draw the line at going against my own better judgement. On this occasion, I think she is right. If you are given a come-out and introduced into Society in the accepted manner, then I do not doubt you will take. A husband is what you need.' Even as he spoke, he realised that if some young buck offered for her and she accepted, he would not be happy about it. He did not want to her to leave his protection for someone else's. He pulled himself up short. Whatever was he thinking? He had made himself her guardian and one did not have wayward thoughts and feelings for those one is supposed to protect.

'I am not looking for a husband,' she said, annoyance making her cheeks flush. 'I have vowed never to marry.'

'Oh, Sophie, you are too young to make vows like that,' Harriet said, reaching out and putting a hand on her arm. 'And giving you a ball does not mean that we expect you to accept the first offer that is made. Do we, James?'

He smiled. Sophie angry, Sophie with that heightened

colour and those brown eyes flashing amber fire was the most beautiful thing he had ever seen, with the exception of Sophie asleep in his arms, soft and pliant. 'No, we do not. Sophie, you will have your come-out ball, and if you do not receive a dozen offers I shall be surprised, but whether you accept one of them or not will be your decision. I do not believe in pushing unwilling girls into marriage.'

'But you would be glad to be rid of me. I am an embarrassment to you.'

'When have I said that?'

'You do not need to. I know it. Yesterday—'

'I have told James about our aunt's visit,' Harriet said. 'He agrees with me that she has simply made herself look foolish and giving you this ball will make everyone realise that her suspicions are groundless.'

'Especially if I accept an offer of marriage,' she said bitterly. 'But who would want to marry me, unless…?' She glanced across at the Duke, who was looking uncomfortable. She had hit the nail on the head! 'Unless you paid him to.' Her eyes filled with tears, but she scrubbed angrily at them with the back of her hand. She would not cry. She had ceased being a watering pot when her mama died. 'I will leave at once.' She pushed back her chair and almost ran from the room.

He rose and followed her. She was clambering up the stairs, falling over her dress in her haste. 'Wait, you foolish child. I want to talk to you.' She ignored him and he took the stairs two at a time to catch up with her before she reached her room. She had her hand on the doorknob, ready to open it, when he covered it with his own. 'Sophie, why must you fly into the boughs over every little thing? I never met such an independent article in my whole life.'

She ignored the warmth of his hand on hers, though it was having a very strange effect on her body. She was curling up inside, growing warm and moist, wanting to snatch her hand away and at the same time fling her arms about his neck and beg him to hold her close. She felt as if she was drowning and that the only thing keeping her above water was her anger. 'I am independent because I have had to be,' she said. Even as she spoke she remembered her dream, the feeling of being loved and protected. That was not the dream of an independent woman, nor even of one who wished to be. It was the dream of someone who longed to be loved, a manifestation of her true feelings.

'I know,' he said softly, and she heard again the gentle voice of her dream. So that was it! In her dream he had been her hero, her protector, and that could only be because he had been kind to her and offered her a home. Her unconscious self had made it seem like reality. 'I understand,' he went on, watching her expression change, the puzzlement and then the enlightenment in her eyes as they lit up and then darkened; she had the most expressive eyes of anyone he knew. But he still could not tell what was going on in her head. 'Be assured, nothing on earth would induce me to pay someone to marry you. Nothing. If you find someone you wish to marry, then I will give you my blessing and a small dowry.' He stopped, putting a finger on her lips, silencing the protest she had on her tongue. 'Oh, not so much as to attract fortune-hunters, but enough so that you may pick and choose. Do you understand?'

She nodded, knowing with a sudden insight into her own heart that the only person she would ever wish to marry was the Duke of Belfont himself. It was a revelation that shook her to the core, but one she must never acknowledge, not even to herself, because it was plain as day he wanted to be rid of her. 'Thank you.' It was a whisper.

'Do you ride?' he asked suddenly, making her realise that as far as he was concerned that was the end of the matter. He would have his own way and she wondered why she had ever doubted that he would.

'I did when I was young.' She stopped when she saw his mouth curl in a wide grin. 'Why are you laughing?'

'Sophie, you talk like a grandmother. When I was young, indeed! How old are you?'

'One and twenty.'

'Then what do you call young? When were you last on a horse?'

'When we lived in Austria. They have beautiful horses there and some wonderful places to ride.'

'Hyde Park will be a little dull after that, I think, but, if you would care to, I will take you riding in the park. Do you have a habit?'

'Yes. Harriet insisted on buying me one. I told her it was not in the least necessary, but she would not listen.'

'Good for Harriet. How long will it take you to change?'

'What, now?'

'Yes, now.'

'I have no mount.'

He laughed. 'I have a stable full. Why do you think Harriet wanted you to have the habit?'

She gave a delighted laugh. 'Then I shall be ready in twenty minutes.'

'Make it fifteen. I will be waiting in the hall.'

She rushed into her room and pulled out the new habit. It was in a dark blue kerseymere, cut like a military tunic and frogged in silver. The matching skirt was plain and fell in soft folds about her booted feet. The hat was a black beaver with a high crown and a stiff brim swathed in blue satin ribbon.

* * *

Inside fifteen minutes she was stepping out of the front door, the skirt over one arm so that she did not trip over it, and his hand under her elbow.

On the street a groom stood holding two horses, one a huge black stallion and the other a small bay mare. 'This is Hotspur,' James said, indicating the stallion. He nodded towards the mare. 'And that little beauty is Amber.'

The groom held his cupped hands to help her mount while James jumped lithely into his own saddle. They walked the horses to the park. It was wonderful to be in the saddle again after so long. She remembered as a ten-year-old riding beside her parents at their country home, happy and unaware of the shadow that hung over them. But within a year, the horses were gone and most of the servants.

Her mother had tried to keep the truth from her, but she had known there was something wrong. She had heard raised voices and Mama cried a lot and then they had left England for France. 'A little holiday,' Mama had said. At first she had believed it; she did not go short of food or clothes and they went out and about with other expatriates, but when there was no sign of them returning home, Sophie had begun to realise that they could not return. Oh, Papa was sometimes in funds and, when he was, the life they led was fun. Riding in Austria had been the last time her mother had been anything like happy. After that matters went from bad to worse and they didn't go riding any more.

'You are quiet, Sophie,' he said as they turned to go into the park and were able to ride side by side. 'What were you thinking of?'

'Oh, nothing,' she said airily. 'I am enjoying the ride.'

'Good.' He turned to look at her. She had a natural

grace, a straight back and a good seat. She had been well taught. And that habit was magnificent. Harriet had given him an account of everything she had bought, even though he had told her there was no need to stint. If he was going to set himself up as Sophie's guardian, he did not want people to think he was a pinch-penny, he had told his sister. He did not want to be ashamed of her as he had been when she had first entered his drawing room in that dowdy lilac dress she must have had two or three years. He was not ashamed of her—he was proud of her. Proud as a peacock! He smiled at his own foolishness.

'Your Grace, we are well met,' called a familiar voice, forcing him out of his reverie.

Ellen was riding towards them, accompanied by Alfred. He cursed under his breath, but doffed his hat as they drew level and pulled up. 'Lady Colway. Alfred.'

'James.' Alfred bowed his head. 'Miss Langford.'

Sophie inclined her head, watching him, wondering if he were about to make another scene, but he seemed content to stay in the lady's shadow. She was magnificent, from the long feather curling round the brim of her hat, down to the mulberry velvet riding coat and spreading habit, to her polished boots and the harness of the white-socked bay she rode.

'So this is the chit, is it?' she said, as she eyed Sophie up and down.

'Lady Colway,' he said, though there was little warmth in his voice. 'May I present my cousin and ward, Miss Sophie Langford.'

'How do you do, Miss Langford,' her ladyship said, smiling as if she were enjoying a private joke. Sophie did not like that smile; there was something tigerish about it. 'We are well met. James, do bring your little cousin to my next rout. Wednesday, eight o'clock.'

'I am afraid we shall be otherwise occupied,' he said coldly. 'Good day to you, my lady. Alfred. Come, Sophie.'

He walked his horse on and Sophie had perforce to follow. She heard the woman chuckle behind her. 'Afraid I will tell her a few home truths, are you, James?'

'What does she mean?' she asked him.

'I have no idea.'

She knew he did, but his face was set and she was wise enough not to press him. But she was curious. What home truths? Something not to the Duke's credit, she guessed. A love affair, perhaps. Why did that idea make her want to weep? He was thirty-four years old and it was inconceivable that he had never had a mistress; there had probably been more than one. Alfred had hinted as much when he had warned her off. Was there more to it than that? Why had the sun suddenly gone behind a cloud and spoiled her day?

Chapter Five

At the beginning of June, Tsar Alexander, Prince Platoff, King Frederick of Prussia, Prince Metternich of Austria and Marshal Blücher, all arrived in London with their respective entourages for three weeks of celebrations. In the absence of Wellington, who was still in France, Blücher, the allied commander who had taken Paris, had become the people's hero and was cheered wherever he went, much to the chagrin of the Regent, who was more likely to be jeered. To make matters worse, the Tsar angered the Regent when he insisted on staying at the Pulteney Hotel with his sister, the Grand Duchess, instead of at Carlton House. It made James's task of protecting the royal visitors even more difficult. Because he was so busy Sophie saw little of him; he came home sometimes, but only to change his linen or pick up his correspondence. Occasionally he managed to take nuncheon with them, but he did not stay longer than to ask her how she did, to which she always replied, 'Very well, your Grace.'

She spent the rest of her time writing or going out and about with Harriet, being introduced to other young people, most of whom viewed her as some kind of exotic animal who had been captured and brought to the confining atmosphere of London in the Season to see how she would behave in civilised company. For the most part she behaved very properly, but occasionally when her inquisitors were being particularly puerile, she could not help saying or doing something outrageous.

On one occasion, they attended a soirée being given by Mrs Jefferson, a friend of Harriet, whose daughter, Ariadne, was enjoying her first Season. Theodore Buskin, another of the guests, had been boasting all evening of his exploits: he had met one of Frederick's aides while out hunting and the man had been excessively polite to him; he had been sparring with Gentleman Jackson, who had said he was a natural; he had danced a waltz with the Tsar's sister's lady in waiting at Almack's and the Grand Duchess, who had been watching proceedings, had bowed towards him.

'I am sure her Highness can never have seen such an elegant dancer in Russia,' Peter Poundell said. He was a thin youth, whose cravat was so high and stiff his chin was perpetually in the air. 'Unless it be a bear.'

Everyone laughed and Theodore's face turned bright pink. Sophie felt sorry for him, even though she thought he was something of a macaroni. 'I believe Russia is renowned for its dancers,' she said, smiling at him. 'You would be in good company.'

'Have you been to Russia?' he asked, glowing with gratitude for her support.

'No, Russia was never on our itinerary.'

'But you have travelled a great deal, have you not?'

'Indeed, I have. Most of my life has been spent travelling.'

'Oh, how I envy you.' Dorothy Fidgett, who had come out the year before, but had not been lucky enough to secure a husband on account of a pronounced squint, sighed heavily. 'If one must stay single, then I would rather it was because one was doing something exciting.'

'It was not always exciting. Sometimes I longed to be settled.'

'Did you not have offers?'

'Not any I would seriously consider. There was one from an artist and another from an Italian count, but I rejected them both.'

'A count! Why? Was he low in the stirrups? Or old? Or ugly?'

'Not at all. I simply did not like him enough to link my life to his.' She did not add that it was her father who had arranged for them to meet and he had been particularly annoyed when he learned she had rejected the offer.

'What did he say when you rejected him? Did he swear undying love? Did he go into a decline?' Ariadne asked.

'No. He left for France and I never saw him again.'

'Oh, how romantic. London must seem very dull after that.'

'Not at all. There are so many interesting people to meet and things to see, especially now.'

'And do you think you will find a husband this Season?'

'I am not looking for one. Marriage does not interest me.'

'How can you say that?' Ariadne asked. 'Every young lady needs a husband or how is she to go on?' She was a pretty girl who did not have a serious thought in her head. Sophie wondered if the Duke might be attracted to someone like that, someone compliant, who would be decorative and cause no contention. Somehow she did not think so, but even thinking about the Duke marrying gave her a heaviness around the heart that she would not allow herself to dwell upon.

'Not me. I had as lief remain single and earn my own living.'

'Good heavens!' Theodore exclaimed. 'How will you do that?'

'I am writing a book of my travels, the interesting things I have seen, the beautiful scenery and buildings and the people I have met. You would be surprised at the strange characters I came across. So, you see, I will be too busy to think about a husband.'

'The Duke will never allow it.'

'The Duke does not rule me.'

'He is known to be looking for a wife…' Ariadne said with a heavy sigh.

'Then I wish him happy,' she said, determined to squash any rumours that might be circulating. It would be mortifying if they thought she was heartbroken when he decided to marry someone else. 'I shall write my book.'

'And will your count be in it?'

'Naturally he will, along with dozens more, high and low, though I shall not name names.'

'Oh, scandalous doings in the courts of Europe,' Peter Poundell said with a laugh. 'I shall look forward to reading it.'

The conversation was interrupted by the arrival of none other than the Duke himself. He stood in the doorway, surveying the assembled company, while their hostess left Harriet, with whom she had been conversing, and hurried forward to greet him. 'Your Grace, you honour us…'

He bowed and smiled, noticing Sophie in the centre of a group of young people. They were fashionably dressed, perfectly acceptable in society, but Sophie stood out like a flame. He did not know why. She was dressed in a pale lemon gown trimmed with matching silk roses round the high waist and down the centre of the front. Perhaps it was its simplicity, contrasting with the fuss and frills of the other ladies, or the straight-backed way she held herself, perhaps it was her perfect complexion or the smile she gave him, which warmed his heart. 'I came to bear my sister and ward company on the way home. The streets are swarming with people chasing all over town for a glimpse of some important personage. I was cheered to the echo though I am certain they had no idea who I was.'

Sophie did not think it at all surprising he should have been mistaken for a visiting royal. He was so particular in his dress, which, though not flamboyant, was certainly outstanding. The cut of his plum-coloured velvet coat, the precision of his cravat, the jewelled fob that hung across his brocade waistcoat, the studied casualness of his hairstyle spoke of wealth, but most of all it was his bearing that made him stand out. It was not pride exactly, but self-assurance, giving him an air of importance, of one used to command and of having his commands obeyed.

'Oh, are you come to take Miss Langford away, your Grace?' Theodore asked, as Harriet crossed the room to join them. 'We were having such an interesting conversation.'

'Miss Langford has been telling us she is writing a book,' Peter added, in a way which she could only describe as mischievous. 'And we are all agog to know who will be in it.'

The Duke looked at Sophie, and although his smile remained fixed, something in his blue eyes told her he was displeased, but she could hardly explain that the reason she had mentioned the book was because they had been quizzing her about her relationship with him and she needed to divert them. 'It was only a passing mention,' she said. 'Everyone has been so kind as to be interested in my travels.'

'Indeed.' The one word was enough to reinforce her conviction she was going to be roasted over it.

'Miss Langford has turned down an offer from a Italian count,' Ariadne put in, making Sophie groan inwardly. 'And he went off to fight for France because of her rejection.'

'I never said that,' Sophie protested. 'I simply said he went to France. His reason for going had nothing to do with me.'

The young people about them looked at each other in perplexity. Perhaps Miss Langford had been humming all along and the Duke knew it. Or perhaps he had a more personal reason for wishing to silence her. Either way they were intrigued.

'I am afraid you will have to remain in ignorance, at least for now,' he said, smiling easily at them. 'I would like to have Lady Harley and Miss Langford safely home before everyone starts leaving their routs and balls and theatre visits and the roads become even more congested as they chase about town to catch a glimpse of this or that royal personage. I fear London has gone quite mad.'

'Then I propose to go mad along with them,' Peter said. 'Shall you join me, Buskin?'

Theodore agreed with alacrity and the two young men, with others who had been on the periphery of the group, set off 'emperor hunting', leaving Harriet and Sophie to take leave of their hostess and accompany the Duke to his carriage.

Surprisingly, the Duke said nothing about Sophie's book; in fact, he hardly addressed her at all, confining himself to speaking to his sister about their forthcoming engagements.

'Lady Myers has invited us to a ball next week,' Harriet told him. 'I know Sophie is not officially out, but I do not think that signifies, considering she was used to attending such functions with her ladyship in Naples. I can see no harm in her going and it promises to be a grand occasion because Lord Myers is well known to so many of our foreign visitors. Shall you go?'

'If my duties allow, then I shall certainly escort you.'

'Good,' she said, much relieved. 'A whole evening in the company of Cousin Alfred and his mother would be the outside of enough.'

'From that I collect he has offered himself as your escort?'

'Yes. I told him I thought you would be going, but then he said we could make up a little party. What could I say but that we should look forward to seeing him there?'

'After the scene his mother made in front of your friends, I wonder he has the effrontery to suggest it,' Sophie said. 'And if he speaks to me, I shall certainly tell him so.'

'You will not,' James put in. 'You will keep your tongue between your teeth and smile.'

She chuckled. 'That might be a little difficult, your Grace.'

'Nevertheless, you…' He stopped suddenly when he realised she had been teasing. 'Oh, Sophie, what am I going to do with you?'

'Nothing, my lord, above what you are doing already, giving me a home and allowing me space and time to write.'

Was that all she wanted from him? he asked himself. Had the few weeks she had been living at Belfont House not made her realise there was more to life than that? Was she sincere in her determination not to marry? Or was she deluding herself?

'Sophie,' Harriet put in, 'Alfred knew his mother had gone too far and has written to apologise for her behaviour and I do not want to cause more gossip by cutting him. I am not asking you to be more than polite.'

'Very well, I shall be excessively polite. One can often achieve more in that way than in heated exchange, and keep one's dignity into the bargain, don't you think so?'

'Indeed I do.'

'Does that mean you will have to invite him to your ball?'

'Your ball, Sophie. It is being given in your honour, but, yes, he will be sent an invitation.'

'And Lady Colway?'

'Certainly not!' James snapped.

'What a pity,' she said with a sigh. 'I was looking forward to being excessively polite to her too.'

He laughed, but in truth the subject was becoming a little too embarrassing and he quickly changed the subject by asking Harriet when she proposed to hold their own ball.

'I think as soon as it can be arranged, don't you? Then Sophie can accept whatever invitations she chooses. There is so much going on, what with the official celebrations, we need to give people plenty of notice or they might find themselves too busy. Of course, if I can prevail upon someone very important to attend, they will drop everything to come.'

He laughed. 'Am I not important enough?'

'You know I meant one of our eminent foreign visitors.'

'Like the Tsar? Or the Grand Duchess?' he queried, teasing. 'Blücher, perhaps, though he told me he is sick to death of being pursued and cannot even dine in privacy; his hostesses sell tickets for people to stand on their stairs and watch him going into the dining room.'

Sophie's laughter pealed out. 'Oh, they never do! You have the right of it, my lord, London has gone quite mad. But I beg you not to go to such lengths. If you insist on having a ball for me, then let it be a quiet one with a few select guests…'

'Nothing would please me more,' Harriet said, 'but I doubt it will be possible. The Duke is too well known and we have been invited everywhere; everyone will expect a return invitation. Besides, you have become a person of interest in your own right and those of our friends who have not already been introduced will want to meet you.'

'I wish that were not so,' Sophie said.

'How can that be?' James queried. 'Everything you have said and done so far invites attention. Talking about writing a book and having offers from counts…'

'It was no more than the truth. I am writing a book. Harriet will tell you I spend many hours in my room working on it. And Count Cariotti really did offer for me.'

Where had he heard the name before? He racked his brain, but could not bring the occasion to mind. Had the man been in England? Had he met him here? Or had he met him in Europe when he had been incognito? How important was it to remember?

'Then, you must have known the Count very well.' It sounded like a casual remark, but Sophie had long since discovered the Duke rarely did anything casually.

'No, I did not. He was Papa's friend, not mine. Papa had many friends of all nationalities.'

'I am sure he had,' he said, leaning back in his seat again. Drinking and gambling companions, he decided, not true friends, men who could turn from friend to enemy in the blink of an eye. He sighed, asking himself what he had done to deserve being saddled with this spirited young lady who attracted attention wherever she went. Even the Regent had heard of her and asked about her. He had begun to wish she was the dowdy schoolgirl he had first taken her for, then she would have passed unnoticed. 'But you are not in Italy now, where intrigue is a way of life. This is London, England, and I am on the Regent's staff.'

'Your Grace, I would not for the world embarrass you. In future I will be the model of maidenly virtue. And if anyone should ask about my book or my lovers, I shall deny all knowledge of them. And I shall be *excessively* polite to everyone.'

It was a statement that made him laugh and she found her own mouth twitching. He might be severe, might act the heavy-handed patriarch, but he could be soft when he chose and he had a wonderful sense of humour. For that alone she could forgive his other foibles.

Their coachman had managed to find a way through the press of people, mainly by cracking his whip left and right and shouting, 'Make way for his Grace, the Duke of Belfont', and now they drew up at the door of Belfont House and James escorted them inside.

He was not at all sure he wanted Sophie to be a model of maidenly virtue, certainly not like the empty-headed Ariadne Jefferson, who believed agreeing with everything he said in little more than a whisper would entice him to offer for her. Being married to Ariadne, or any of this year's débutantes, would drive him insane with boredom. His friends naturally reminded him he could always keep his mistress, that the roles of each were different. A wife was for creating a family, for having his household looked after, for being decorative at official functions; a mistress was for love, for entertainment, for relief from the cares of everyday living. He knew that for most men of his acquaintance the arrangement worked perfectly satisfactorily, but he did not want that.

He wanted wife and lover in one person and that was his difficulty; he had never found one that measured up to his exacting standards. Certainly, Sophie Langford did not. She was beautiful, she was lively and amusing, but she was also independent, outspoken, argumentative. And she was dangerous, like one of Congreve's unpredictable rockets, which often landed on friend as well as the foe. So, why did he find himself thinking of her so frequently, having imaginary conversations with her, even making love to her? That had shocked him enough to make him stay away from home until the torment of not seeing her got the better of him and he went out of his way to seek her out, as he had done tonight. And what had he done as soon as he saw her? He had chastised her, found fault, accused her of jeopardising his position at court, as if he cared a groat for that!

He said goodnight to both ladies and watched them as they climbed the stairs, then he turned and went into the book room, where he poured himself a glass of cognac and sat at his desk to study some papers until the inexplicable disquiet he felt subsided and he could go to bed and sleep. He read until his eyes ached, some of it dry reports about his work, and in the end he cast the sheets of paper to one side and sat, sipping his cognac and allowing his thoughts to roam.

He was back in Dresden in 1812, when Napoleon was planning his campaign against Russia and his troops were gathering from all over Europe to begin the march, including the Italian army whose route took them across the Alps into Austria. Was Cariotti among those? Napoleon had come to Dresden to meet the Emperor and Empress of Austria, the parents of his second wife, and was greeted with flags flying and bands playing. Prince Metternich, the Austrian foreign minister, was known to have doubts about the wisdom of allying himself with Bonaparte, but he set them aside as princes, dukes and counts, with their wives and retinues, enjoyed banquets and receptions, attended mass in the cathedral and went hunting in the royal forests.

James was among them, pretending to be Jack Costerman, half-French, half-English, whose loyalty, so he maintained, was most decidedly on the side of his French mother. He had infiltrated the French high command and was trusted with secrets that no other agent had been able to discover, all of it relayed to Richard Summers by way of a network of contacts. Where was Sophie then? Where was her father? Could he possibly have been seen and recognised by him? But Langford was dead, so did it matter any more?

It might, he told himself. With all the foreign dignitaries in London, nothing decided about post-war settlements, and Napoleon Bonaparte, supposedly defeated but living on Elba, too close to France for comfort, anything could happen. Then he would be needed again and if his cover were broken... 'Oh, Sophie, Sophie,' he murmured. 'Was it fate that brought you to my door? Or something more sinister?'

When he finally climbed the stairs he could not resist turning towards her door, remembering the last time he had done that. It had been his undoing; he had discovered an aching need to make love to her that he could not possibly assuage and still keep his honour. Again there was a light under her door and, before he could stop himself, he had taken the two or three steps needed and knocked lightly, not really expecting a response.

He was taken aback when the door was opened and she stood facing him with the lamplight behind her. She had taken off her evening gown and was wearing a flowing undress robe of blue silk. Her hair had been unpinned and cascaded down over her shoulders.

'Your Grace, what is wrong?'

'Nothing.' The sight of her set his pulses racing. He felt an almost irresistible urge to reach out and touch the curl that hung beside her cheek and wind it round his finger to draw her towards him so that he could kiss her. The effort not to do so was so great he clenched his fists by his sides and forced himself speak normally. 'I thought you might have gone to sleep again with the lamp burning.'

'No, I was not sleeping. I was working on my book.'

'That damned book!' he exclaimed. 'You will ruin your health over it. Now go to bed or you will not be fit for anything tomorrow.'

'Then I shall sleep in. You may call it a damned book, but to me it is a lifeline.'

'I never heard such balderdash. There is no necessity for you to work at all. I have offered you a home—'

'For which I am grateful, but that cannot go on for ever.'

'Why not?'

'Your Grace, you will marry one day. Your wife cannot be expected to house a poor relation unless it be as a servant—'

'Servant?' His voice was scornful. 'You would be no good as a servant, I can assure you of that.'

'There you are then! I must become independent.'

'Fustian! You will marry yourself. Already you have admirers…'

'Admirers? Do you mean Theodore Buskin and Peter Poundell? I would have to be desperate to consider either of those. They would be worse than the Count, who at least knew how to dress elegantly and amuse a lady.'

'Then if you are so particular I will find others. I will introduce you to the whole of London—'

'Are you so desperate to be rid of me?' she asked.

'No, damn you!' His voice was a hoarse whisper. 'I want you here where you belong.'

She was taken aback by his vehemence, but quickly recovered herself. 'Do you think that being a Duke means you may speak to me in terms you would not use to your lowliest menial?' she asked coolly.

'I ask pardon for that,' he said, genuinely sorry for his outburst. 'But you are driving me to distraction.'

'Why?'

'Why?' he repeated, wondering himself. Could what she said and did affect him so badly he so far forgot himself as to use language he ought never to utter in a lady's presence? He felt himself losing control, and always being in control was something on which he prided himself. Was he afraid for her or for himself? 'Because you seem unable to grasp the rudiments of life as part of my household—'

'Household, my lord? But you have just said I would never make a servant.'

'I meant my family and you know it. As one of the family, you should conduct yourself in a way that does not bring notoriety to the family name. And telling the world you are writing a book because I am too penny-pinching to accommodate you is hardly the way to go on.'

'I never said that! Why does everyone twist what I say? I am becoming afraid to open my mouth at all.'

'Then pray keep it shut.'

She glared at him, her eyes defiantly bright, her mouth half-open, as if she had been going to add something and then decided against it. He reached out and put a finger under her chin, lifting it gently to close her mouth. Then, before he could stop himself, he had drawn her towards him and was kissing her. He felt her go rigid with shock; though he knew he ought to apologise and withdraw, he could not. The taste of her lips was exquisitely sensuous; it aroused him in a way no other woman's lips ever had.

He wanted to crush her to him, to carry her over to the bed so invitingly empty behind her, to possess her totally. And as the kiss deepened, he felt her relax. She was no longer rigid, but compliant. Her arms had come round his neck, her fingers were tangling in his hair. It did more than any resistance or anger on her part to make him realise what he was doing was totally reprehensible. He let her go and stepped back.

His move was so abrupt, the withdrawal of his supporting arms so sudden, she felt her knees giving way. Fearing she was about to swoon, he reached out and grabbed her, holding her upright against his body to stop her from falling. The feel of her soft curves under the flowing robe set his senses reeling all over again. His body betrayed him and surely she must know it? But how could he release her? He never wanted to let her go. Was that why he had been so adamant she must give up her determination to be independent, because he wanted her, desired her, loved her? Good God! Could that be true? But if it was, he had ruined it by his disgraceful behaviour. A gentleman would immediately apologise and offer marriage, and he had always considered himself a gentleman. He had never in his life forced himself upon a woman; most of those he had bedded had been only too pleased to oblige him. Sophie was different, so different she would hurl his proposal back in his face. He leaned back to look at her.

Her face was charmingly pink and her eyes, though bright, had lost their anger, replaced with perplexity. He smiled crookedly. 'Sophie, I am sorry. It came to me suddenly as a way of silencing you and I could not resist the temptation.' As an apology it left a great deal to be desired, but he was still reeling with the shock of recognising the strength of his desire and could not find the words.

She looked back at him. There was nothing of the austere duke about him now, nothing of the autocrat; his blue eyes were like the morning mist before the sun breaks through, soft but not clear enough to fathom. Why had he kissed her like that? It could not have been because he had any feeling for her; he had only the moment before been roasting her, telling her how inadequate she was, talking to her as if she were a child. But there had been nothing childlike about that kiss. It had been sweet beyond anything she had ever dreamed of, but then wasn't he a master of *l'amour*? Hadn't Alfred Jessop said how dangerous he was? And she had been fool enough to succumb!

'Is that how you go about silencing everyone who has the temerity to disagree with you?' she demanded.

'No, only the ladies.' It was said with a rueful grin.

'Then Cousin Alfred was right to warn me. He said you were an incorrigible rake, who gambles with people's lives and whose path is littered with broken hearts.'

'And, of course, you believed him.'

'Not until now. Goodnight, your Grace.' She stepped back and closed the door before he could see her tears.

He had destroyed her dream. Oh, she knew those protective arms carrying her to her bed and the gentle voice bidding her go to sleep had been a dream, but the aftermath had been a glow of contentment, a feeling that someone cared and it had been comforting to imagine the arms belonged to the Duke himself. But something he had said when he first knocked on her door, nagged at her mind. And then it came to her. He had said he was afraid she had left her lamp burning *again*. She had thought she had forgotten putting out the lamp and getting into bed on that occasion, but she hadn't. He had done it. He had been in her room; it had not been a dream, but reality. And now he had ruined it, ruined not only the dream but her hopes for the future. She could not stay here now, could not pretend nothing had happened. And, until she found some-where else to live, she would make sure her bedroom door was kept locked.

Never in all his life had James done something for which he was so deeply ashamed. It was unforgivable and he had no idea how to put matters right, except to offer for her, to say he had meant to do so before stealing a kiss. He raised his hand to knock on the door again, but let it drop to his side. Now was not the time. He turned on his heel and went back to his own quarters, unaware of the broken heart he left behind him.

Sophie hoped desperately that he would not be at the breakfast table when she went down the following morn-ing. How could she face him? What could they possibly have to say to each other? Would he be able to tell from her face she had spent a sleepless night, alternately rag-ing and weeping? Should she cut him or pretend nothing had happened. Did one dare cut a duke, especially if he was your sponsor? On the other hand, to pretend nothing had happened might make him think she was accustomed to being kissed, even welcomed it. The shameful thing was that, just for a moment, she had. She had responded with a warmth that had taken her by surprise. Her whole body had glowed with it, until she was a molten heap of desire with no will of her own. Her legs had not been able to sup-port her and he had had to hold her up, making matters a hundred times worse. She would never be able to look him in the face again.

She entered the breakfast parlour, her heart in her mouth, ready to turn tail if he were there. Harriet was sit-ting at the table alone, though the place at the head of the table bore evidence that he had been there: his chair pushed back, a used plate, an empty cup. Harriet looked up from reading her correspondence when Sophie entered. 'Good morning, Sophie,' she said, just as if nothing had happened, as if the world was still smoothly turning. 'Did you sleep well?' Then, 'My dear, whatever is the matter?'

'Nothing.' She pulled out her chair and sat down, but the thought of eating choked her.

'Forgive me if I do not believe you. You look dreadful.'

'I did not sleep well, that is all.'

'And why did you not sleep well? You are surely not brooding over that set down James gave you?'

'Set down?' She had forgotten what that had happened before that kiss. It had wiped everything else from her mind.

'Yes. You know he does not mean to be hard on you. You said yourself his bark is worse than his bite.'

'That was before—' She stopped, unable to go on.

'Before what? Sophie, please tell me.'

'I can't,' she said, her face fiery and her eyes downcast. 'It is too shameful.'

'I cannot conceive of anything you might do which you could not tell me about. Unless…' She paused. 'What did he say to you?'

'It wasn't anything he said.'

'Something he did? Oh, Sophie, you are alarming me.'

'He kissed me.'

'Oh.' She looked thoughtful. 'He is very fond of you.'

'It did not seem like that to me. He was demonstrating his power over me. It wasn't fair!'

'No, it certainly was not and I shall tell him so.'

'No! Oh, please say nothing. I shall find somewhere else to stay.'

'Sophie, you must not think of such a thing. To begin with, every bed in London is taken up this Season and in any case it will start the most dreadful rumours. James has made himself responsible for you and everyone knows it.'

'Responsible! He should have thought of that before—'

'I agree.' She reached out and took Sophie's hand. 'My dear, you must not take it to heart so. No damage has been done and I will wager James already regrets it bitterly.'

She looked puzzled when Sophie burst into uncontrolled laughter. Harriet might say no damage had been done, but it had; her whole body and soul was in torment from the revelation that she loved him—she, Sophia Langford, who had sworn she had no time for men at all, loved the Duke of Belfont to distraction, and to be told he regretted kissing her made it infinitely worse.

'You will feel better about it in a day or two,' Harriet said. 'Promise me you will do nothing precipitate like running away.'

'I have never run from anything in my life!' Sophie, the independent intrepid traveller, was suddenly resurrected. 'If and when I go, I will give you due warning.'

'Good. I do believe the weather is set fair. Shall we take a carriage ride in the park? The fresh air will restore you.'

Sophie did not think anything would restore her to the girl she had been. She had thought that looking after her father and enduring his up-and-down moods and coping with the strange fellows with whom he consorted and insisted on bringing home had made her worldly wise, but it had not. She knew nothing, nothing at all, about men. But she had become very fond of Harriet and did not want to hurt her. 'I think I should like that,' she said.

Nothing more was said about that kiss and James was not mentioned at all as they set off in the open carriage, parasols up against the sun. But he could not be forgotten because everyone they met seemed determined on asking how he did and if either of the two ladies had been invited to any of the official functions with him. 'It must be gratifying to be so close to the court at an exciting time such as this is, Lady Harley,' one lady simpered, as their carriages came to a stop together, the press of vehicles making progress impossible. 'It must be exceedingly tiring.'

'Oh, it would be,' Harriet replied with a smile. 'That is why we do not attend them if we can avoid it. Miss Langford and I prefer to visit friends.'

This reply did not seem to please the lady. She sniffed audibly. 'It is a pity Lady Colway does not share your dislike of his Highness's hospitality, my lady. She appears on every occasion and her poor husband sick at home.'

'I am sure her ladyship's affairs are of no interest to me,' Harriet said as the traffic untangled itself and they were able to proceed. 'Good day, my lady.'

'That will silence the critics who wonder why he does not always accompany us,' Harriet said. 'In any case, they only wish to know if I have any court gossip to pass on, which I would not do even if I knew anything.'

'You mean about Lady Colway?'

'Oh, she is not to be considered, Sophie. James once had an interest in her, but it did not last and I am glad of it. It did not take her long to find someone else.'

'Cousin Alfred?'

'Alfred? What makes you say that?'

'We met them together, the Duke and I, when we were out riding. She asked his Grace to bring me to her soirée, but he refused.'

'I should think so too!'

This talk of the Duke and Lady Colway was not helping Sophie's peace of mind. She found herself wondering if the Duke kissed the lady as he had kissed her and imagining them in each other's arms. It was sheer torture.

As soon as they arrived back at the house, Harriet ordered refreshments and then produced a pile of cards, which she put on the dining-room table together with pens and ink and a long list of names. 'Now, let us sit down side by side and write out these invitations to your ball,' she said. 'I have decided to make it the last day of June. The weather should be good then and it will be daylight until quite late and we can utilise the garden. A large tent, perhaps, and coloured lights…'

'Harriet, I wish you would not refer to it as my ball. It puffs me up too high and makes me feel uncomfortable. And it will be prodigious expensive. I wonder the Duke allows it, considering his poor opinion of me.'

'Poor opinion! What nonsense! He is very fond of you.'

'How can that be? He is for ever roasting me. And, if he is not roasting me, he is—' She stopped, unable to bring up the subject of that kiss again, though it never left her mind for long.

'Oh, Sophie, do not mind that. He will undoubtedly apologise and explain.'

Sophie did not see what good explanations would do, or apologies either; the deed had been done and her life had been changed for ever. She told herself she was glad he stayed away from the house, but she could not make herself believe it.

She did not see him again until the evening they went to the opera at Covent Garden. She suspected he had been staying away on purpose to avoid her and she had gone from being angry to longing for him to come. She wanted to see him, speak to him, try to ascertain from a look or a gesture just how he felt about that kiss. Did he realise the effect it had had on her? Had he felt anything at all himself? Or was she just another broken heart left on the trail behind him?

The opera was unimportant—what was important in the eyes of those fortunate enough to obtain tickets was that the Regent and his illustrious guests were to be there in the royal box. Everyone was dressed in their grandest and began arriving long before the performance was to begin. Sophie was in a gown of floating gauze, open down the front to reveal an underskirt of green satin trimmed with rows of matching velvet. The elbow-length satin sleeves had undersleeves of lace cascading over the backs of her hands. The *décolletage* was lower than she had ever worn before and made her feel half-naked. She filled it with a scarf of gauze and her mother's pearls and had to admit that, when she looked in the long mirror in her room, it became her very well.

'Oh, you look beautiful, Miss Langford,' Rose said when she had finished dressing her hair in a simple Grecian style. 'You cannot fail to be noticed.'

Sophie did not want to be noticed; it was the very thing the Duke had complained of. But when she tentatively suggested to Harriet she should wear something less attractive, perhaps her lilac muslin or her plain black mourning gown, her cousin would not hear of it. 'My goodness, do you wish to shame us, Sophie?' she said. 'You are a Dersingham and we have always been in the forefront of fashion.' She was dressed in amber taffeta, which gleamed gold as she moved. She wore diamonds at her throat and in her hair, which had been dressed in a complicated style of twisted coils. 'Now, let us be off. We must take our seats before the Regent and his party arrive. It would be the height of bad manners to arrive after them.'

Nothing had been said about the Duke escorting them and it seemed they were to go alone, for he had not appeared. Sophie was both relieved and disappointed, which was typical of the muddled way she felt these days, one minute elated, the next deflated. It was taking its toll of her mental strength as the longing in her heart did battle with her determination to put him from her mind. Unfortunately her heart was winning and she berated herself for it. 'What about the Duke?' she asked, as they made their way to the carriage. 'Will he sit with us or the Regent?'

Harriet paused in the act of stepping into the carriage to look back at the girl, then smiled. As far as her plans were concerned, all was not lost. 'He will have to be in the Regent's party, but no doubt he will come to our box in the interval. You will have your chance to speak to him then.'

Sophie climbed in and settled herself beside her cousin. 'I am not at all sure I want to. We will only quarrel.'

Every seat in the theatre seemed to be taken and Sophie was glad they had a box, where she had a good view of everything that went on, both on the stage and in the audience. They had barely taken their seats when the royal party arrived and made their way to boxes on the other aside of the auditorium. Both men and women were resplendent in colourful clothing, jewels flashing, but Sophie had eyes only for James, following behind his Highness's immediate entourage. He was in burgundy silk, with knee breeches and white stockings. There were ruffles at his wrist and at his neck, where a diamond pin gleamed in the folds of lace. He was carrying a *chapeaubras* under his arm and talking to Captain Summers who walked beside him. The audience rose and cheered.

'Oh, how magnificent he looks,' she murmured.

'The Regent?' queried Harriet, picking up her opera glass.

'No, the Duke.'

'Yes, to be sure.' She leaned forward as the crowd cheered louder than ever. 'Goodness, there is the Princess of Wales.' She pointed to a woman in a black wig, her gown and throat glittering with jewellery, who was making her way with her attendants into another box. 'Now, what will happen? He can hardly order her out.'

The Regent, with great aplomb, stood and, smiling, made a stately bow, pretending the cheers were for him. 'Oh, how clever of him!' Harriet said, as the cheers died down and everyone resumed their seats for the performance.

Sophie did not care about the Regent's troubles; she was watching James, aching for him to notice her and give her one of his lopsided smiles. She had forgiven him that kiss; how could she not when it had given her so much pleasure? But she could not tell him that because he had never asked for pardon. To him it was an everyday occurrence, not worth mentioning again, and when she saw Lady Colway take her place beside him and whisper something that made him smile, her heart plummeted still further. He could smile at his mistress when he could not spare her a single indulgent glance. Cousin Alfred had been right; his Grace was a rake, a man who did not give a second thought to those he used. And the lady in the park had been right, Lady Colway was everywhere and that was undoubtedly how the Duke liked it.

When he came to their box during the interval, she could not bring herself to do more than bow her head in recognition and then try to ignore him while he talked to Harriet. But his nearness as he pulled up a chair to sit beside them, his breeches-clad thigh almost touching the fullness of her gown, was having a devastating effect; she was shaking so much she had to hide her hands in her skirts and concentrate on watching the audience, who were drinking and eating oranges and apples and throwing the pips and cores at each other. And then she caught sight of a figure she knew.

It was the Count Cariotti, she was sure of it. Had he seen her? What was he doing in London? If they should meet, what ought she to do? Could she pretend she had never met him? Or had forgotten him? Or remember and behave as if he had merely been a friend of her father? And then she recalled that she had been foolish enough to tell that gaggle of young people about him; they would make much of it if they put two and two together.

'Do you not agree, Miss Langford?' James's voice hauled her back to him.

She shook herself. 'I am sorry, I was wool-gathering.'

'Indeed? Then am I to assume you were not interested in what I was saying?'

'Yes. No. I mean… What were you saying, my lord?'

'It is of little consequence. Go back to your dreaming.'

'His Grace was commenting on the opera,' Harriet said, trying to soften the blow of what appeared a set down. 'He asked your opinion.'

'Oh, it is well enough, but comes nowhere near those I have seen in Italy.'

'No, one must suppose those would be superior. Did you attend many, Miss Langford?'

He was addressing her formally again, which proved he thought nothing of her, that he had kissed her because he felt like it and because he could, knowing she would not dare complain. 'No, not many, your Grace.' They could not afford to pay for visits to the opera, but they had been once as the Count's guests. It was the night he had proposed and been rejected. Papa had been furious and would not speak to her for a week. And the Count had disappeared. Now he was here and she prayed they would not meet.

Chapter Six

Sophie was shaking with nerves, had been all day as Harriet endeavoured to amuse her until it was time to dress for Lady Myers's ball. She had seen so little of the Duke in the last week that she had begun to wonder if, after all, he would not be escorting them, but Harriet had told her firmly that he would not break his promise, even though it had been made before that encounter outside her bedroom door. The thought that soon he would return from his duties at Carlton House or St James's Palace and she would be once again in his company, subject to his scrutiny, recipient of his criticism, object of his laughter, was almost more than she could bear.

Delaying going downstairs until the last possible moment, she sat at her dressing table and surveyed herself in the mirror. Her smoky blue-green gown was trimmed with white flowers from which floated long satin ribbons. The small puffed sleeves were tied with ribbon bows. Her mother's pearls finished the ensemble. She could not fault it for simple elegance, but she wished she did not look so pale, with dark rings under her eyes, which all Rose's ministrations with a powder puff could not disguise. And her eyes, she realised, were dull, as if she was short on sleep, which she supposed was not far from the truth.

She attempted to smile at her reflection, but decided it looked false. Would he notice? she wondered, thinking of the Duke. Everything she thought, said and did had him at the core of it and she did not seem able to stop herself. He was autocratic, frequently uncivil, and a rake into the bargain, she told herself over and over again, but it did no good because even thinking of him made her limbs ache with longing. And she had seen his gentler side, knew him to be generous and compassionate and it was that side of him she loved. But it was a hopeless love, she knew that, she was not duchess material; she was too unconventional, too independent, too outspoken, and he certainly had never treated her as anything but an inconvenience, which he must endure as head of the family. Except when he had kissed her. It was that which had caused her the sleepless nights.

Hearing the sound of voices in the entrance hall, she sighed, slipped her feet into her shoes and stood up. Time to go. She took a deep breath, left her room and descended the stairs, keeping her back straight and her head up. The Duke and Harriet stood in the vestibule, ready to go. Before he had even said a word to her, she felt herself go on the defensive; he must have realised it, for he bowed briefly and conducted them out to the waiting carriage without speaking.

It was not incivility that kept him silent, but the overwhelming knowledge that she was the most beautiful, the most desirable and the most exasperating creature he had ever encountered. He could neither treat her with cousinly affection, ruling her for her own good, nor kiss her as if she were one of his light o' loves, and yet he had tried both. He had kissed her to prove that he could and it was the most foolish thing he had ever done. Looking at her coming down the stairs towards him, he had seen a lovely woman, a proud woman, her head held high as if he were beneath her contempt. He smiled grimly as he helped her into the carriage. He had used his position to humiliate her and she was right to put her nose in the air and ignore him.

The Myers's residence was crowded, the noise of laughter and music overwhelming as Sophie stood beside Harriet and the Duke, waiting to be greeted by Lord and Lady Myers. She was not unaware of the sighs of admiration they were attracting; Harriet in a deep rose-pink-and-white striped gown, the Duke in a black evening tail suit, with a pure white waistcoat and cravat. On anyone else it would have looked severe, but on his superb figure it made him stand out from the overdressed dandies who gaped at him. Sophie permitted herself a little smile, guessing that half the young men would be in black and white the next time she encountered them at an evening function.

'The Duke of Belfont, Lady Harley and Miss Langford,' the footman announced as they reached the door to be greeted by their host and hostess. The men bowed and the ladies curtsied.

'Your Grace,' Lady Myers said, preening. 'We are honoured that you have been able to leave your duties with his Highness to attend our little gathering. And, Sophie, how becoming you look.' She stood back to survey her friend. 'But looking a little downpin, I declare. Perhaps the rush and tear of society life is a little too much for you.'

'Not at all,' she responded. 'Lady Harley takes good care of me.'

'Good. Now, I think you know most of the young people, do you not?'

Sophie looked about her; there was the usual crowd she met at almost every function, including Peter Poundell and

Theodore Buskin, both flamboyantly dressed, and Ariadne and Dorothy, who looked more pasty faced every
time Sophie saw her. The poor girl was being hauled about
by her parents from one function to another in the hope
she would take, when Sophie was sure she would rather
stay at home curled up with a good book. Ariadne, still
simpering, still hopeful, was demure and unremarkable in
white muslin.

But there were also strangers there, many of the men
in foreign uniforms, covered with decorations, and the ladies in huge skirts and even taller wigs, courtiers of a previous age, still trying to pretend they mattered. And among
them, taller than most, she spied Count Cariotti, dressed
in peach satin and a great deal of lace. She turned away
quickly, hoping he had not seen her, and followed the
Duke and Harriet into the room.

The young people greeted her enthusiastically as she was
drawn into their circle, leaving the Duke and Harriet to find
their own friends. In no time at all, her dance card was fill-
ing up and the Duke had not asked to write his name on it.
Disappointment battled with pride. She could, of course,
save him a dance, but that would make her look foolish if
he never asked to stand up with her, and so she allowed her
card to fill, glad that the Count seemed to have disappeared.
Alfred was one of the first to claim a country dance.

'You look very fine tonight, Miss Langford,' he said,
as he took her hand to lead her into the set. He was in pale
blue and yellow, his dark hair smoothed back and tied with
a black ribbon.

'Thank you.'

'I heard Lady Myers say you look tired. I must say, I
agree with her.'

'It is hardly civil of you to find fault with a lady's appearance,' she said stiffly.

'My dear, I was not finding fault. I am simply concerned for your welfare. After all, you can hardly be used to the fast pace of society life in London and it is unfair of his Grace to expect you to—'

'The Duke has nothing to do with it,' she said, annoyed by his familiar way of addressing her. 'I hardly see him. He stays at Carlton House a great deal of the time.'

'Is that where he is? Now, I had thought he had found a more comfortable bed with a certain lady…'

'Mr Jessop, if you insist on talking about the Duke, whose affairs do not interest me in the least, then I shall feel obliged to leave you to find another partner. And be assured that I am no stranger to society. I used to go out and about with Papa in Italy where the pace is every bit as fast.' This was not exactly true because her father spent most of his time with his gambling friends and she had been left to her own devices. It was Lady Myers who made sure she went out sometimes.

He gave her an oily smile. 'Enough said, eh?'

The dance took them away from each other for the next movement and she was glad of the time to try to regain her composure. Enough had certainly been said to convince her Alfred meant mischief, but Harriet had warned her of his motives, so she should not have been surprised, although she did wonder if Harriet had been right in saying the Duke had finished with Lady Colway.

Her partner came towards her and bowed as they linked hands to step down between the lines of other dancers in the set. 'If it is not society, then it must be working on your book that has caused your fatigue,' he said. 'How is it coming along?'

'Very well.'

'And have you decided who will grace its pages?'

'Do you mean will I include you?' she queried. 'Have

you done something of great moment that must be left to posterity?'

'No, I did not mean me. I am too ordinary.'

She laughed aloud. 'Very few people are ordinary, Mr Jessop. We all have a tale to tell.'

'And will it be set entirely in Italy?'

She did not particularly want to talk about the book, but it was better than talking about the Duke. 'No, I shall write of other places we visited—life in France after the Terror, and Austria under Napoleon, for instance.'

'And will it be published in England or will it be too hot for English publishers to handle?'

She laughed. 'I have yet to find a publisher.'

The dance ended and he offered his arm to escort her back to Harriet, who was sitting beside Lady Myers. James stood behind them, surveying proceedings in what appeared a detached manner, but she was not deceived; he was watchful. She was almost relieved to be claimed by her next partner. Determined to prove she was not tired, she threw herself into every dance, laughed and prattled as if she did not have a care in the world and could stay up until dawn and still be ready for more. Every now and again she caught a glimpse of the Count and made every effort to keep out of his way, which, added to everything else, was a terrible strain, and by the time the supper dance was announced she was almost dead on her feet.

'Come, Sophie, this one is mine,' James said, stepping forward and holding out his hand.

'But Mr Buskin has signed my card.'

'Mr Buskin will not mind.' He frowned meaningfully at the young man who was making his way towards them. 'I cannot allow you to dance a waltz with anyone else.'

In a dream she took his hand and allowed herself to be led on to the floor. The music was a background to a dream, like the one she had had before, when someone she liked to pretend had been the Duke, had been gentle and kind and protective. He held her firmly, but not too tightly, as he led her expertly in the steps. At first she was vaguely aware that they were being watched, but as the music took over she forgot there was anyone else in the room. There was simply two people in perfect harmony.

He held her the requisite twelve inches from him and looked down at her. She did look wan and he supposed he was the cause of that, but even so she was achingly beautiful and he wanted to crush her to him, to kiss her as he had done once before and to tell her she was brave and resourceful and he loved her. He could not do so in a crowded ballroom, but he would as soon as they could be alone. Quarrelling with her was hell, but making up would be heaven. But he must not rush her, must not frighten her, must give her no opportunity to doubt his sincerity. For the moment, it was enough that she seemed to have forgiven him. He did not speak and neither did she.

He smiled a little wryly; perhaps she was obeying him and keeping her mouth shut. He hadn't meant she should not talk to him. He wanted to hear her voice, to gauge how she was feeling, what she was thinking. 'Are you enjoying the ball, Sophie?' he asked as the music drew to a close.

'Yes, thank you.' She dropped a deep curtsy as the dance ended.

So formal and so little. Perhaps he had not been forgiven after all. He bowed and offered his arm. 'Shall we go in to supper?'

The ballroom came into focus again; the colourful gowns and evening suits, the glittering jewels and bright faces, the sparkling chandeliers helping to make the room overwarm, all brought her back to the present, to the realisation that she had abandoned poor Theodore to dance with the Duke and they had managed it without speaking until the very end. He had not found fault, had not commented on her looks, had not roasted her; on the other hand, he had not said anything complimentary either. Did that mean dancing with her had been a duty, not a pleasure? She put her fingers on his sleeve and together they followed the general exodus to the dining room.

Supper was eaten at small tables placed about the room and he led her to one occupied by Harriet. They had no sooner seated themselves than Alfred arrived with his mother and took their places at the same table. Waiters brought them food and wine, but Sophie could not eat. She was sitting between two men who disturbed her for very different reasons and they drove all wish for food out of her head. The Duke seemed in a jovial mood as he joked with his sister and aunt, but Alfred was glowering and she could guess the reason; he did not like the Duke paying attention to her and she had better find a way of disabusing him of the idea that the Duke would ever offer for her or that she would accept.

'Miss Langford tells me her book is so scandalous she might have to have it published abroad,' Alfred said, apparently to no one in particular, but Sophie, who had gasped with astonishment as his statement, knew it was directed at the Duke.

'Mr Jessop, I said no such thing,' she retorted. 'It was you who suggested that.'

'You did not deny it.'

'It was too fanciful to need denying. I beg you, speak of it no more.'

'And I am not begging,' James said sharply. 'I am insisting. The book is not to be mentioned again. It is only being done for Miss Langford's amusement and not intended for publication.'

Sophie, taken aback, turned to look at him, but he refused to meet her gaze. Oh, he knew what he was doing; he was publicly belittling her. 'My lord,' she said, in a voice that froze his blood, 'do you suppose because I am young, and a female into the bargain, I am incapable of writing a publishable book and you seek to save me the embarrassment of rejection? You are wide of the mark if you do, because I have received an education second to none for that purpose. In truth, I am more fitted to be an author than I am to be a wife.'

'A blue stocking,' Mrs Jessop chuckled. 'James, I hope you will take careful note of that. No one likes an educated woman who answers back, certainly no man of any standing would marry one. Learning in a lady goes against all sensibility and politeness.'

Alfred laughed aloud, having achieved his aim of sowing dissent, but Sophie had managed to make her point that she was not looking to trap the Duke into marriage. But her evening was ruined. She pushed her chair back and stood up. 'Please excuse me,' she said, and walked majestically from the room. At least that was how she hoped it appeared from her back, glad that they could not see her face. The ballroom was on the first floor and she debated whether to go up to the room set aside for the ladies' *toilette* or go down and out through the conservatory to the garden. The ladies' room might very well be populated by young ladies chattering away like a flock of magpies. She decided on the garden.

It was cooler out of doors; the lights from the terrace vied with a pale moon to light her way towards a small arbour, which she remembered from the time she had been staying with Lady Myers. Behind her she could hear the musicians beginning again after the interval, but she had lost interest in dancing. Her life stretched before her, lonely and desolate. She could see herself living alone in some dismal apartment, growing old with only her writing and perhaps a cat for company, the love of her life married to someone else.

'Sophie, please return to the house.' The voice, easily recognised, was polite but far from pleading. He expected to be obeyed.

'I prefer the night air,' she said, controlling the urge to turn and face him, to look into his eyes, to let him see the misery in her own. 'And my own company.'

'Oh, very well, sulk if you must, but you are making yourself look very foolish.'

'I am not sulking!' She swung round, stung by his words. 'Foolish, is it, to want to make myself independent and rid you of the burden of having to support me?'

'Did I say it was a burden?' He was standing before her outlined by the terrace lights behind him, his face in shadow. His expression was inscrutable, but she could see his eyes, searching her face, demanding an answer.

'Not in words, my lord, but I know.'

'How do you know? Can you read my mind?'

'Yes.'

He threw back his head and laughed 'Then tell me what I am thinking now?'

'You are wishing you had never set eyes on me, that I have been trouble ever since I arrived and, if it were not for your sense of family pride, you would wash your hands of me. Well, I shall save you the inconvenience and take myself off.'

'You are wrong,' he said softly.

'That is no more than I would expect you to say. You would never admit that anyone else could be right.'

'I had not realised your opinion of me was so low.' It was a statement, not a question, and she did not trouble to deny it.

'Can you blame me? First you kiss me as if I were some lightskirt whose reputation is already lost, and then you humiliate me by pretending my book is so worthless no one would ever publish it. I wonder at you making such a fuss about it, if that is what you think. While it lies in my desk drawer it can do you no harm.'

'No, so long as that is where it remains.' He paused. 'Sophie, it is not your competence I question, rather the opposite. I am concerned that you may inadvertently have hit upon something of interest to the state…'

'War secrets, you mean?'

'Perhaps.'

'Fustian! Who would be interested in anything I have to say? I am a foolish girl with delusions of fame and fortune, is that not so? And the war is over.'

'For the moment,' he said grimly.

'Oh.' She paused, thinking of Napoleon's threat to return. 'But it is only a travel book, all about the architecture, the countryside and the customs of the people.'

'Then why did you allow people to think there were scandalous secrets in it?'

She grinned. 'To make them buy it, of course.'

'Oh, Sophie.' He reached out and lifted a curl from her cheek and wound it about his finger. She stood frozen, wondering what was coming next. If he kissed her again… Oh, that he would! No, no, she could not bear it because she would give herself away. 'I wish—' He stopped. He wished they had met in less turbulent times, before she left England with her no-good father. Perhaps she might have been saved the life she had led and been brought up more conventionally. But then Sophie would not be the Sophie he loved. He stopped, smiling at his own foolishness; she had been only ten years old when she left England and he had been a young man of three and twenty, sowing his wild oats, already a soldier. Would he have deigned to notice a gawky little second cousin? She was not gawky now, she was eminently desirable and he desired her. The back of his finger caressed her cheek. She shivered suddenly and visibly.

'You are cold. Come back indoors. We will dance together again just to show we are the best of friends still.'

'And save face,' she said flatly. 'Yours and mine.'

'If you like.' He took her elbow and guided her back to the house, knowing that once again he had made a mull of everything. It was a state of affairs to which he was unaccustomed; until now he had always been in command, of his life, his loves, his own emotions, and he did not like this feeling of inadequacy.

A dance was in progress as they entered the ballroom and they made their way on to the floor without speaking. He was aware of the glances made towards them and could almost hear the gossip: they had been out in the garden unchaperoned, something must have happened out there, she was looking flustered and even he was not behaving with his usual aplomb. He endeavoured to engage her in conversation, though the dance was a little too quick to make that easy. 'Sophie, smile, please, pretend to enjoy my company, even if you do not.'

She gave him a smile that was so false he almost cringed. 'Oh, I forgot, your Grace, we are the best of friends.'

'Is that not possible?'

'No.' How could he talk of friendship? How could he be so urbane about it?

'I am indeed sorry to hear that. I had hoped we might begin again, forget our differences and live in harmony...'

'So long as I do as I am told and do not embarrass you by talking about my book or revealing that I can read and write and have a brain which can think beyond trivialities.'

'I never said that. Now you are the one twisting words.'

'Words can hurt, my lord, more than blows.'

'I know that, and if any of mine have hurt you, then I beg pardon.' He paused, smiling at her in a way that turned her heart over and made it beat as if she had been running for her life. 'And if any other action of mine has hurt you, I apologise for that as well, and beg your forgiveness.'

He was talking about that kiss, she knew, and how could she hold that against him, when all she wanted was more of the same? 'I forgive you.' It was said in a whisper.

'Then are we friends again?'

'If that is your wish.'

'Of course it is.' His wish was that it could be more than friendship, much more, but he refrained from saying so. He had made a little headway; it would not do to spoil it by being too precipitate. And there was all the time in the world to court her, to make sure she understood his true feelings before he offered. He would offer; he had made up his mind to that.

The dance ended and they made their way back to where Harriet was sitting with Mrs Jessop and Alfred. 'I think Harriet needs rescuing, don't you?' she said, laughing up at him, something that was noted by all and sundry.

They had almost reached her when a tall figure interposed himself between them and executed a flourishing bow. 'Miss Langford. Sophie. It seems we were destined to meet again.'

Sophie gasped; in all the excitement, she had forgotten about the Count. He stood before her now, tall, older looking than she remembered, but still darkly handsome. 'Count Cariotti, how do you do?'

'I do well enough,' he said in perfect English. 'And you

seem to have fallen on your feet.' He looked at James, apparently at ease in a situation she found disturbing, though she could not have explained why. 'Will you not present me?'

She turned to the Duke. 'Your Grace, may I present Count Antonio Cariotti. You remember, I told you he was a friend of Papa's. Count, the Duke of Belfont.'

The two men bowed warily to each other and murmured, 'How do you do.' James was prepared to end the encounter, but the Count had other ideas. He turned to smile at Harriet. 'And this must be Lady Harley.'

'Allow me to present my sister, Lady Harley,' James said. 'And Mrs Jessop, our aunt.'

'I have already made the acquaintance of Mrs Jessop,' he said, smiling at the lady in a way that worried Sophie. It was almost conspiratorial. 'My friend, Alfred, has already made me known to his charming mother.'

Mrs Jessop smiled back and nodded her plumed head. 'So kind,' she murmured.

Another dance was starting. The Count bowed and offered Sophie his hand. 'Will you do me the honour of standing up with me?'

She glanced at her card where Alfred's name was written neatly against the number of the dance. She looked towards him, but he simply smiled and nodded. 'I bow to the superior claim,' he said.

There was nothing for it but to comply. She took the hand offered to her and stepped back on to the floor.

James watched them until they were swallowed in the crowd of other dancers, then he turned back to Alfred. 'Superior claim?' he queried, one eyebrow raised.

'Yes, did you not know? The Count and Miss Langford were in love and he once offered for her, but her father thought she was a little too young and they ought to wait, and then the circumstances of the war separated them, but now he is here and the war is over, he will resume his courtship. He considers himself as good as betrothed to her already.'

'I was told she rejected him.'

'Oh, she said that to save her pride. He had gone away and she did not know the true reason. No doubt he will be explaining that to her now.'

James looked at the couple as they danced; they were in animated conversation and he began to wonder…

'Why have you come to London?' Sophie demanded.

'Why should I not? My mother was English.'

'But you fought with the French.'

'The war is over. And Italy was only ever an unwilling partner of Napoleon, not a staunch ally.'

'Then why did you go to France?'

'Can you believe I was heartbroken at your rejection of me?'

'No. I do not believe you have a heart. You pauperised Papa with your gambling and I find it difficult to believe he was always so unlucky…'

'Are you accusing me of cheating?'

'If the cap fits…'

'If you were a man, I would call you out for that.' It was said with a charming smile. 'But as you are undoubtedly the most beautiful woman in the room, I will forgive you.'

'You will not put me off with silken words,' she said. 'You have not answered my question. Why are you here?'

'I came to claim you.'

'Gammon!'

'You have certainly learned some strange expressions since returning to England. What does gammon mean?'

'Rubbish. Nonsense. It means you are roasting me and, before you ask, that means teasing, not sincere.'

'Oh, but, my dear, I am perfectly sincere. Your father gave you to me.'

She looked up into his face. He was wearing a self-satisfied smile that she longed to wipe from his face with the back of her hand. 'For what consideration?'

'Why should there be any consideration? He and I were friends; we spent a great deal of time in each other's company. I came to know him through and through, learned that he would promise anything for money, but he did not always keep his promises. It was a very bad trait he had.'

'You bought me!' She stumbled and he put out a hand to steady her, though she shrugged it off.

'No money changed hands, I do assure you.'

'What then?'

'Nothing. He promised information for the return of his vowels, but then he failed to deliver…'

'He died.'

'Yes, sweetheart, he died.' He paused. 'But you are alive.'

Suddenly she remembered the circumstances of her father's death, so sudden and violent. He had been out playing cards as usual and had been making his way home, when he had fallen down in a drunken stupor and been set upon by thieves, who took the money he had won and left him for dead. Or so those who found him told her. Was he killed because he could name names and not for the money he carried? The Count had gone to France almost immediately afterwards. She was silent for a moment, trying to pull herself together, to retain her presence of mind and not accuse him. 'I know nothing.'

'Oh, I think you might. Your cousin, the inestimable Alfred Jessop, tells me you are writing a book and I think, maybe, you know more than you think you do.'

'For heaven's sake, what about?'

'Places, people, things done, things said, all very innocent, of course, but lethal in the wrong hands.'

So the Duke had been right; her book was a source of danger. And yet there was nothing in what she had written so far that could be construed as a state secret, either English or French. 'That is ridiculous nonsense.'

'Then why is the Duke so anxious to shut you up? He will go to any lengths to find out what you have written, you know. I do believe he might even consider marrying you.'

Suddenly she was back in her bedroom, drowsing over her desk, and the Duke was creeping across the carpet. How surprised he must have been to find her there and not in her bed. He had carried her to her bed, but had he afterwards read what she had written? What had she been writing that evening? Something about Napoleon's visit to Dresden, the people who were there, his affability when all the time he was planning to invade Russia. And the discomfort of his host and hostess, his wife's parents. She remembered writing that her father had said Napoleon had only married Marie-Louise to make sure of Austria as an ally, but it would not be enough; Austria would, in the end, defy him. And Papa had been right. But surely there was nothing subversive about that?

'Everyone is uncommonly interested in my book,' she said levelly, though her head was whirling with other possibilities. Had the Duke been intending to try to see more when he knocked on her door and ended kissing her? Was his present affability, his apology and offer of friendship, a ruse to learn more? Could she trust him an inch? 'I hope that means it will sell well and I shall become rich by it.' She was surprised how light her voice sounded.

'You would do well to abandon it.'

She knew he was right. If she publicly announced she had given up the idea and destroyed the offending manuscript, then she might be left in peace. But what peace? What other means of earning a living could she use, for earn a living she must? Another consideration was that she had yet to show it to a publisher and his decision could very well make up her mind for her. As soon as she had something worth submitting, she would do something about that.

'You are thinking about what I have said,' he murmured, misconstruing her silence. 'That is good. And think of this too: I consider myself betrothed to you, have done so ever since your father gave me his blessing. You do not need to be independent. I will take care of you. Being Countess Cariotti will give you a position in society you could never otherwise have.'

'In Italy.'

'Wherever you like. We will stay in England if that is your wish.'

She felt numb, as if all emotion had been driven from her body, leaving her a shell of flesh and bone with a heart that could beat but could not feel. It was not his statement that he considered them betrothed—she could easily refute that—but the knowledge that the Duke was not all he seemed. 'Why do you want to marry me?' she asked dully.

'Why do most men propose? You are comely, far more so than when I first proposed. You are sensible and not given to frivolity, and I think you will make an excellent wife and mother to my children.'

'But you do not love me.'

'What a droll idea. Is it necessary to love one's wife?'

'For me it is.'

'Then I love you.'

The statement was so patently insincere, it was comical. She threw back her head and laughed. He looked puzzled and then slowly smiled.

James saw it though he was not near enough to see the lack of humour in her eyes, the blankness in them as if a lamp had gone out inside her. He saw only a laughing girl and a handsome man looking decidedly pleased with himself. His heart dropped like a stone to depths he had never plumbed before. He turned on his heel and left the room, making for the card room where he involved himself in serious play until it was time to escort the ladies home. As soon as he had done that, he went out again and sought relief and solace in the arms of Ellen Colway.

Ellen, estranged from her sick husband, who preferred to remain at his country home, lived during the Season in their London house in Clarges Street, where she held court, entertained and generally amused herself. James had once been her most frequent visitor. He knew, because she had told him so, that she was only waiting for her husband to die to become the Duchess of Belfont. It was an idea that had never appealed to him, but as her husband's malady seemed not to be serious, he had not bothered to disillusion her. She was a talented and amusing lover and, until he had found her in bed with his cousin, that was all he required.

'James, dear heart, I knew you would return to me,' she said, coming forward in a diaphanous undress robe that concealed nothing of her voluptuous figure. Her maid, who had answered the door to him, was used to his coming and going and had withdrawn to allow him to make his own way to her boudoir. 'But why have you kept me waiting so long?'

'You know why.'

'Alfred. Pooh, he is nothing. A nobody. I amuse myself with him, nothing more. But now, I think, you have forgiven me.' She took his hand and led him to the adjoining room and her huge four-poster bed.

He was still smarting from seeing Sophie with the Count, still angry that she had never told him the extent of their relationship or he would never have come, would never have been drawn into re-igniting their affair. He looked from her to the rumpled bed, his nostrils filled with her heady perfume, and knew he could not do it. 'Excuse me,' he said. 'But I do not think I forgive you, after all. I am sorry I wakened you.' And with that he turned and left, but not before he had heard her rejoinder.

'You will be far sorrier, James Dersingham.'

Dawn was breaking as he found himself in the street, too late to go to bed, too early to begin his duties at Carlton House. He went home only long enough to change into riding clothes, then made his way to the mews where he kept his horses and asked for Hotspur to be saddled. It was while he was waiting that he noticed Amber was not in her stall. 'Where is she?' he asked the groom, nodding at the empty stall.

'Miss Langford took her out, your Grace, half an hour since. Tom accompanied her on the roan.' Tom was his son, a young lad of nineteen who was an exceptionally good rider, the Duke had often used him as a jockey when he entered horses at the races. 'Was I wrong to allow it?'

'No, if Tom is with her, I doubt she will come to harm.'

He mounted and trotted off towards Hyde Park, keeping a sharp look out for her, though why he bothered he did not know. She did not appreciate his care of her, was determined to go to the devil in her own way. So be it.

'Miss Langford, good morning.'

She smiled at Theodore, who had pulled up beside

her as she drew up from a canter across the grass and rejoined the Row. It would have been an enjoyable ride, out in the early morning air before anyone was about, if it had not been for the heaviness that weighed about her heart. The Duke was an ogre, a petty dictator, a philanderer who was exactly as Alfred Jessop had painted him. He used people. Last night in the carriage going home he had not spoken a word, had sat stiffly correct and escorted them into the house, saying only a brief goodnight.

She had heard him go out again almost immediately and guessed there was only one place he would go at that hour. She had flung herself face down on to her bed and thumped her clenched fists into the pillow over and over again, wishing it was his body she was hammering. At dawn, unable to lie still or stay in the house, she had gone to the mews and asked for Amber to be saddled. She managed a smile for Theodore as Peter Poundell rode up to join them. 'As you see.'

'Then allow us to escort you.'

'I do not wish to keep you from your ride.'

'Oh, we do not mind in the least, do we, Peter?'

'Not at all,' the young man said, bringing his horse up to her other side so that she was flanked by the two men. They walked their horses, talking as they went.

'Miss Langford, the latest *on dit* is that you were once betrothed to Count Cariotti,' Theodore said after they had remarked upon the weather and the young men had praised her mount and her handling of the mare.

'The gossip, as usual, is mistaken.'

'Is he not the count you told us of, the one who proposed and went to France?'

'He is, but I never accepted him.'

'He is a handsome fellow. Can't hold a candle to the Duke, of course…'

She pulled up sharply, making Amber dance a little so that the young men were obliged to give her a little more room. 'Gentlemen, you cannot have been paying attention when I said I intended never to marry.'

'Oh, we did not think you meant it,' Theodore said. 'Every young lady wishes to marry. What else is there for her to do?'

'Only write books,' Peter put in. 'But we know the Duke will never allow that. He has said the book is for your amusement only.'

'The Duke, like the gossips, is wrong.' She was relieved to see Ariadne and Dorothy approaching on two ponies, sitting stiffly, walking their mounts as if they were on parade, which she supposed they were. They were in almost identical dark green riding habits and tall hats with tiny veils. 'I see Miss Jefferson and Miss Fidgett approaching us. Shall we join them?'

The five young people stopped a little to one side of the ride so that they did not impede other riders. The conversation revolved around the weather; gossip about the Regent, who, it was said, intended to pack his wife off to live abroad so that he never had to set eyes on her again; and the fact that Princess Charlotte had disappointed her father in breaking off her engagement to William of Orange when she learned she would have to leave England. As an exile herself Sophie could understand that. The ladies were interested in the gossip, but the men were more interested in boasting.

'Nothing can beat driving a coach and four over Finchley Common and foiling a High Toby,' Peter was saying.

'Have you done that?' Sophie asked him.

'Yes. Last week, I took *The High Flyer* from Whetstone to Highgate.'

'I am surprised the coachman allowed it.'

'Oh, most of them will hand over the reins if they know they'll be given a handsome tip. It relieves the boredom of their occupation.'

'And were you really held up by a highwayman?' Ariadne asked.

He looked sheepish. 'Well, there was a horseman riding hard by us, but we outran him.'

'A coach cannot outrun a determined horseman,' Theodore said disparagingly. 'I'll wager he was an ordinary rider going about his business.'

'He was sinister enough to frighten the passengers.'

'Gammon! It was more likely the passengers were terrified of being driven by a wild man. I have seen some of your driving.'

'I am as good with the ribbons as you,' Peter said, becoming heated. 'I'll wager a hundred guineas I can beat you in a race. You name the time and place. We find our own horses and vehicles.'

Theodore could not ignore the challenge. 'Done,' he said. 'Whetstone to Highgate on Sunday, driving a coach and four.'

'Agreed.' The men shook hands.

'Why, here is the Duke,' Ariadne said suddenly, making Sophie jump out of her skin which, in turn, made Amber prance. She pulled herself together to control her mount as Ariadne said, 'Good morning, your Grace.'

He pulled up and inclined his head in their direction. 'Ladies, gentlemen, good morning.'

'We are well met, your Grace,' Dorothy said. 'Mr Buskin has just wagered he can beat Mr Poundell driving a coach and four from Whetstone to Highgate on Sunday. Who do you think will win?'

'I think they will both break their necks,' he answered laconically. 'And probably the horses' necks too.'

'Then you will not bet on the outcome?'

'Certainly not. It is foolhardy in the extreme.'

'I have never yet reneged on a wager,' Theodore said. 'And I do not intend to start now. I will be there.'

"And so will I,' Peter said. 'It a matter of honour.'

'Then I suggest you take the precaution of taking advice from my coachman,' James said. 'There is nothing Sadler does not know about driving a four-in-hand. Now, come, Sophie, Harriet will be made anxious by your absence.'

He turned his horse, waiting for her to follow, which she did half-reluctantly; she knew she was in for another roasting. They had been riding for perhaps two minutes when he said, 'Where is Tom?'

'I sent him home for his breakfast.'

'You will not do that again. In the first place he should not have been taken from his work to escort you—'

'I did not ask him to follow me.'

'I am aware of that. Fortunately, Sadler knows I would never let you ride out alone. Nor will I. In future, if you wish to ride, you will ask me to accompany you.'

'Then I will have to give up riding, for it is certain you will never have the time.'

'I will try and make the time.'

'I think a certain lady might have something to say about that.'

He turned towards her, his face like thunder, but then thought better of what he had been about to say. Instead he said, 'That remark was unworthy of you, Sophie.'

Oh, she had been so right when she said one could achieve more with politeness than with anger. He had managed to put her down very successfully with his soft answer when what she had wanted was to have a blazing row with him, to tell him she knew about Lady Colway, to shout and rave, elicit some response. She looked down at her gloved hands on the reins and leaned forward to pat Amber's neck. Horses could be trusted, men could not.

Chapter Seven

If James had intended to have more words with Sophie
as soon as they were in the privacy of Belfont House, he
was prevented from doing so because Lady Myers was ensconced in the drawing room, taking tea with Harriet. It
was an ungodly hour for callers and he wondered what had
brought her, as he stood in the doorway and bowed politely. Sophie left him there and went upstairs, no doubt
relieved to escape. 'Lady Myers, good morning. Please excuse my riding clothes. I will go and change.'

'Oh, please do not trouble yourself on my account,
your Grace. I will be on my way as soon as I have imparted
the news I bring.'

'News?' he queried, perching himself on an upright chair
just inside the room, uncomfortably aware that he should
not be bringing the odour of horses into the drawing room.

'A message from Lord Myers,' she said. 'He thought it
best that I should be the bearer, considering I call frequently on Lady Harley and Miss Langford and no one
will think anything of my coming to say goodbye before
we leave for the country. Lord Myers intends to spend a
week or two in the quiet of our Hertfordshire house, set-

tling his affairs, before he takes up his new post in India. Where, naturally, I shall accompany him.'

This was of little interest to James, who listened politely and waited for her to come to the point.

'Lord Myers, as you know, is acquainted with a great many people,' she went on. 'Some of them of doubtful character whom he has met on his travels. It behoves him as a diplomat to listen and observe…'

'Indeed, I am sure the country is indebted to him.'

She inclined her head in acknowledgement. 'It has come to his ears that there is to be an attempt on Wellington's life when he returns to this country.'

'Whatever for?' Harriet asked. 'He is a hero, beloved of the whole country.'

'Yes, he is.' Lady Myers turned to answer her. 'If he were to die the country would be plunged into mourning and would certainly not be prepared to repulse Bonaparte should he make an attempt to regain his throne. The French tyrant fears no one as much as Wellington and he would give anything to have him out of the way.'

'Is the intelligence credible?' James asked her.

'Lord Myers thinks so, sufficiently to alert you. I collect you are responsible for the Duke's safety during the celebrations.'

'If he allows it,' he said. 'I am informed he makes little of the risk. He has been heard to comment that he has survived worse in the Peninsula than a crowd of his own countrymen and women bent on enjoying themselves and he will not be hedged in by petty restrictions.'

'And there, according to my husband, lies his danger.'

'Does Lord Myers know more? Names, times, places?'

'No, only that the plot is in the making and probably led by a foreigner, here as part of the celebrations.'

'I see.' Why had his mind suddenly flown to Count Cariotti? He had no possible grounds for suspecting him. It was simply that the man had been so much in his head because of Sophie; it was jealousy on his part, the desire to be rid of him, to have Sophie for himself. His honour and sense of fair play made him discount the idea almost immediately, but the news was worrying.

The Regent was due to hold a reception at Carlton House in honour of the Duke and had commissioned a huge hall 136 feet in diameter to be built in the garden, connected to a series of supper tents by covered walkways. The builders were already at work and James was heavily involved, something Lord Myers and half of London already knew. He would have to step up security measures and that meant even less time at home. His inbred sense of duty battled with his desire to be with Sophie, to prove he was not the ogre she thought him to be, to make her see how much she meant to him. Duty won. 'Please thank Lord Myers for the information,' he said, getting to his feet. 'I know I can rely on you not to pass on what you have told me. We do not want to alert the culprits that we are on to them.'

'No, indeed not. You may trust me, your Grace. And it goes without saying Lord Myers will say nothing. If we hear more, we will find a way of letting you know.'

He bowed and left the room to hurry upstairs to change and go out again.

He met Sophie on the stairs. She had changed into a light morning gown and was coming down to pay her respects to Lady Myers. She looked tired; there were dark rings around her eyes, but she seemed to have regained her self-assurance. She paused as he approached her, waited but did not speak.

'I regret I have to leave you again,' he said, stepping on to the same stair but, as the stairs were wide, there was at least three feet between them. It might as well have been a chasm.

'Of course, you must not neglect your duty, your Grace.' And with that she went on down, leaving him feeling somewhat dissatisfied and wondering whether there was a touch of irony in the way she had spoken.

The Duke was not the only one to feel dissatisfied. Sophie was also cast down. His Grace had simply looked down his haughty nose at her as if she had so far displeased him he had given up even trying to reason with her. In the absence of love, or even friendship, between them, she had perversely been looking forward to a good wrangle, a war of words in which she could let fly all her frustration and make him angry. She could cope with his anger, or at least she thought she could, but not his silent reproach. And now he was going out again and he would probably not come home for days, preferring the company of his mistress.

She went on down the stairs and joined Harriet and Lady Myers, who offered no explanation as to why his Grace had gone out again so soon, but chatted inconsequentially about the latest *on dit*, the weather and what Lord Myers might expect to find in India, all of which drove Sophie to distraction. What did his Grace say to you? she wanted to ask. Why has he gone out again? Why do I make him so angry? Why can't he love me just a little? Can't he see that it is because of the way he treats me that I keep saying and doing the wrong thing and getting into a coil? If only he would love me, I would do anything, anything at all to please him.

Of course she said none of these things, but sipped the cup of tea Harriet had handed her, expressed an interest in everything that was being said and, having done her polite duty as she saw it, excused herself and retreated to her room where she pulled out her manuscript and set determinedly to work.

She was right about the Duke not returning home, an absence that did not seem to bother Harriet. Sophie spent some of her time keeping her cousin company and listening to her plans for her come-out ball, for which she could rouse no enthusiasm, though she hid it bravely, and the rest working on her book until Mrs Jefferson and Ariadne called on Friday afternoon to ask if the two ladies would like to join the party she was organising to go out to Highgate on the following Sunday to witness the end of the carriage race.

'We are going to take our barouche and there will be ample room for you and Miss Langford,' Mrs Jefferson told Harriet. 'That is, if the Duke is not to take you.'

'I think he will be too busy,' Harriet said, then to Sophie. 'Should you like to go, Sophie?'

'Yes, if you go.'

'Then we will.'

They completed the arrangements regarding the time they would set out, the contribution each would make to the picnic they meant to have while waiting for the protagonists to appear, and talking about who else would be going—that seemed to be half the population of London. Word had gone round and what had started as a mere wager between two hot-headed young men was turning into a grand occasion. And according to those who prided themselves on predicting such things, the weather was set to be fair.

The predictions were right and even at the early hour they set out, the sun was hot. Sophie wore her coolest muslin, a pale lemon with white spots, a wide neckline and tiny sleeves. Her hair was pinned up under a wide-brimmed straw hat. In one hand she carried a fan and in the other a parasol. Her reticule, which hung on a cord from her wrist, contained nothing but a handkerchief and a phial of violet water.

Their road, already packed with other vehicles, took them out to Islington Spa, a charming village with a pond beside a green dappled by the shadow of several tall elms. They paused here to take a drink and allow the gentlemen who were riding beside the coaches to rest their horses, then were on their way again. When they breasted the hill at the top of Holloway Road and looked back, they had a fine view of London spread out before them. Sophie remembered that aspect from when her parents had first brought her to London. She had been innocently excited, a child travelling to a new place, unaware that travelling was to be her lot for the next ten years and more, that the simple life she was leaving behind was to be lost to her for ever. She looked back and tried to recall how she had felt, but growing up and the years in between got in the way.

They continued through the village of Highgate and drew up on the outskirts of Finchley Common, where a grassy area made a grand viewing arena. It was already lined with open carriages from which the occupants hoped to witness the end of the race. Some enterprising salesmen had set up their stalls and were selling favours and trinkets, currant buns, ale and lemonade, and others were taking wagers, shouting the odds. As they arrived Sophie heard one shouting. 'Three to one on *The Winged Chariot.*'

'Which one is that?' she asked Ariadne who sat beside her.

'Mr Buskin's. Mr Poundell has called his equipage *The Yellow Peril.* Shall you risk a wager?'

'No, certainly not. I abhor gambling.'

'Oh, surely there can be no harm in putting a little of one's pin money on the outcome? It adds to the excitement.'

'I think it is exciting enough, when either or both men could be killed or injured.' She could not condone gambling, however innocent it appeared. She had seen where it could lead. That first small wager was the harbinger of untold misery.

'Fustian! I am going to put five guineas on Mr Poundell.'

'Five guineas! Surely you do not carry so much about with you?'

'I do today. I have double that in here.' And she lifted the hand from which hung her reticule.

Sophie was shocked at the amount. She could and often did keep house in Italy for a month on its equivalent, and a great deal less in that last year when her father's luck, never good, had run out altogether. Thinking of that time, she was sharply reminded of her confrontation with Count Cariotti at Lady Myers's ball and quickly thrust it from her. She did not want to remember. 'And if you lose it?'

'Oh, Papa will ring a peal over me, but I can soon turn him round my thumb and he will give me some more.'

The difference between Ariadne and herself could not have been better illustrated. The Duke had paid for her to be as well dressed as her friend and had made sure she had enough to eat, but it seemed not to have occurred to him that she might need money, a few coins in her reticule to spend on fripperies, though not gambling, definitely not on gambling. Knowing herself as well as she did, she knew her pride would have made her refuse even if he had offered, but she was painfully aware that the little money she had brought from Italy and changed into English coins had all but run out and the sooner she earned her own living the better. She should have stayed at home and continued her writing instead of coming out to enjoy herself. The pleasure of the day was fading fast.

They stopped the coach at the end of the line where they had a good view of the road leading to the finish and nothing would do but Ariadne must get down and put her bet on. 'Come with me,' she begged Sophie.

Harriet and Mrs Jefferson were content to sit and talk, so the two girls left them and strolled, arm in arm, to the man who was shouting the odds. He took Ariadne's money and wrote her name in his book, after which they decided to see who, among their friends, had arrived. They all seemed to be there and they stood about talking to them, speculating on who might win.

'Mr Poundell has the most experience,' Ariadne said. 'He often takes over the ribbons on stage journeys and the passengers do not know if he is driving or the regular driver.'

'Yes, but his vehicle is an old stagecoach he borrowed from William Chapman who took it out of service some time ago, and Mr Buskin is using his father's new travelling coach…'

'Then I think Sir Henry is a bigger fool than his son to indulge him,' Sophie put in.

'Not only that, he has wagered a thousand guineas on his darling son and heir coming in victorious,' someone else added, ignoring Sophie's remark.

This was too much for Sophie and she turned away to watch a troupe of acrobats who were entertaining the waiting crowds.

'Why, if it isn't the little blue stocking.'

Sophie, struck by the strident voice, turned to face the speaker, only to find herself being scrutinised by Lady

Colway. From beneath a large silk parasol, her brown eyes raked Sophie from head to toe. 'Who would have thought such pretty nothingness could harbour such a vitriolic spreader of tales…'

'I beg your pardon?'

'Oh, it is not my pardon, you should beg, but his Grace's. You have done nothing but humiliate and embarrass him from the minute you arrived. Why did you come? Was it to see how much you could squeeze out of him?' She stood in front of Sophie, blocking her way back to the carriage.

'No, certainly not. Please let me pass.'

The woman ignored the request. 'No, I had forgot, you are going to make a name for yourself as a writer of scandal. But let me warn you of the dangers. You will lay yourself open to litigation if you mention me and the Duke of Belfont.'

'Indeed? Is truth not the perfect defence in law?' It was said sweetly; she refused to raise her voice, but it was evidently an answer her ladyship had not been expecting.

'Truth needs proving.'

'Oh, I do not think I shall have any trouble in that direction.'

She tried to push past, but Lady Colway seized her arm in a painful grip. 'You will ruin yourself by that, if you have not already done so. When I am the Duchess of Belfont, you may be sure I shall take care you are never received in polite society. You will sink to the level you evidently aspire to, unrecognised except by purveyors of illiterate rubbish and their ignorant readers.'

'*When* you are Duchess of Belfont, you may do as you please.'

'Oh, I shall be, never fear. Clarence cannot last much longer and James and I have a long-standing arrangement.

It will take more than a silly little fortune hunter to come between us.'

'Oh, I am sure it will. Now, please allow me to pass.' She pulled herself out of the woman's grasp, almost ran back to the carriage and scrambled up beside Harriet. Thankfully Mrs Jefferson had left her and was talking to her husband, who had ridden up and dismounted nearby.

'Sophie, whatever is the matter?' Harriet asked. 'You look positively distraught. And where is Ariadne?'

'She is talking to Dorothy and some others we met. They were making wagers and I do not approve of gambling.'

'That I can understand, but surely you do not need to be so agitated about it.'

'Oh, I am not agitated about that. I was accosted by Lady Colway, who informed me she is to be the Duchess of Belfont. It seems she and the Duke have an understanding.'

Harriet laughed. 'She is romanticising. My brother would never marry her, even if she were not ineligible on account of having a live husband.'

'How can you be so sure? I know they are still lovers and she told me Lord Colway is mortally sick.'

'He has been mortally sick for years. What else did she say?'

'That I would be taken to law if I mentioned her or the Duke in my book.'

'I did not realise you meant to do that.'

'I do not. The book is about my travels in Europe, places and people I saw, nothing scandalous at all.'

'Did you tell her that?'

'No, I did not. Why should I justify myself to her?'

Harriet looked as if she were about to say more, but Mrs Jefferson came back to join them with the news that the carriages, racing neck and neck, had been seen on the road a couple of miles to the north. All conversation ceased as people craned their necks to catch a glimpse of the combatants, hoping their own favourite would be the first in view.

'It's Buskin!' someone shouted as the noise of galloping hooves heralded the arrival of the leading coach.

Along the road came *The Winged Chariot*, its tired horses being goaded into further effort by the whip Theodore cracked over their heads. The watchers cheered and then went wild with excitement as *The Yellow Peril* hove into view and appeared to be overhauling its rival. Sophie gave thanks that both drivers, horses and carriages had survived in one piece.

But her thanks were uttered too soon. Peter was gaining inexorably and, five hundred yards from the finishing line, had brought his equipage level with Theodore's. They were wheel to wheel on the narrow road, when a mail-coach, innocently going about its business in the opposite direction, appeared over the brow of the hill and came upon the crowds, some of whom were in the road and had to jump out of its way. It would have ploughed into the oncoming vehicles if someone, with great presence of mind, had not ridden up beside the coach and yelled at the driver to pull up, at the same time grabbing the reins of the leading horse and jumping at full gallop from his own mount to the back of the leading horse. It was an act of courage and strength that had the crowd gasping.

It was then, as she watched in horror, Sophie recognised the gallant horseman as the Duke of Belfont. It took superhuman strength to haul the horses to a stop, but, between the Duke and the coach driver, they managed it before the oncoming coaches, with their drivers desperately trying to pull up, were on to them. Sophie was down from

her seat almost before the mail's wheels had stopped turning, determined to make sure the Duke had not been hurt.
She was just in time to see him slide from the back of the
horse and Lady Colway throw herself into his arms, a
very public demonstration of their relationship. Sophie
stopped and stared as his arms went round his lover. She
could not look. Turning her back on them, she faced chaos
as people ran hither and thither, trying avoid the oncoming coaches.

Theodore, slightly in the lead, had seen the road ahead
of him blocked by the mail and the people surrounding it,
and swerved off the road in one direction, scattering the
stalls, while Peter had taken the other, rattling over the
rough heath, bouncing up and down until the ancient carriage could take no more and the axle broke, sending one
wheel hurtling away down the hill on its own, missing several bystanders by a hair's breadth. The coach came to rest
on its side, its remaining wheel still spinning.

The whole episode had taken only seconds, but the
confusion among the onlookers, as they ran hither and
thither, lasted much longer. Sophie, who was standing
quite still, staring at it all, wishing the earth would open
and swallow her, so that she would never again have to
witness the man she loved cradling another woman in his
arms, found herself taken by the arm and propelled back
to the Jeffersons' coach by Harriet.

'Get in,' she said. 'And sit still. I am going to see what
I can do to help.'

'I'll come too.'

'No, it is not fitting. I forbid it.' She nodded towards
Ariadne, whose father was helping her back to the carriage
in a swooning state. 'Stay and talk to Ariadne.'

The two girls were left sitting side by side in the coach,
both benumbed by what had happened. Ariadne had seen

Peter thrown from his carriage and several people hurt in the crush as they tried to avoid the coach; Sophie had seen the man she loved, the man who had undoubtedly saved many lives by his courage, fall into the arms of his mistress. It should have been her arms! It was to her he should have turned... Tears pricked at her eyes.

'Oh, Sophie, it was awful,' Ariadne wept. 'Poor Peter. If he should die...'

'Is he like to?'

'I don't know. I cannot bear it.'

Sophie was distracted from her own misery long enough to look hard at the girl beside her. 'Ariadne, have you developed a *tendre* for Mr Poundell?'

'Oh, yes. But Papa does not approve. Peter does not have a title, you see. He had hopes the Duke of Belfont would offer for me.'

'And you did not?'

'No, he is far too grand for me. I should be for ever doing the wrong thing or being silly. I collect he does not like silliness.'

In spite of herself, Sophie managed to smile. How true that was and how silly she had been. The Duke of Belfont was looking to someone more mature, more able to please him, than an awkward second cousin who had turned out of the blue and thrown herself on his mercy. 'Then we must pray all is well and your papa relents.'

It was some time before order was restored and the on-lookers, who had come out to have a little fun, turned slowly for home, some of them bearing scratches and bruises caused more by the panic than the accident. Ariadne was allowed to see Peter, who had sustained a bump on the head and a badly bruised shoulder and was laid out on the seat of Theodore's coach, which had managed to come to a stop without damage. Theodore himself was un-hurt, but he had learned a sharp lesson and was very sub-dued.

'Sir Henry is going to drive them both back to town himself,' Ariadne told Sophie when she returned to the carriage. 'And all bets are off.'

'I should think so too. So, your money was refunded?'

'No, the rogue cut and ran in the confusion, taking everyone's money with him.'

Sophie wanted to say, 'It serves you right', but decided that would be unkind. 'I am sorry.'

'I do not care about the money as long as Peter is not badly hurt. And you are right, I think Papa will relent. At any rate, I think he has given up on the Duke after today's disgraceful exhibition. Everyone is talking of it.'

'He was extraordinarily courageous,' Sophie said, feeling she ought to defend him, even though she knew what Ariadne meant and was still smarting herself. The whole day had taken on the aspect of a nightmare, a quality of unreality, as if she might wake soon and discover it had all taken place in her imagination.

'Oh, no doubt of it, and the men are all clapping him on the back and calling him one hell of a brave fellow, but that doesn't mean they approve of the way Lady Colway flung herself at him. Having a mistress is all very well, but she ought to be kept discreetly out of sight.'

Ariadne's choice of words surprised Sophie, but she supposed she was only repeating what the gentlemen had said. If her mother had been present and not discussing the matter with other ladies, standing in a huddle waiting to be carried away in their respective carriages, she would undoubtedly have reprimanded her. 'It wasn't the Duke's fault.'

'It does not matter whose fault it was, it was as good

as a public announcement. It will take a very brave or a very blind woman to marry him now.' She sighed. 'Of course, the fact that he is a Duke might have some bearing on the matter.'

Sophie did not want to talk about the Duke—she especially did not want to talk about whom he might marry—and looked away, wondering where Harriet was. She had not returned since she had gone off to help the injured, bidding her stay in the coach.

When Harriet found him, James had taken off his jacket and was helping bind up a nasty cut sustained by a young lad who had tried to flee Theodore's out-of-control coach and horses and fallen in a prickly bush. He was thankful that no one had been badly injured, though it had been a very near thing. The mail had been stopped in time and, once the frightened horses had been calmed, had gone on its way. The grateful thanks of its occupants had done little to make him feel better about what had happened. If he had not decided on a sudden whim to join his sister and Sophie and enjoy a few hours free of his duties, he would not have been riding up the hill at almost the same time as the mail and would not have been there to avert a dreadful accident. His arms had almost been pulled from their sockets when he jumped from his own mount to the other horse and they had been hurting like hell and almost numb when he finally brought the whole equipage to a shuddering stop. He had not, at first, seen Ellen running towards him and had been almost bowled over by her, then had had to lift his aching arms to stop her flinging them both to the ground. He had thrust her away, but not before he had seen Sophie running towards him and then stop suddenly, her lovely eyes betraying her shock. Then she had turned and walked away from him.

Everyone had been staring. Half the *ton* had witnessed him with his arms about his one-time mistress and the other half would soon hear of it. He would be damned and what he had forecast would come about. Lord Colway would learn of it and be forced to see what he had conveniently refused to see before, that his wife was cuckolding him. James wondered vaguely what the fellow would do, but his real concern was for Sophie and Harriet; gossip tainted everyone it touched.

His sister had always been steadfast and loyal, even when their father had railed at him for not marrying and providing the next heir. The nagging had gone on so long he had joined the army to escape it and made matters worse. Eldest sons, particularly only sons, did not go off to war and risk leaving a huge estate with no head. He had survived a wound and returned home to take up his filial duties and those the Regent imposed on him just before his father died. It was at court he had met Ellen. He had had no compunction about making her his mistress simply because he was not the first lover she had taken; she already had a certain reputation. It was his misfortune that she fancied herself a duchess and would not let go, even when he had caught her in bed with Alfred.

Alfred, of all people! He assumed she was hedging her bets, knowing Alfred was his heir. He had been surprised that he had not felt hurt, so much as anger. And then Sophie, his beloved Sophie, had exploded into his life and changed everything: the way he looked at life; his thoughts on marriage, which he had previously equated with being shackled; what constituted pleasure, what pain; his duty. And now that had all been scattered to the wind because Ellen Colway had publicly proclaimed their relationship. She could not have known the opportunity would come her way, but when it had, she had seized it with alacrity. The acrimonious row they had had afterwards had made him feel slightly better, but only slightly. The damage had been done.

'Well?' Harriet demanded as he finished what he was doing and reached for his coat. It was not at all like his sister to be angry, but she was angry now.

'Well, what?'

'How are you going to get out of this coil? What are you going to do about that demi-rep?'

'Nothing. It will blow over.' They walked slowly back towards the carriage as they talked.

'Only if you keep away from her and then it might take a very long time.'

'Sis, I did not know she would be here. I was coming to join you.'

'That may be, but why did you let it happen? Everyone saw you put your arms round her.'

'She flung herself at me, nearly knocked me off my feet. I had to grab hold of her. If I had stepped aside, she would have fallen to the ground. Surely you understood that?'

'If I did, it isn't the interpretation other people are putting on it.' She paused. 'Is she still your mistress?'

'No, she is not, has not been for some time.'

'Then you must say so publicly and hope you will be believed.'

'Harriet, that would be ungallant.'

'Then, for heaven's sake, offer for someone else and be done with it.'

'She will not have me and I cannot blame her.'

'Who?'

'You know who.'

'Sophie.'

'Yes. Sophie. To her I am a tyrant and a rake.'

'That's because you behave like one. Can you not show her your gentler side? I know you to be loving and tender-hearted, concerned for all your people, even those who do not deserve it. Why make an exception of Sophie?'

They were approaching the carriage where Sophie sat beside Ariadne, waiting for Harriet and Mrs Jefferson to return, but he did not think she had seen them coming. She was staring into the middle distance as if what she saw there was infinitely preferable to what she could see close at hand. Her face was still, but he had never seen her look so sad. Did that mean she cared? But it was too late, wasn't it? He had damned himself for ever in her eyes. 'She has made an exception of herself.'

'You mean because she does not conform? I think, in the present situation, that might be a good thing. The usual débutantes will not do. I collect Mr Jefferson saying that Ariadne had had a lucky escape.'

He laughed.

Sophie heard his laughter and turned to face them. How could he laugh when he had behaved so abominably? Did he not care that he had compromised his sister and she would not be received in anyone's drawing room after this? Did he not care that he had broken her heart? She glared at him, hating him.

He recoiled from the venom in her eyes, but it happened only inside him; outwardly he was his usual confident self. He stopped beside the carriage and bowed. 'Miss Langford, Miss Jefferson.'

Ariadne giggled and turned her face away; Sophie had more courage, she put on a sugar-sweet smile. 'My lord, we are indeed honoured that you have torn yourself away from more amusing company to see us safely on our way.'

He refused to rise to the bait. 'It is my pleasure, Miss Langford.' He assisted Harriet into the carriage, while Mr

Jefferson helped his wife in the other side, then he bowed again and went off in search of his horse.

The journey back was as uncomfortable as it could be. No one spoke. Sophie was not sure whether Mrs Jefferson was deliberately cutting them or whether she genuinely could not think of anything to say. Ariadne looked as if she were daydreaming, no doubt about Peter Poundell, and speech would only spoil it. Sophie looked at Harriet, sitting opposite her, and Harriet looked back and smiled reassuringly. Her composure was admirable and steadied Sophie.

She found herself wanting to defend the Duke and that did not accord with her fury at the way he had behaved. She was not furious on her own behalf, she told herself, but for Harriet, who did not deserve to be ostracised by society. She could not understand him. He had risked his life to save others, had been hailed a hero and then spoiled it all by embracing his mistress in public. Why had he come when he had been so against the idea of the race in the first place? Because he knew Lady Colway would be present and he could not resist the lady's allure, she answered herself.

The journey came to an end at last and Harriet and Sophie were set down outside Belfont House. They thanked Mrs Jefferson and turned away, glad to be home.

'What a day!' Harriet said, as they handed their hats and parasols to the maids, ordered the footman to bring tea and went into the drawing room, where Harriet flung herself on a sofa, kicked off her shoes and put her feet up.

'It will have repercussions, I think,' Sophie said, sitting opposite her.

'No doubt of it.'

'Shall you mind? Being cut by your friends, I mean.'

'My real friends will not cut me.' She laughed lightly. 'Do not look so woebegone, Sophie, we are not about to lose our position in society. It is one of the advantages of being a duke, you can get away with things lesser mortals would be condemned for and he will soon be forgiven. Whatever the ladies might privately think, they will follow their husbands and, while the men might say he was a little unwise, they will not condemn him. In their eyes he is a fine man who saved the lives of a great many people, among whom were their wives and perhaps their children. Besides, none of it was James's fault. That foolish woman threw herself at him and, short of allowing her to fall to the ground, he had to steady her.'

'You always defend him.'

'I would not if he were in the wrong. Can you not forgive him?'

'What has it to do with me? It is not my forgiveness he needs.'

'Oh, but it is, my dear, yours most of all.'

'I do not understand.'

'I think you do.'

Before Sophie could ask her to explain, the footman arrived with the tea tray and the conversation ceased while he set it down on the table and arranged the china cups on their saucers. Sophie noted there were three of each. 'I'll see to it, Collins,' Harriet said.

He bowed and withdrew, standing aside at the door to admit James. 'You are just in time for some tea,' Harriet said cheerfully.

He lowered himself into a chair rather gingerly. 'My lord, are you hurt?' Sophie asked, though she had vowed never to speak to him again.

'A little stiffness, Sophie, nothing more, thank you.'

'I am not surprised, after that Herculean effort you made,' Harriet said, handing him a cup of tea. 'This will revive you. Or would you rather have something stronger?'

'No, this is just what I need.'

Silently they sipped their tea.

'Was Hotspur hurt?' Sophie asked, to break the silence, which she found oppressive.

'No, but he was certainly distressed.'

'As we all were.'

The allusion was not lost on him; he knew what she meant. 'Indeed.'

'It is fortunate you arrived when you did,' Harriet put in quickly, worried what Sophie might say next. 'Your courage will not be forgotten.'

'I would that it could be, along with what happened afterwards.'

'I am sure you do,' Sophie said, unable to keep quiet; it was a serious flaw in her character her mother had warned her about many times. 'But perhaps, now the boot is on the other foot, you may realise how I feel, being so misunderstood.'

He turned to smile at her, the rueful smile of a scolded man wanting to make amends. '*Touché,* my dear. I stand rebuked.'

She discovered, to her consternation, that her heart was softening. How could she be so weak as to surrender at the first glimmer of a smile?

'There!' Harriet said, going to the table to replace her cup. 'I knew you could not remain at odds with each other for long.'

Sophie smiled; she was too fond of Harriet to contest that statement, but she did not think anything had really changed. That he had not planned or wished for the encounter with Lady Colway she conceded, but that did not alter the essential facts: Lady Colway was his mistress, and he disapproved of ladies writing books. The book was more important than ever now. She excused herself and went up to her room to work on it until it was time to change for supper.

'I hoped you intend to stay at home tonight,' Harriet said, after Sophie had gone. 'I think a little show of domesticity is in order…'

'To placate Sophie?' Why did he feel his ire bubbling up again? He was the Duke of Belfont, a man of great wealth, a modicum of talent, a man admired by princes, beloved of the ladies, a man who did his duty, however irksome; he did not need to justify himself to anyone, least of all a chit of a girl. He could come and go as he pleased. 'She is hardly a model of maidenly reticence herself.'

'Her mistakes are made from ignorance, yours from pride.'

'You would defend her.'

'That is exactly what she said to me about you. I see the good in both of you, while I deplore the not-so-good.'

'You are an angel and I wish others would follow your example.'

'Offer for her, James. You know that is what you long to do.'

'And risk being given the right about? And what about that Italian fellow?'

'He is not to be considered any more than Ellen Colway is.'

'You make it all sound so simple.'

'I am sure you are clever enough to make her see the advantages. Besides, it will silence your critics and put an end to Lady Colway's tricks.'

He laughed suddenly. 'Oh, is that all! And when am I to do this?'

'At our ball. It will be an ideal opportunity.'

'You mean to go ahead with it, then?'

'Yes, more than ever. We must show the world that the Dersinghams cannot be put down by a vindictive woman.'

It was unfortunate that Sophie had come downstairs again to fetch her reticule, which she had abandoned on a table and only remembered when she reached her room. She was standing outside the drawing-room door, her hand on the knob to go in, when she heard the last part of the conversation. She forgot what she had come down for and fled back upstairs. She did not hear James add, 'Do you think she will have me?', or Harriet's answer, 'Yes, she loves you. And you love her, don't you?'

'To distraction.'

'Then tell her so.'

Sophie did not appear for supper that night.

Sophie only went down next morning when she was sure the Duke had left the house. Even so, she had to face Harriet. She found it hard to believe that Harriet, who had welcomed her as a cousin, bought her clothes, taken her out and about, introduced her to her friends and defended her, could be so devious. Sophie was so badly hurt she wanted to scream out, yell abuse, call Harriet names and wondered at her own restraint. Pride, that's what it was. To say anything meant admitting she listened at doors. Keeping quiet meant pretending nothing had changed between them. Could she do it?

Harriet was in the little sitting room on the ground floor, which she favoured because it had long windows that looked out onto the garden. She was not looking at the garden when Sophie entered, but going through a large pile of correspondence. 'What did I tell you?' she ex-claimed when Sophie entered the room. 'These are all ac-ceptances. Everyone is coming to our ball.'

'Oh.' Sophie sat down opposite her and picked up one of the cards. 'Lord and Lady Mountjoy are delighted to ac-cept,' she read, wondering who Lord and Lady Mountjoy might be. And there was another, Mr and Mrs Jefferson and Miss Jefferson were also delighted to accept. So were Sir Henry and Lady Buskin and Mr Theodore Buskin. And it went without saying that Mrs Jessop and Alfred would be there.

'Are you sure they are not all coming to crow?' she asked.

'Of course not. And even if they are, it does not mat-ter. We are stronger than they are. Together we will face them down and, who knows, we might have some good news to impart.'

'You mean you hope someone will offer for me, in spite of my reputation as a purveyor of illiterate rubbish for ignorant readers.'

'Whatever made you say that?' Harriet asked, genu-inely shocked. 'Is that how you see yourself?'

'It is how the world sees me, according to Lady Col-way.'

'Oh, give her no mind. I heard she has gone back to her husband. Now, come and sit beside me and tick the names off on my list. Then I must make sure everything is in hand for the supper and that the flowers will be delivered on time. I am really looking forward to this ball. We haven't had one at Belfont House since my own come-out and that was ages ago.'

Sophie wondered how Harriet could be so cheerful. But then she could afford to be; she imagined she had ar-ranged things very neatly. But she was in for a shock because Sophie Langford was not going to succumb like some vapid schoolgirl, Sophie Langford had more guts than that; Sophie Langford was going to stick to her guns and remain single.

Chapter Eight

James was entertaining a handful of close associates in a private room at White's. They were supposed to be playing cards; indeed, the table around which they sat had cards laid out and there was a pile of coins and a glass at everyone's elbow, but gaming was not the purpose of the meeting. He had called them together to discuss the return of the Duke of Wellington the following week. They were all serving officers or men like James who had served with distinction and were now trusted with undercover work. They had successfully protected the royal visitors and ensured their visit to London was without incident and, though the Regent had not specifically asked them to do the same for the Duke, they felt duty-bound to watch out for him. Not only had some of them served under him, but they knew that if anything happened to him the consequence could be dire.

Without mentioning Lord Myers, James told them he had heard of a possible attempt on the Duke's life. 'The intelligence comes from an impeccable source,' he said. 'And, though no names have been mentioned, one springs to mind.'

'Cariotti,' Richard said. 'Though there is no proof, none at all.'

'Do you mean that macaroni who is dancing in the shadow of the Austrian delegation?' Major Bowers asked. 'He is a fop.'

'But a dangerous one,' Richard said. 'I have come across him before, when we were working behind the lines, and, since he has been in London, I have been making enquiries. His mother was English and he started out by spying for the British government, but when it looked as though Napoleon might be victorious, he changed sides and became a double agent. He was well trusted by Bonaparte.'

'But so many changed their allegiance in defeat and no one thinks the worse of them for it,' Lord Carstairs, husband of Harriet's good friend, put in. 'Why do you think he is implicated in a plot to kill the Duke?'

'I have no evidence except that my source mentioned a foreigner here with the distinguished guests of the Regent,' James said.

'There are many of them.'

'True, but Cariotti has something to hide. And I am sure he thinks Miss Langford knows his secret and is going to reveal it in her book. He is doing his best to stop her.'

'Miss Langford?' Bowers queried. 'But what can she know?'

'I have yet to find out. Perhaps nothing. But her father might well have done. Perhaps the man thinks Lord Langford passed on information to his daughter.'

'Not only about Cariotti,' Richard murmured. 'She might have learned something of our own operations.'

'Is that of any consequence now?' Carstairs asked. 'The war is over.'

'I am not convinced of it,' James said. 'Boney has threatened to come back. I would like to preserve my cover if I can.'

'You are too involved in society to be rushing off to war

again,' one of the others said. 'And the Regent values you too highly to let you go.'

James smiled. If he was needed he would go, but if he did not it would not be because the Regent thought he should remain at home, but because a certain young lady had agreed to marry him. The prospect of sharing the rest of his life with her was one he contemplated with infinite pleasure. He loved her, her happiness was paramount, especially if it resulted in his own, but he had yet to convince her of it. She was stubborn and there was that foolish vow not to marry, which he would have to overcome. And that book.

'You will have to get a sight of the book,' the Major said, echoing his thoughts. 'She is living in your house, under your protection. It should not be difficult for you to insist on examining it.'

'And what reason should I give for wanting to do so?'

'God, man! Do you need a reason?'

'I think I do. It is common courtesy, after all.'

'Then you had better think of one. You are supposed to have a winning way with the ladies, use it.'

James bit back an angry retort, which would not have helped. Instead he changed the subject. 'In the meantime, we must do what we can to protect Wellington. There will undoubtedly be great crowds to cheer his coming, ideal conditions for an assassin. He must be surrounded by our people every step of the way. Richard, can you organise your company to be at Dover to ride close to his coach, as we did when the French king arrived? I will arrange for local militia to meet him when he arrives in London and escort him to his home. If an attempt is made, we will be ready.'

'If Cariotti is at the bottom of it, I doubt he will make the attempt himself,' Richard said. 'He will hire assassins, disillusioned soldiers have come home to nothing but penury.'

'If apprehended, they will be offered an amnesty to name names.' He paused. 'Now, unless anyone has anything to add, I beg to be excused. I have a ball to attend.'

The arrangements had all been made; a huge tent had been put up in the garden and a ballroom floor laid in it which had been polished until it was like a mirror. Shuttered lamps with coloured glass had been strung in the trees, ready to be lit at dusk; the food had been delivered and an army of servants employed to help the chef and the regular staff prepare and cook it. Extra footmen had been taken on and arrayed in the Belfont livery. Flowers were being arranged in huge vases all over the house and a large orchestra had arrived. Sophie could hear them rehearsing through the open window of her bedchamber.

She was supposed to be resting before Rose came to help her into her ball gown, but, though she was lying on her bed, she was feeling far from restful. Not only was it uncomfortably hot, but her head was whirling. All this fuss, a fortune being spent, all so that the world might know that the Duke of Belfont repudiated his mistress and was taking as his bride his nobody of a second cousin. Gossip must be silenced at all costs; his Grace must be saved the embarrassment of being asked to leave court in the middle of the most important Season since his Highness had been made Regent. But why choose her, when there were others falling over themselves to be his duchess?

Could that be because none of them would accept him, after what had happened? To be a duke and be rejected must be the ultimate humiliation. But Harriet had told her firmly that what had happened would make no difference;

he could do almost anything, flaunt all the rules and still be called a jolly fine fellow and welcomed everywhere. He would be accepted simply because he was a duke. Which was right? And did it matter? She meant to refuse him. Not that she wanted to humiliate him; she could not do that after he had taken her in and spent so much on her, but she would have to find an opportunity to prevent him from asking. All her efforts to persuade Harriet to cancel the affair had failed.

'I cannot,' Harriet had told her. 'It would not look well and would give rise to prodigious gossip, especially if we could give no good reason for cancellation. Conjecture would invent one, you may be sure.' She had paused and looked closely at Sophie. 'Why are you so against it? I thought you were looking forward to it.'

'I told you, I do not like to be puffed up. I do not want to have the eligibles standing in line to offer simply because I am the ward of the Duke of Belfont and they might gain some advantage being married to me. I intend to remain single and will have none of them. It is not fair to them to encourage speculation.'

She could not tell Harriet the true reason, that she knew the Duke intended to propose, not because he loved her, but to silence his critics and to take people's minds off his affair with Lady Colway. Marrying Sophie might also serve to placate Lord Colway, who would undoubtedly have heard what had happened. However much she loved the Duke, however much she longed for her love to be returned, Sophie did not intend to be used in that fashion. A marriage made under those circumstances was bound to fail and they would both be made miserable. She was already more miserable than she had ever been in her life before and bearing it in silence was using up all her reserves of stoicism.

'There will be more if we cancel at this late stage,' Harriet had told her. 'And no one is going to put pressure on you to choose a husband. It would be the last thing I would do…'

'Is it?' she asked dully. 'And the Duke?'

'He will not either. The ball is to introduce you to society, to enable you to accept other invitations, to make new friends. And to tell the world you have our support whatever you choose to do.'

'Even if I stay single and spend my life writing books?'

'Even then.' She had smiled reassuringly and reached across to pat Sophie's hand. 'But you will forgive us, dearest, if we hope for something more for you.'

What else could she do but smile back and pretend all was well? But it left her with a serious dilemma. The ball was going ahead; more than half the *ton* had accepted invitations. There was even some talk of the Regent putting in a brief appearance if he was not too busy entertaining his illustrious guests. How could she make sure the Duke did not follow his sister's advice and propose? Perhaps he would not.

No, of course he would not, she told herself suddenly. Why would a wealthy duke, who, according to his sister, could do almost anything without anyone thinking anything of it, stoop so far as to marry a nobody with nothing to recommend her? She had been a nuisance to him ever since she arrived and though he might wish she would marry someone else, he would never marry her himself. She lay on her bed and laughed aloud; what a fool she had been to believe he would, never mind worry herself sick over it.

Revitalised, she sprang up and went over to the cupboard in the corner of the room and fetched out the gown she was to wear. It had been made for her before the ill-fated trip to Finchley Common and at the time she had been pleased and excited at the prospect of wearing it, had even laughed when the Duke had asked what it was like, telling him it was a secret until he saw her on the night.

The overdress, open from the high waist, was in a shimmering pale blue spider gauze that revealed the underskirt of ivory satin, which was heavily embroidered with gold thread and seed pearls down the length of the front and around the hem. The sleeves were of the same spider gauze, very full and caught just above the elbow with ribbons and from there floated freely. The boat-shaped neckline was severely plain, but she had a shawl of the spider gauze to drape over her shoulders. It was by far the most expensive gown she had ever had and she was unlikely to wear it again; it did not accord with the life she had mapped out for herself. She would persuade Harriet to send it back to the shop, along with other extravagances, because, after this night, she must put self-indulgence from her and concentrate on making a living.

She was holding it up against herself, stroking her hand down the soft fabric, daydreaming a little, when Rose came to help her with her *toilette*. She carried a small narrow box in her hand.

'Miss Langford, I am come to help you dress and to give you this.' She held out the box, whose lid was painted with tiny mauve pansies. 'His Grace stopped me on my way up and instructed me to make sure you had it.'

Sophie's hand shook as she opened the box; it was strange that even talking about the Duke, or touching something he had touched, set her quivering with nerves. Inside, nestling in tissue, was a fan. The handle was made of carved ivory with a silken cord to hang it from her wrist. Opening it revealed an embroidered picture of a country house set in parkland. Though she had not been there since she was a little girl, she knew it was Dersingham Park. She stood and looked at it, lost in wonder at the workmanship. There was a folded piece of paper in the lid. She opened it and read James's simple message. 'This was my mother's. I would be honoured if you would accept it with my affectionate best wishes for a successful come-out. Belfont.' It was all too much for her and she burst into tears.

Rose gaped at her in perplexity. 'Miss Langford, please do not cry,' she pleaded. 'You will ruin your complexion.'

And that made her laugh so hysterically between her sobs that Rose became alarmed and rushed off to find Lady Harley.

Harriet had been in the middle of dressing and arrived in a hastily donned dressing gown. 'Sophie, whatever is the matter?'

Sophie had stopped her wild sobbing and was standing by the window, looking out over the garden where workmen and servants hurried to and fro between the house and the marquee. She stood very still, her hands holding the fan, as if afraid to move in case it started her off again.

'Sophie.' Harriet hurried to put an arm about her shoulder. 'What is it? What has happened?'

'This.' She raised the fan but did not look at her friend. 'The Duke sent me this.'

'Has he? Oh, how thoughtful of him. But surely that is not making you sad?'

'Oh, can't you see? It is just one more thing to add to all the others…'

'I don't understand. Do you not like it?'

'It's lovely.' A huge sigh of a sob escaped her. 'But I already owe him so much and there is no way I can repay him, except—' She stopped suddenly.

'Except what, dear girl?'

'Do whatever is asked of me. Marry whomever you choose for me. Give up my book. Give up being me.'

'Nonsense, no one has asked you to give up being yourself. I cannot think what has got into you, Sophie. I would never have taken you for a watering pot and all over nothing at all. Now, dry your eyes and let us have no more tears. Our guests will be arriving soon and you must be there to greet them. Rose will bathe your face and help you dress. I will come for you when it is time to go downstairs.' She bent and kissed Sophie's cheek. 'Be happy, my dear, that is all I wish for you.' And then she was gone.

In a daze Sophie submitted to Rose's ministrations, had her eyes bathed in witch hazel, put on her petticoat and white silk stockings, had her dark hair intricately arranged in coils and ringlets interwoven with strings of tiny pearls, slipped on her ivory satin slippers and was finally helped into her dress.

'There, miss, you will undoubtedly be the belle of the ball,' Rose said. 'Though that is only as it should be, considering it is being given in your honour. You must consider yourself very fortunate to have the Duke and her ladyship to sponsor you.'

'I do, Rose, I do.'

'Then could you not smile a little more?'

Sophie looked in the mirror and saw an elegant young lady, fashionably dressed, not bad looking; in fact, quite handsome, but pale. Too pale. She pinched her cheeks viciously and ventured a wobbly smile at her reflection.

'That's better!' Rose said, evidently relieved, then, as a knock came at the door, added, 'Here is Lady Harley.'

Sophie turned as Harriet, dressed in a gown of pink-and-white striped silk and a matching turban, came into the room. Sophie curtsied. 'I am ready.'

'Oh, you look lovely. You will be a great hit, I know it. Now, let us go and join James.'

It was time. She picked up her reticule and the fan, took a deep breath and followed Harriet out on to the landing and down the stairs.

He was waiting at the foot of the stairs, talking to Captain Summers who had arrived early. Alerted by Richard, James turned and looked up as they descended slowly, step by step.

'By God, James,' Richard murmured. 'I would never recognise her as the same chit we met at Dover. She takes one's breath away.'

James smiled wryly. Sophie certainly robbed him of breath and, for a moment, of speech. He simply stared. It was not only her beauty, though that was striking—it was her poise, her maturity, and those huge wondrous eyes that seemed to him a little sad. But her step was firm and she was smiling.

She reached the bottom step. He bowed. 'Magnificent,' he said, which was inadequate to express what he was feeling, but with Richard beside him, grinning from ear to ear, and footmen standing about listening, it was all he would allow himself. Later, perhaps…

She curtsied, stiff with the effort to keep herself under control. But magnificent described him as well. He had chosen a deep midnight blue for his short-waisted tailcoat and a lighter blue silk for his breeches. Beautifully tailored, they showed off a physique that was honed to perfection. His waistcoat of white grosgrain, starched muslin neckcloth, white stockings and black shoes were worn with an air of casual elegance that belied the hard work of Talbot, his valet. 'Your Grace.'

She took her place between the Duke and Harriet as the sound of a coach drawing up outside reached their ears.

The first encounter had been successfully negotiated and nothing untoward had happened, nothing but a quick glance, no doubt to assure himself that she would not disgrace him and that his gift was safely suspended from her wrist. It had been formal, almost impersonal, which was all to the good, she told herself as she prepared to greet their guests.

The first arrivals were Alfred and his mother. Mrs Jessop looked her up and down and gave a snort of reluctant approval before passing on. Alfred, in the black and white adopted by James at Lady Myers's ball, stopped in front of her. 'Miss Langford, you look majestic. What a pity the Count could not be here. But never mind, I will do my poor best as a substitute. May I?' He lifted her dance card and wrote his name against two dances, one of which was a waltz.

'No, I am afraid that dance is mine,' James said, taking the pencil attached to the card, striking out Alfred's name and substituting his own against the waltz and also adding it to the opening dance. 'Choose another one.'

Sophie, standing beside him, smiled her fixed smile and said nothing as Alfred obeyed.

Alfred and Mrs Jessop were quickly followed by more guests, arriving in twos and threes, some in larger groups, some singly, until the ballroom and reception rooms on the ground floor of Belfont House, substantial as it was, was a heaving mass of humanity, all talking at once.

'Good God, Harriet,' James exclaimed. 'Have you invited the whole of London?'

'Not quite,' she said blithely. 'But I did not want to find that, after all our efforts, guests were thin on the ground.'

'Then I am thankful for that great tent, or we would have been hard put to squeeze them all in. How many more, do you think?'

It was a question echoed by Sophie. The ball was going to be a great crush and how they were to find room for dancing, she did not know. And it was all being done for her sake. Or was it? Was it not to prove that the Duke of Belfont could do as he pleased? He could flaunt his mistress and take whom he liked as a wife and when he issued an invitation, he expected people to turn up.

'I think they are all here now,' Harriet told him. 'We can safely leave our post and join our guests.'

James took Sophie's hand and tucked it beneath his arm, but even that small touch sent her senses reeling. She took a deep breath and bade herself keep a cool head.

'Sophie, you look charming,' he whispered as they strolled after their guests to the garden where the orchestra was tuning its instruments on a dais at one end of the marquee. 'I am proud of you.'

'Thank you, your Grace. Thank you also for your gift.'

'You like it?'

'It is very fine. I collect the picture is of Dersingham Park.'

'Yes, my father had it made for my mother to celebrate the first anniversary of their wedding. He gave her something on every anniversary.'

'Then I am surprised you could bear to part with it.'

'I wanted to give you something special and it seemed appropriate.'

'Appropriate?' She felt her frayed nerves getting the better of her and furiously brought herself under control.

'Yes, I wanted to mark your coming out with something out of the ordinary. I know it is usual to give jewellery, but I did not think it would serve. I came late to my guardianship of you and the circumstances were unusual; it seemed more fitting to give you something else, something that might have more significance than jewels.'

His words, carefully chosen, were almost her undoing. They showed him to be tender, considerate, thoughtful, all things she had known and acknowledged before that foolish race between Theodore and Peter. Had he changed so much? 'Then I shall treasure it, my lord.' She meant it too; the fan would always remind her of him, of the man, not the Duke, of his kindness and generosity. When she was busy scratching out a living with her pen, she would have it beside her.

It was only slightly cooler in the garden, where the heat of the day lingered into the twilight. She still had her hand on his sleeve and he had put his other hand over it, as if to keep her at his side. The master of ceremonies announced the opening dance as they arrived and James led Sophie on to the floor to start the proceedings. She was aware of the comments of the people standing on the sidelines and heard one matron say, 'They make a handsome couple, I'll wager he won't remain a bachelor much longer.' He must have heard it, too, but he gave no indication of it as they wove their way in and out of the others in the set. They executed the steps, smiled at each other and at their guests as they faced them in the figures, apparently at ease, but both could feel the tension between them, communicating itself through the air they breathed and the touch of their fingers. Sophie found herself almost holding her breath, waiting for him to say something, wondering how she could find her voice to reply, but the dance ended without a word being spoken.

He took her back to where Harriet sat with Lady Carstairs, bowed to Sophie and stationed himself behind his sister's chair to watch the proceedings.

Sophie's next partner was Theodore Buskin, bouncing around like a puppy, and then Peter Poundell, recovered from his injury, though he admitted to being a little stiff.

She stood up with Captain Summers, elegant in his regimentals, and then Alfred came to claim her for his country dance.

'You are definitely in looks tonight,' he said, as they executed the opening steps. 'But a little wooden, I think.'

'Wooden, Mr Jessop?'

'Yes, but you may relax now. The Duke has gone and you are no longer being observed.'

So, he had left the floor. She allowed herself a fleeting moment of disappointment and then rallied. 'If the Duke was watching us, then it was only to make sure I am enjoying myself. I am, after all, his ward.'

He laughed. 'Is that what he calls you?'

'What else should I be?'

'That is for you to decide, my dear. But collect I did warn you not to allow yourself to be drawn into his spider's web of deception. If he were not a duke, he would long ago have been ordered from court and not only because of his outrageous behaviour with another man's wife. There are other mysteries…'

'Mr Jessop, I beg you to desist. I do not want to listen to gossip.'

'Oh, it is not gossip. It is fact. He spent years abroad, years in which no one knows what he was up to. Oh, they believed he was fighting for his country, but believe me, he was not with Wellington. He disappeared in the middle of a battle and only reappeared when his father was dying.'

'How disappointed you must have been,' she scoffed. 'No doubt you were hoping he was dead.'

'My time will come, never fear.'

'Oh, do not doubt it.' She did not allow him time to decide what she meant, but turned and left him standing in the middle of the floor, excusing herself to the other dancers, 'Forgive me, I am a little too hot and feel faint.'

She made her way out of the awning, where it had indeed been uncomfortably hot, and made her way down the garden. It was dark now. Moon and stars were hidden by clouds and the only light came from the lanterns strung between the trees and they swung eerily in the slight breeze which had arisen in the last few minutes. The heat was still oppressive and she wondered if there might be a storm. It would cause consternation if there were.

She found a bench in an arbour and sat down to fan herself, wondering why Mr Jessop had taken the trouble to make those accusations against the Duke. He had as good as called him a traitor. Where had he obtained his socalled facts? Not for a minute did she believe them to be true, though they could be very damaging if that dreadful man repeated them to others, far more damaging than gossip about his Grace and Lady Colway. What could she do? What did Alfred Jessop expect her to do? Tell his Grace? What would he say? Would he be angry, hurt even, that she appeared to give the tale enough credence to repeat it?

She ought to go back to the ball, which was, after all, being given in her honour. She could hear the music and chatter, an occasional laugh, and dimly through the shrubbery, she could see the lights under the awning. She could also hear the wind in the tree tops and, in the distance, some way off still, a faint rumble of thunder. But the weather was the least of her concerns as she tried to calm herself and make the effort to go back and pretend to be enjoying herself.

James, who had gone to claim her for the waltz which was next, had just been in time to see her leave the floor and disappear down the garden path. Where was she going? And why? Surely she would not be so indiscreet as to arrange an assignation? Who with? And if she had gone to be alone, why? He followed, treading carefully, keeping in the shadows.

He found her alone, sitting on the bench, almost in the dark. The light from the nearest lantern, swinging backwards and forwards in the shadow of some branches, made her dress shimmer like moving water, but she sat very still, her closed fan in her hand. He could not see her face properly, but her eyes were huge and bright. What was she thinking about? A past love? The Count Cariotti, perhaps? How he hated that man! He moved forward silently.

'Sophie.' He spoke quietly, but his voice startled her so that she jumped to her feet with a cry of alarm. 'Don't be afraid. It is only I.'

'Oh.' She was glad of the seat behind her knees and thankfully sank back onto it. 'You startled me.'

He sat beside her, so close one knee was touching her skirt and his breath was warm on her cheek. 'I am sorry, it was not my intention. What are you doing out here alone?'

'I came out to think.' His nearness was making thinking impossible. Her traitorous body was betraying her and she leaned towards him. Before she knew what was happening, he had taken hold of her chin and was tipping it upwards so that she was looking up into his face. She could not see his expression, but his eyes were scanning her face, looking from her eyes to her mouth and back to her eyes. Those few seconds of intense scrutiny seemed to go on for ever. And then he kissed her.

It was a lingering gentle kiss, meant to soothe, not to startle, and though her brain, the part of it still able to think coherently, registered how skilled he was, it was totally eclipsed by the singing joy in her heart. She loved him and whatever he did, whatever he had done in the past, could not erase that. She turned in his arms and put her own about his neck, utterly lost to propriety.

It was some time before he could bring himself to break off the pleasure. 'Sophie, you witch, you have made me forget myself. I have done this in quite the wrong order. Talk first, kisses later.'

She moved a little away from him to regain her composure, knowing she had made a complete cake of herself. 'Talk, my lord?'

'Yes. You said you came out here to think and that must mean you have a problem. May I know what it is?'

'What to do for the best.'

'And what conclusion have you reached?'

'I haven't reached one.'

'Are you concerned for your future?'

'A little, perhaps.' She was fiddling with the fan, opening it a little way and shutting it again.

'Do not be. I want to take care of it, to take care of you.'

So he intended to go through with it, after all. She rallied. 'If I am a good girl and do as I am told.'

'Oh, Sophie, why do you say that? You make me sound like a tyrant.'

'No, my lord, but I think you like to be in control of those around you.'

'If I do, I have singularly failed with you, my darling. You go your own sweet way.'

She noted the endearment, but would not let herself be influenced by it, for that was no doubt what he intended. 'But you would have me marry, when I am resolved to remain single.'

'Why, Sophie? Why so adamant? Are you afraid?'

She managed a weak smile. 'Of you, my lord?'

'Good God, there is no need to fear me. I meant of marriage. Or others. The Count Cariotti, for instance. I collect he fancies himself betrothed to you.'

'That is all it is: fancy. I have never given him any reason to think I would marry him, quite the contrary.'

'Why does he think otherwise?'

'I do not know. I wish I did.' In the background, growing nearer, the thunder rumbled, though neither paid it any attention.

'Can it have anything to do with the book you are writing?' He was careful not to sound as if her answer were important. He had to know if she had heard of Jack Costerman and if she had mentioned the name in her book, if only in passing. That was all it would take for Cariotti to put two and two together and report to his masters, which meant Jack Costerman, alias James Dersingham, would be of no further use to his country.

'No. Why should it?' She countered sharply. That book was still the centre of discord, a great wall that came between them, a barrier to their understanding of each other. But she could not demolish it. Without it, she had no protection.

'You have perhaps written about him, slighted him perhaps, put him with people he would rather not be associated with.' He dare not put the name of Jack Costerman into her head.

'I do not think so. He was a friend of my father, one with whom he used to play cards. I am not sure, but I believe Papa owed him money and died before he could repay it…'

'Gambling debts cannot be collected after death, Sophie. He has no claim in law. You need not be afraid.' He took both her hands in his and tried to sound reasonable. 'Sophie, I think you would be wise to abandon that book.'

She gave a brittle laugh and frantically tugged her

hands away, breaking the cord that held the fan to her wrist. 'So that is why you came out to find me? That is why you soften me with flattery and kisses, only to lay down the law about my book. If you wish to find out what I have said about you, then you must wait until it is published, along with everyone else. And after what you have said and done, you may be sure it will be little to the good.'

She stood up and faced him, her eyes glittering and her breast heaving at the magnitude of what she had said. It was unjust and petty and untrue, and yet she could not bring herself to retract it.

He rose too and took her shoulders in his hands and looked down at her, magnificent in her anger. Perhaps he deserved it, forcing kisses on her, making little of something she obviously felt to be important, but why the venom? And was he going to allow her to make a fool of him? The whole *ton* knew he had said the book was not to be taken seriously. 'Sophie, I did not come out here to scold you or lay down the law. I came to claim my waltz.'

'It is over now.' She meant more than the waltz.

'Yes, but there will be others.' He paused, wondering whether to go on. The happy atmosphere of a few minutes before had gone, been squandered by mention of the Count and that book. He had never intended either to get in the way of his declaration, a declaration of undying love and a proposal of marriage that came from the heart, but somehow they had. How could he have been such a blundering fool? 'Sophie, there is something I wish to ask you—'

'No.' The one word was said very forcefully and accompanied by a great flash of lightning that lit the sky, outlined the trees and the marquee and the people dancing and made nonsense of the light from the feeble lamps. It was followed almost immediately by a rumble of thunder that reverberated as if heaven itself reflected her fury.

'We must go inside.' He took her hand as the rain began, large spots here and there, soon followed by a deluge.

They joined their guests as they deserted the marquee and rushed back to the house. Some were screaming, some trying to hold reticules, handkerchiefs, dance cards, over their heads to protect their elaborate coiffures. James held on to her as they all squeezed their way into the house. He was obliged to leave her in order to restore calm and order, but not before he had whispered, 'We will finish our conversation on another occasion, Sophie, and I will have an explanation for that emphatic denial before I had even uttered the question.'

The ladies were shepherded up to bedrooms by the maids, where towels were found for them; the men taken to the dining room or the gun room where they divested themselves of their coats and sat in shirt sleeves, downing bumpers of brandy. The storm continued unabated, matching the storm in Sophie's heart as she went up to her own room and flung herself in a chair by the window to watch the flashes and see the marquee collapse in a heap of canvas and broken poles. He had been on the point of a proposal, hadn't he? Could she have held out against him, if he had?

He had spoken gently, kissed her tenderly, given her a present he had taken a great deal of trouble choosing. In any other circumstances she would have been crying out in ecstasy. Why then did he have to spoil it all by mentioning the Count and her book? Set against her passion for him, it was nothing, a tawdry piece of conceit. If he had never mentioned it, she might have given it up. Now, she was more determined than ever.

She was wet to the skin, her hair hung down in sodden

strands; she ought to take off her clothes and find something dry to put on. She lifted her arm; the cord from her fan was still encircling her wrist, but there was no fan. It was out in the garden, being ruined in all that rain. She sprang up and made for the door, pushing past Rose, who had come to help her, ran down the stairs and through the house, passing servants carrying jugs of hot water, towels and dressing robes, and out into the rain again.

The garden was awash, the lamps put out. Unable to see the puddles, she paddled through them and made her way back to where she had been sitting with the Duke. The fan was not on the bench. She sank to her knees, feeling the ground about it, muddying everything, her lovely dress, her stockings, oblivious to the mud, rain, thunder, even the cold, for the temperature had dropped considerably. The fan was nowhere to be found. It was his gift, his special gift, and she had promised to treasure it. Instead she had lost it. Her salt tears mixed with the rain that continued unabated. Perhaps she had dropped it on the way to the house. She turned back, still on hands and knees, feeling her way, but the rain and mud hampered her.

James, warned by Rose that Miss Langford had dashed past him and gone out again, went looking for her and found her crumpled on the wet path. 'Sophie! In God's name, what do you think you are at?'

She lifted her head, but though she tried to rise, her wet skirt tangled itself in her legs and she fell back again. He bent to pick her up and cradled her in his arms. 'My love, what possessed you to come out again? You will catch your death of cold. Let us get you back inside and into bed with a hot brick and a tot of brandy.'

'My fan,' she murmured. 'I dropped it.'

He was running with her towards the house. 'You came out again and risked life and limb to look for that?'

'Yes.'

'How foolish of you. Compared to your life, it is nothing, a mere bauble. I could easily have another made.'

'But it will not be the same. You said it was special…'

'As you are. I pray there are no repercussions to this night's folly. If you were to be taken ill…' He could not finish, the prospect was too awful to contemplate and he needed his breath to carry her inside and up to her room.

She felt warm and safe in his arms, and oh, so very, very tired. She was hardly aware of being carried through the house, of being put on her bed and handed over to the ministrations of Rose and Harriet, who was appalled at the state she was in. She was only half-conscious as they stripped the filthy garments off her and carefully washed her clean before tucking her into bed. She did not hear the guests leaving, all laughing now over the extraordinary end to the evening, something that would be remembered and talked about for years, even exaggerated until it became part of the folklore of the *beau monde*. Some even joked that the Duke had arranged the storm on purpose to entertain them. Sophie, the belle of the ball, was sleeping the sleep of the utterly exhausted.

She was unaware that Alfred Jessop had been witness to the touching scene in the garden and had heard every word that passed between them. Not only that, he had picked up her fan and carried it triumphantly back to his mother, whose comment as she put it in her reticule was that something would certainly have to be done about the chit.

Chapter Nine

Sophie sat silently watching as the man who had introduced himself as John Murray scanned the first few chapters of her book. She had slipped out of the house without being seen and walked alone to the publisher's offices, not at all sure how to go about persuading him to see her, an unknown writer with no introduction; after all, she was no Byron or Miss Austen, both of whom had taken the reading public by storm.

As it happened, she did not need an introduction because Mr Murray always kept his ear to the ground and knew all the latest *on dit*. He knew she was the ward of the Duke of Belfont, recently returned to this country from a long sojourn abroad, and making quite a hit among the *beau monde*. He had not only agreed to see her, but had come from his inner office to greet her.

It was two weeks since her ball, two weeks since the terrible storm that had wrecked the tent and played havoc with the garden, but that had been nothing to the havoc in her heart or the confusion in her head. One minute she was remembering the Duke's gentle words, his loving kiss, the present of the fan, still missing in spite of an extensive search, his concern that she might be ill from her soaking; the next she recalled him quizzing her about her book, as if that was all that mattered to him, asking questions about Count Cariotti. The Italian was nothing but a poseur and a cheat, of that she was sure. She was less sure about her suspicions that he might have had a hand in her father's death. Nothing could be done to prove it and the Duke could not have known about it, so why was he interested in the man? It might be flattering to think he was jealous, but Sophie did not believe that; he was too composed, too cool for such heated emotions. And if that were the case, was he capable of love?

Whatever the rights and wrongs of that, the Duke had shown his colours, had proved that all he was interested in was what she had put in her book. Had that anything to do with Lady Colway and his wish to protect his mistress, or Mr Jessop's hint that he had something to hide, something not to his credit? The book would certainly not reveal that because she knew nothing of it.

She had even considered destroying the manuscript, which would certainly have pleased the Duke, but when it came to doing it, she could not. It was the key to her independence. Now, more than ever, she needed to leave Belfont House. She would have done so the day after the ball if she had not felt too unwell, shivering one minute, hot the next, with a head that, for all its muddled activity, felt like wool. It was thanks to Harriet and Rose looking after her so well that she had made a swift recovery.

Harriet. Of course she would support her brother, do whatever he asked of her, even suggest a marriage of convenience, if she thought it would serve his purpose, but Sophie had come to love her for her friendliness and generosity and what seemed like treachery was all the harder to bear. The only solution was to take herself out of it, away from the daily torment and to do that she had to be able to earn a living. She had decided it was time to show the book to a publisher.

'This is very well written,' he said, when she thought he would never speak. 'But a little too mundane, I think. You need to spice it with a little gossip, a few famous names, something to make the reading public talk about it. Nothing scandalous, you understand, but titivating. Now, if you could do that…'

'Won't that lay me open to legal action?'

'Let me worry about that. We have skilled lawyers.'

'I am not sure I meant it to be that kind of book.'

'It is the kind that makes the money.' He paused. 'Go away and think about it.'

'Thank you.' She stood up and held out her hand for the manuscript, trying to hide her disappointment.

'No, I shall keep it,' he said. 'I will look at it in more detail and let you know how I think we can make something of it. I am not rejecting it out of hand, but you will need to work on it. You do have a copy?'

'Yes. I have my original work.' She had spent some time making the careful copy of the few chapters he had in his hand and, in view of everyone's unhealthy interest in the manuscript, had wrapped the original in a parcel and hidden it in the chimney in her room. The weather had been far too hot for fires.

'Good. I suggest we meet again in two weeks' time, if that is agreeable.'

'Yes, of course.'

'There is one thing, Miss Langford. Does the Duke of Belfont know what you are about?'

'Oh, yes,' she said, thinking of the many conversations they had had on the subject, but most of all picturing him creeping about her bedroom while she slept. 'He is fully conversant with my intentions.'

She bade him goodbye and set off back to Belfont House. She should have been pleased with progress so far, but she felt somehow deflated. She had not expected Mr Murray to fall on her book with cries of joy at having discovered a genius, but the fact that he wanted her to do what everyone thought she had already done, and fill it with scandalous gossip, was a little worrying. It wasn't that she didn't know any gossip—her father, in his cups, had often been indiscreet—but the fact that the Duke thought her knowledge dangerous. By dangerous did he mean legally scandalous? Or something more sinister? Mr Murray seemed not to be concerned about scandal; he knew how far he could go.

She had hoped to ask him for an advance, in order to make a start on finding somewhere to live, but she had soon realised this was over-optimistic. She would have to remain at Belfont House at least for the time being. The best she could do was try to avoid the Duke, keep to her room and work on the amendments Mr Murray had suggested.

The streets had been reasonably quiet when she set out, but while she had been in the publisher's office, the crowds had begun to gather and, as had been happening all summer, they were intent on seeing some celebrity or other. Not only the pavements, but the road itself and every balcony was packed. She had not gone far when she found herself being pushed this way and that by what would have seemed like a mob intent on a lynching. They were running down the road alongside a carriage that was having difficulty making its way through them. Unable to make progress in her chosen direction, and finding that even standing still was impossible if she did not want to be pushed to the ground, she found herself propelled along with them.

'What is happening?' she asked a woman who was pushing past her, holding up her skirts and showing several inches of silk-clad calf.

'Can't you see? It is the Duke of Wellington, home from the war.'

Sophie had never seen the Duke, and could not resist trying to peer into the coach. He did not seem to be a big man, his dress was far from ostentatious and he was looking decidedly alarmed. For a man known for his coolness under fire, this puzzled Sophie. Could everyone have been mistaken and this was not the hero of the Peninsula? She had visions of the poor man being dragged from the coach and torn to pieces.

'He will have the coach over if he is not careful,' she said, nodding towards one man, who had grabbed the lamp brackets and was hanging on for dear life. 'And the horses are terrified enough to bolt.'

'If you are so lily-livered, why come? Take yourself off and let those of us who want to cheer him on.'

It was easier said than done. The crowds were so thick they had stopped the traffic. Carriages, carts, pedestrians came to a standstill. People cheered lustily, others yelled angrily at each other, horses neighed and reared. A curricle was overturned and its occupant disappeared under its wheels. A barrow of apples was upended and the produce rolled underfoot. Sophie felt herself slipping on the squashed fruit. Terrified of being trampled to death, she seized the first thing to hand, the rough sleeve of the costermonger.

'Hey, le' go o' me,' he shouted, pushing her away.

Somehow she managed to keep her balance and then forced her way through the crowd to a side street, where it was quieter, though there were some people hurrying towards the melee. She walked quickly in the opposite direction. The noise grew fainter, but she kept going. It was not until she realised she had lost her direction that she stopped. She was at a busy crossroads that she did not recognise. Uncertainly she looked about her. It was evidently a poorer part of the city—the houses were huddled together, the people were raggedly dressed, the children barefoot, the roads running with filth. And the stench was decidedly unpleasant. Aware that she was being stared at from open doorways, she turned and tried to go back the way she had come.

She could hear the clamour faintly in the distance. Was the coach still in the same place or had it moved on? Wherever it was, it was likely to be in a part of the town she knew and she would be able to find her way home from there. She set off steadfastly, trying not to run and show her fear.

'Miss Langford!'

She looked up to see Alfred Jessop approaching her. She was so relieved to see someone she knew she did not stop to question what he was doing there, or the fact that she did not like the man. 'Mr Jessop, how pleased I am to see you.'

'I am honoured.' He stood and appraised her, smiling a little, so that she became aware she had lost her hat, her hair was in disarray and her sleeve had been torn. 'But what are you doing here and in such a pickle too? Where is your escort?'

'I do not have one.'

'I am surprised at Cousin Harriet allowing you out without one.'

Now that she was no longer alone, she felt safer and able to sound confident even if she was still quaking a little.

'Harriet was resting when I left. We are to go out this evening.'

'And the Duke? Where was he?'

'I have no idea. He does as he pleases.'

'And so do you, it would seem.' He paused, but when she made no answer he went on. 'Independence is all very well, Cousin Sophie—I may call you Cousin Sophie, may I not?—but London at any time is dangerous for a young lady on her own, and with the unruly crowds, it is doubly so. Allow me to escort you.' He turned and offered her his arm.

'Thank you.' She accepted his offer with a smile of gratitude.

'Now,' he said, as they walked, 'tell me what you were doing in a place like Seven Dials. It is the most notorious slum in London and I am surprised you were not set upon.'

'I have nothing on me worth stealing, a few coins in my reticule, that is all.'

'A few coins! They would kill for those. And for the clothes you are wearing.'

She shuddered. 'Then I am doubly glad I encountered you. But if it is as bad as that, what were you doing in such a place?'

'Taking a short cut, my dear, avoiding the crowds. But you have not explained your own presence.'

'I was on my way home and encountered a great crowd chasing after the Duke of Wellington's carriage. They were frightening and I lost myself trying to escape them.'

'Easy to do, when you do not know your way about and when the mob sets its mind on causing mayhem, it can be very dangerous. Did they harm him?'

'Not while I was there, but it was very frightening.'

He patted the hand that held his arm. 'There, my dear, you are with me now and I shall see you safely home.'

'Thank you.'

He turned and looked at her. 'But what were you doing out in the first place? You did not think to go and see Wellington yourself, did you?'

'No, I had no idea he was arriving today and I would not have gone if I had. I see no virtue in rushing about just to get a glimpse of someone of note. I had business to contract.'

'Business, Miss Langford? Surely the Duke looks after your business affairs?'

She smiled. 'Not this. I went to see a publisher.'

'About your book. I had no idea it was so near completion, but now I understand why you crept out alone. You knew his Grace would not approve.'

'It is not for him to approve or disapprove.'

'He would not agree. He thinks of himself as your custodian. At least until you marry, then of course that delightful duty will fall to your husband.'

'Custodian? You make the Duke sound like a prison warder and he is certainly not that.'

'No? But he does wish to control you.'

Whether she agreed with that or not, she felt constrained to defend him. 'No more than any good guardian would.'

'Good guardian. Is that what he claims to be? I think he is most remiss in his duties if he makes no provision for your safety. Anything could have happened in the crowd.' She was wondering where this was leading when he added, 'What did the publisher say about your work?'

'He suggested one or two changes I might make, but otherwise he was complimentary.'

'Then I must congratulate you. But what do you suppose Cousin Harriet will have to say when she learns you have defied her brother and gone ahead? She will see that as a betrayal. She idolises James, you know.'

'I know, but I must do what I think best.'

'And what will she say when she sees the state you are in?'

'I shall have to explain what happened, shan't I?'

'You could try.' He sounded as if he did not think she would be believed. 'But I have a better idea. I have a friend whose home is nearby. I could take you there. You will be made welcome and can tidy yourself before we proceed. I must confess, we are attracting attention.'

She realised that they had come to an area of town where the houses were clean, the knockers bright, the windows shining, and most of the people coming and going were well dressed, but once again she was being stared at. She prayed no one would see her and recognise her. 'Thank you,' she said.

He took her arm and hurried her along the street before she could change her mind and the next minute was knocking on the door of a tall narrow house on the corner of Piccadilly and a road she recognised as Duke Street. It was not until the housekeeper conducted them up to the first floor and ushered them into a small parlour that she realised she had been duped. Count Cariotti was sitting in a chair by the window, reading a newspaper.

He rose at once and bowed to her. 'My dear, this is an unexpected pleasure.'

Dismayed, she turned to go, but Alfred blocked her way. 'Do not be in such haste, my dear cousin, you need to calm yourself and tidy your clothes before you can be seen out again, surely you realise that?'

'I thought you were bringing me to a married lady. I would never have agreed if I had known.'

He shrugged. 'It makes no difference.'

'Indeed it does. Have you no honour?'

'Honour does not come into it when there is so much

as stake,' the Count said. 'But as you set so much store on a married lady, let me tell you my housekeeper, Mrs Davies, is a widow of impeccable character.'

'What is at stake?' she demanded, not at all interested in the status of his housekeeper.

'Oh, everything, my dear. I need to be accepted in English society and I think you can help me with that.'

'How?' She knew the answer, but she asked the question as if she did not. She wanted him to put it into words so that she might know what she was dealing with.

'Marriage, my dear. It was what your dear father wished.'

'I do not believe my father wished anything of the kind. You cheated him and then tried to coerce him into something dishonourable when he could not pay. Did you think I did not know?'

His glittering eyes told her that she had come upon the truth and that frightened her, though he continued to smile urbanely. 'The world of serious gaming is a harsh world, my dear. If he could not stand the pace, he should not have embarked upon it.'

'On that point, Count, you and I agree. But it makes no difference now. I cannot pay his debts.'

'Oh, but you can. I want you and I want that manuscript. That will be my recompense.'

'For what purpose? There is nothing in the book you need concern yourself with. As for marriage, why wish to marry someone who is so reluctant?'

'Oh, I do not think you will be reluctant when the time comes. But for the moment, I am in no hurry. Alfred, take her home, there's a good fellow.'

'She had better tidy herself,' Alfred said. 'We were inviting some strange looks on the way here and I do not want my reputation to go out of the window along with the Duke's if we are recognised.'

'You have a point.' He rang the little bell on the table at his elbow and the housekeeper appeared immediately. Sophie wondered how much she had heard. 'Take the lady to the guest bedchamber and provide her with whatever she needs to make herself respectable,' he told her.

The woman sniffed her disapproval, but conducted Sophie up a flight of stairs to a bedroom. 'I'll go and fetch hot water,' she said. 'You will find towels on the stand and combs and brushes on the dressing table.'

As soon as she had gone Sophie stepped up to the mirror to look at herself and what she saw shocked her. She looked as bad as she had after the storm; her hat was gone, her hair undone and there was a tear in the sleeve of her jacket. There was nothing she could do about the tear, but she could try to do something with her hair. And the quicker the better. The sooner she was out of this house and safely home again the happier she would be.

She was brushing her hair when Mrs Davies returned with hot water, which she poured into the basin on the stand. 'Shall I send the girl up to help you?'

'No, thank you, I can manage.'

The woman left and Sophie set about washing the grime from her face and pinning up her hair. She could not manage it as Rose did, but at least it was tidy. Then she opened the door softly and peered out onto the landing. There was no one about. She crept down the stairs, pausing outside the door where she could hear the two men talking in low voices. She hesitated, but decided it would be too dangerous to stop and listen. She continued down to the ground floor, relieved there was no one about, and silently let herself out of the front door.

'Where was she going?' James demanded of Harriet, who was pacing backwards and forwards in the drawing room, pulling at the corners of a lace handkerchief, tearing it to shreds in her agitation.

He had come back from witnessing the tumultuous reception afforded the Duke of Wellington to be told Sophie had left the house without an escort. His first thought was that she had gone riding alone again, even though he had forbidden it, but Rose, when she was summoned, assured him she was not dressed for it.

'She was wearing a day dress and a short jacket and ordinary bonnet and shoes, your Grace. I thought she was going out in the carriage with Lady Harley, and thought nothing of it, but then I saw her ladyship coming downstairs. Even then I supposed they had come back together...' She began to sob hysterically.

'Oh, do stop crying,' he snapped. 'How long had she been gone when you realised she was missing?'

'Over an hour and a half,' Harriet answered him because Rose seemed incapable of it. 'From the time she left Rose about noon until I asked where she was at half past one when luncheon was served.'

'Good God! Today of all days. Anything could have happened to her.' The capital was in a fever of excitement over the return of Wellington; everyone had been out on the streets or watching from overcrowded balconies. The Duke was safe, though it had been a near thing. He had been cheered all the way from Dover to London, but the expected attack had not come while he was on the road, perhaps because the would-be assassins were aware of the presence of Captain Summers and his troop of guards riding close alongside. The capital was another matter. Word had got out that the great man was approaching Westminster Bridge and the citizens had turned out *en masse* to greet him, so that his coach was reduced to a crawl.

And then some bright spark had thought of taking the

horses from the traces and pulling the carriage themselves and, to James's dismay, the whole equipage was brought to a halt. It was then Wellington lost all patience with them and, against James's advice, left the carriage and demanded a horse. Lord Carstairs was mounted beside James and immediately offered his own mount. His Grace mounted up and disappeared into the crowd at a gallop, with James speeding after him. Once they had left the crowd behind, they slowed their horses to a walk, like two gentlemen out for an afternoon's ride, and thus they had arrived safely at the Duke's home.

James had declined refreshment and turned back to the rendezvous he had arranged with Richard if things should not go according to plan. Carstairs, left without a mount, had climbed into Wellington's carriage and completed the journey, only to be fired on as it approached Piccadilly. The gunman, an unemployed ex-soldier, had been arrested and was being held for questioning, though, according to Richard, he was refusing to talk.

'Is Carstairs hurt?'

'No, thank God.' Richard grinned suddenly. 'We never thought of using a decoy, did we? And yet it worked.'

'Yes, this time, but I do not think that will be the end of it. There is still the Regent's reception and the guest list is long and includes some strange people. We need to have the ringleader behind bars as soon as possible. See what you can get out of the prisoner. I must go home. I have an evening engagement.'

He had come home, feeling cheerful at having delivered the Duke safely to his wife, and was looking forward to taking Sophie to Almack's ball. It promised to be a grand affair and James was hoping that he might renew his courtship of Sophie, so violently interrupted by the storm. But this time he meant to speak to her before they left and not rely on finding an opportunity during the dancing.

He knew it was going to be a tricky interview because she had not yet given him an explanation for that emphatic 'No!' Nor had she explained why she was in the garden in the first place. And why had they not found that fan? He hoped and prayed his earlier suspicion—that she had arranged to meet someone—was unfounded. To come home and learn that she had ventured out alone had sapped his euphoria until he was both extremely anxious and very angry.

'Has no one any idea where she might have gone?' he asked Harriet after Rose was sent weeping from the room. 'Did she ask anyone to accompany her? Collins? Sadler? Tom, even?'

'It appears not. I sent Collins out to look for her.'

'I'll go and look for her myself; when I find her, by God, I'll ring the loudest peal over her you ever heard. I will have to find some way of curbing her, even if it means packing her off to Dersingham Park for the rest of the summer.'

'I am sure she would not have meant to go far,' Harriet said, trying to defend her cousin, though very worried herself. Sophie had been behaving very strangely lately, keeping to her room even after she had recovered from her chill, not wanting to join her on outings. She had been so open before, so ready to confide, now she hardly spoke more than politeness demanded. Harriet wondered what she could have done to upset her. Surely it was not bad enough to drive her away?

'Whatever she meant to do, she has been gone over two hours. Anything could have happened.' He did not want to dwell on the possibilities, but he could not help himself. He imagined her lying injured in the road, no one knowing who she was, robbed, abducted, raped even. It was more than he could stomach and he turned on his heel. 'I must find her and, by God, if anyone has harmed her, they shall pay with their lives.'

He had not quite reached the door when it was opened and Sophie entered. She appeared to be cheerful and unharmed. His relief exploded into anger. 'Where in damnation do you think you have been?'

She stood and stared at him. His face was white, his blue eyes icy. This was not the mild man who had given her the fan and kissed her so tenderly. This was a frighteningly furious autocrat not used to being thwarted. If she had been ready to apologise for being gone so long, to explain that she had not realised the crowds would be so dense, the words stopped in her throat. If he could be angry, so could she.

'I have been out,' she said. 'And when you calm down sufficiently to listen, I shall tell you where I have been.' She paused when she saw that she had startled him; he was unused to anyone answering him back. It gave her a tiny amount of satisfaction, but not much.

'Oh, Sophie!' Harriet, half-laughing, half-crying with relief, ran to embrace her. 'We have been so worried…'

'I am sorry for that, Harriet, but I had thought to be back long before now. The crowds were so thick—'

'You mean you were caught up in that mad crush to get at the Duke of Wellington?' James demanded. 'It is a wonder you were not trampled to death.'

'Well, I was not,' she retorted, as Harriet tried to lead her to a sofa to sit down, a gesture she resisted. She could better defend herself standing.

'But I perceive your jacket is torn,' he said. 'And your hair is a mess. And where is your hat?'

'I lost it.'

'Good God! Is there no end to your folly? I had not thought you so caught up in the madness as to join in that ridiculous hero worship.'

'Of course I did not. I had no idea it would happen.'

'What would happen?' Harriet asked.

James answered his sister. 'The mob went wild. They tried to take the horses from the Duke's carriage and pull it themselves. It was pandemonium for a while, but he escaped on horseback. It was fortunate he did, because someone took a shot at the carriage from the crowd…'

'Oh, Sophie!' Harriet remonstrated. 'You could have been killed.'

'I came to no harm,' Sophie said.

'But why did you go out without saying a word to me of your intentions? I would have accompanied you.'

'I preferred to go alone.'

'Where?' James demanded.

'To see Mr Murray, the publisher.' How she kept her voice calm Sophie did not know, but she managed it, even injecting a hint of sweetness. 'You will be pleased to know he was complimentary about my work.'

'You mean he is going to publish?' James's anxiety over her safety switched to the book. That damned book was the barrier to any kind of relationship with her. Major Bowers had advised him to find it and read it himself, advice he had been reluctant to follow. It would be an invasion of her privacy, like reading someone's private letters. But if he had handled her more gently, talked to her about it, perhaps she would have volunteered the information he wanted. Now he feared it was too late.

'He suggested a few changes, which I intend to work on. I am to see him in two weeks' time and put them before him and then he will give me an advance and I will be able to find somewhere else to live.' She was not at all sure about the advance, or even how much it would be, but she was not going to admit it. If she was ever to have any peace of mind, she must stop this erratic beating of her heart and be practical. But, oh, how difficult it was.

'Somewhere else? Why would you wish to live anywhere else?'

'I should have thought that was self-evident. I have said all along, I mean to be independent.'

'Gammon! You wish to be a thorn in my side, that is what you wish.'

'No, but if I am such a burden to you, then the sooner I leave the better, then you may go on in your own untroubled way.'

'And where do you propose to go? Into some dismal lodgings on your own, for I am sure no one else will put up with you.'

'James!' Harriet protested when Sophie stepped back with the shock of his words. She knew he was angry, but how could he say something so hurtful when only a week before he had been kissing her as if she meant something to him, had rescued her from the rain and, according to Harriet, had paced up and down outside her door when he thought she was ill? But now he had shown his true colours; he no more wanted her than her uncle, Lord Langford, did.

'I am not without friends,' she said. 'Though why you should care, I do not know, unless you are worried for your reputation.'

'My reputation! You foolish girl, it is yours I am concerned about. There is already talk about that book, everyone expecting scandal, and then boasting you had turned down an offer from Count Cariotti—'

'It was not a boast. I did turn him down. But what has that to do with anything?'

On the point of forbidding her to speak to the man again, he stopped suddenly. 'Did you have an assignation to meet him this afternoon?'

'No!' The words were shouted, though she felt terribly guilty. It wasn't her fault she had been inveigled into visiting his house, but if the Duke ever found out about it, he would undoubtedly believe the worst.

'James,' Harriet protested again. 'Do calm down. Being angry with each other will not help. And I am quite sure Sophie would never be so foolish as to meet a man alone.' She rose and put her arm about Sophie, who had suddenly lost all her self-control and was quietly sobbing. 'It is only worry for your safety that makes him seem unkind, my dear. Come, we will go up to your room and you shall rest. If you like, I will have a tray sent up and you do not need to come down for dinner.'

She led Sophie from the room, leaving the Duke frustrated and still fuming. He was taken aback when a few minutes later Sophie stormed back into the room and flung a sooty paper parcel into his lap. 'Here, seeing you set so much store by it, you had better read it.' And before he could make any sort of reply, she had gone again, slamming the door after her.

He sat and looked at it for several seconds before he could bring himself to undo the tape. And then he began to read…

By the time he had finished he was smiling. It was good, very good; her descriptions of places and people were pin sharp and witty, but there was very little that could be called scandalous. But probably without her realising it, it did reveal what her life must have been like with her father. Poor Sophie, to have to look after a grown man who behaved like a child, and one with a temper to boot, and somehow find the wherewithal for both of them to live, must have taken all her resources of strength and character. No wonder she was so independent! He was filled with admiration for her and remorse that he had not tried to understand her better. But he could make it up to her, would do so at the earliest opportunity.

The last thing Sophie wanted to do was to go to Almack's. Yet another ball was more than she could face. 'My dear, you need not go if you do not feel up to it,' Harriet said. She had brought Sophie's tray up to her room herself after Sophie had stripped off her torn and stained garments and rested on her bed for an hour. She had only picked at the food before thrusting it aside. Every mouthful she owed to the Duke of Belfont and it stuck in her throat. 'But it is an honour to be given vouchers and it will set the seal on your acceptance in society…'

'I do not see that acceptance in society matters. Once I am gone from here, society will not concern itself with me.'

'Gone from here. Oh, Sophie, do not be so foolish. This is your home. We do not want you to leave us. We have come to love you.'

'We?'

'The Duke and I.'

'How can you say that? I am a nuisance to him and make him angry whenever we meet.'

'His anger masks his concern. He worries about you. I know he was looking forward to escorting you to the ball tonight.' She paused, deciding on another argument. 'And you know, if you want to be a success as a writer, being part of society will help you…'

Sophie gave a weak laugh. 'You mean they will furnish me with more material?'

'That, too, but I meant writers need readers and it is no good looking to the illiterate poor to provide you with those.'

She managed a wry smile. 'Oh, you would have made a splendid advocate, Harriet. I am almost persuaded.'

'Then make your peace with James and come with us.'

Could she? Did she want the Duke to think that he had entirely defeated her, which he would if she shut herself away? Had he? Why, when she loved him so much, was she so quick to defy him? Could it be something to do with her parents? Her mother had adored her father, had given up everything, her family, friends, comfort, to follow him about the continent. Even when he was at his drunken worst, railing at his own misfortune and keeping her short of housekeeping money, Mama had made excuses for him. Though Sophie had loved her father, she had come to see him as the weak, selfish character he was and was in despair for her gentle mother. Was she simply fighting against the same thing happening to her? Was that why she must continually demonstrate her independence? But the Duke was nothing like her father, except that he did like to have his own way—in that they were very alike.

She smiled suddenly. 'Very well. If you are sure the Duke still wishes it.'

'Of course he does. Now, do try and eat a little of that cold chicken or you will not have the strength to dance, and then I will send Rose to help you dress. Wear the blue taffeta.'

It was weakness, not strength, that made her accept; she did not have the strength of will to turn her back on the Duke. She wanted to be with him, even when they were fighting. And sometimes, when they were not fighting, he was so thoughtful, so kind and gentle, so very much her idea of what a real man should be. When he was like that, he could make her forget her papa, Count Cariotti and Cousin Alfred; they were not men, they were muckworms.

It was with some trepidation she went down to join Harriet and James in the withdrawing room. She had taken trouble with her appearance, but she knew she looked paler than usual and, with his usual discernment, he noticed it.

'Sophie, you do not look quite the thing,' he said gently. 'If you would sooner not go out, then we will have a quiet evening at home amusing ourselves.'

Why this evidence of his solicitude should make her hackles rise, she had no idea. She was being as contrary as it was possible for anyone to be. 'I would not dream of it,' she said. 'I have been looking forward to this evening ever since it was first mentioned. After all, not everyone is invited to join the ladies at Almack's and I am interested in finding out why an invitation is so prized.'

'Then let us hope you are not disappointed.' He bowed, his lips twitching a little. She was a feisty one, this cousin of his; no one could keep her down for long and his love and admiration grew until he thought his heart would burst. In view of what had happened that afternoon and the dreadful things he had said to her, he had decided not to tell her what was in his heart; she was in no mood to hear a proposal from him. And who could blame her? He had behaved like a tyrant when all he had wanted was to take her in his arms and hold her close, glad that she was safe. He could not forgive himself, so how could he expect her to forgive him? Somehow he had to re-establish himself in her good offices before he laid himself open, for that was what it amounted to: open to disappointment, to rejection, even to ridicule. He was a proud man and the thought that he had finally given his heart to a woman, offered marriage and been turned down was more than he could contemplate.

He offered his arm and she took it, trembling a little at his nearness, but still angry. He had said some terrible things, accused her of goodness knows what and yet there was no remorse in him, no apology was forthcoming, no comment about her book, so she supposed he had not bothered to read it. And that hurt.

'I could knock your heads together,' Harriet said suddenly. 'Are you going to spend the whole evening being coolly polite or are you going to kiss and make up?'

They looked at her and then at each other and then he laughed. It was the first genuine laughter Sophie had heard all day and she found herself smiling. 'What about it?' he asked her. 'If I apologise humbly for my excessive rudeness this afternoon, shall you forgive me?'

'I forgive you.' What else could she say?

'Then let us kiss and make up.' And with that, he bent and put his lips to her forehead in avuncular fashion, but it was enough to set her limbs on fire. Slowly she was beginning to understand her mother; loving someone meant setting aside all doubts, forgiving their faults, cherishing them for what they were, even when their love was not as strong or even non-existent. That was how she felt about the Duke of Belfont.

All three were smiling as they went out to the carriage and they were still smiling as they drew up at the door of Almack's premises in King Street. It was the most exclusive club in London, where admittance was by vouchers in the gift of seven *grandes dames* of society, who reserved the right to refuse whom they pleased. The dress code was strictly adhered to and gentlemen were only admitted if they were wearing knee breeches. Anyone in trousers was sent on his way no matter who he was. Consequently James was dressed very formally in dark blue coat and white knee breeches with white silk stockings and black buckled shoes.

Sophie was surprised to find herself in a large room almost devoid of furniture with a bare floor. It was well lit, which only served to highlight the poor decoration, though she was bound to admit, as the evening progressed, that the music was good. She danced twice with the Duke and once with Theodore Buskin, even more boyish in his formal wear. Lord Carstairs claimed her for another and so did Alfred.

'I do hope he does not ask me to stand up with him,' Sophie whispered when she saw him enter.

'If he does, I am afraid you must not refuse. It will be noted and talked about.'

The last thing Sophie wanted was to engender any more gossip and so, when he came to claim a dance, she curtsied and took the floor with him.

'Why did you rush off this afternoon, without waiting for me to escort you?' he asked.

'I did not want to trouble you with having to escort me. You had already complained that I was drawing unwelcome attention.'

'Did you tell the Duke of our encounter?'

'I saw no reason to, he was worried enough about my long absence as it was.'

'But he does know where you went?'

'Of course.'

'And did it not trouble him?'

'Why should he be troubled by a simple travel book? I have given it to him to read.'

'Have you, indeed?' He paused. 'And what did he say?'

'Nothing—why should he?'

'No, he would not. And I will wager you did not tell him about your visit to the Count this afternoon.'

'I felt foolish at being so easily gulled and decided not to. And if you are a gentleman you will say nothing of it.'

'Then, my dear, it is our little secret.' He smiled and added, 'For the moment.'

The dance came to an end, she curtsied and took the arm he offered to return to her place beside Harriet. On the way they passed several matrons sitting on the side-lines, gossiping among themselves.

'My dear, I heard that Lord Colway has handed in his accounts and she is a free woman at last.'

'Then no doubt his Grace of Belfont will be standing at the altar as soon as the mourning period is over.'

'She might wish it, but I think not. She was married to Colway for fifteen years and never gave him a child, let alone an heir, and Belfont needs an heir. He would not risk marrying someone he thought might be barren. He might keep her as a mistress, but marry her, never. Twenty guin-eas says he will marry that little hoyden he brought back from Italy…'

Alfred chuckled. 'Did you hear that, little cousin?'

'I pay no heed to gossip,' she said stiffly, though she was considerably shaken. Why were people linking her name with the Duke's in that fashion? In public he had never been more than a reluctant guardian. It was how he saw himself, in spite of sweet kisses in private that were far from avun-cular.

'Would you marry him?'

'He has not asked me, nor will he, so the question does not arise.'

'That is an evasive answer if ever I heard one. I think mayhap you would jump at the chance to be a duchess and put up with the mistress.'

'Never! And I thank you not to pursue the subject. I am heartily sick of it.'

He complied only because they had joined Harriet and James. James had watched the changing expressions on Sophie's face as she talked to Alfred—the animation, the anger, the pensiveness—and wanted to ask what they had been saying to each other, but decided he could not. He had to redeem himself in her eyes and he would not do that by quizzing her all over again. He smiled and offered his hand. 'Come, Sophie, I believe this is my dance.'

The rest of the evening passed in a blur for Sophie. James was his most charming and considerate self and that only exacerbated the ache in her heart. Was he building up to a proposal? Was Alfred right? Would she turn a blind eye to a mistress in order to marry him, not to be a duchess, simply to be his wife? Or was he simply happy that, at last, his real love was free to marry him?

It was not until they returned home that she learned the answer. They drove to South Audley Street in near silence, both so engrossed in their thoughts that they answered Harriet's chatter in monosyllables, but when they entered the house he asked Sophie if he might speak to her in the drawing room. 'There is something particular I wish to put to you,' he said. 'I will not keep you long.'

Chapter Ten

Sophie, almost in a panic, turned to Harriet for support, but she simply bade them goodnight and climbed the stairs to her room, leaving James to usher Sophie into the withdrawing room.

'Sit down, Sophie, please,' he said, indicating a sofa, and, when she obeyed, perched himself on the edge beside her, tucking his long legs under him. She clasped her hands in her lap and waited, hardly daring to breathe.

'Sophie, my dear,' he began, wondering why he was finding it so difficult. Never before had he declared his love for a woman earnestly with the intent to be believed. He had played at it, had had mistresses, had dallied here and there, but nothing serious. The ladies themselves had known that, had been more than ready to play his game because he was a generous lover and none, except perhaps Ellen, had minded when the affair had come to a natural end. Ellen he would have to deal with later, but now he must concentrate on making Sophie believe his sincerity. 'We have not known each other very long, have we?'

She gave a cracked laugh. 'Long enough to sharpen each other up.'

'True, but that might be a measure of our regard for each other.'

'How so?'

'If we did not care, we would not do it, would we?'

'My lord, I wish you would not prevaricate. If you have brought me in here to ring a peal over me, then do it and have done. It will soon be dawn.'

'I do not want to scold you. That was not my intention. I wish never to be at odds with you again.'

'Oh, then it is to be a final roasting. I am to be a good girl and not go out alone, not ride alone, and not publish my book, then there will be nothing to be at odds over. Is that what you were going to say?'

'No, it is not.' He took her shoulders in his hands and felt her flinch. Good God! Surely she was not afraid of him? 'My intentions were, and are, otherwise. As for the book, I am glad you showed it to me. It is exceedingly well written and I enjoyed reading it.'

'Thank you. You are no doubt relieved that there is no scandal in it about you or your mistress. You may set her mind at rest.'

'I never thought there was.'

'She did. She threatened me. She said when she was the Duchess of Belfont, she would make sure I was never received in society.'

'She will never be the Duchess of Belfont.' He paused. The conversation was not going the way he had planned and he had to bring it back to the matter in hand and it was not that book or Ellen Colway. 'Sophie, please listen.' He took a deep breath. 'You remember when I first kissed you?'

'Yes.' How could she forget when the pleasure and the pain were engraved on her heart? 'I collect you have already apologised for that, though I have heard no apology for creeping into my room when you thought I was asleep.'

'You were awake?'

'Awake enough to know who held me in his arms.'

'You fell asleep at your desk.' Why, oh, why was she so determined to stop him saying what he wanted to? Surely she had guessed what he intended. Any other young lady would have put two and two together long before and would have met him halfway; she was raising barriers.

'And you would not have known that if you had not entered my room. I suppose you wanted to take a look at my manuscript.' She gave another cracked laugh. 'All you had to do was ask and I would have shown it to you. There was no need for all that creeping about in the middle of the night.'

He dropped his hands from her shoulders, fuming with frustration. 'I saw your light and supposed you had fallen asleep with the lamp still alight and I feared an accident. I should perhaps not have entered myself and sent a maid instead, but everyone else had long since retired. For that I apologise. Now, can we please go back to what I was saying…'

'Please do.' She clasped her hands in the blue folds of her skirt and hoped he had not noticed how they were shaking. If he did not soon say what he wanted to say, she would scream.

'On that occasion, when I kissed you, I said I had gone about it in the wrong order and that we should have talked first. Now I am trying to remedy that situation.'

'I am listening.'

'Sophie, do you see me as a tyrant?'

'Sometimes, though I am persuaded by Harriet that it is done for my own good. Sometimes you seem a cheerful and considerate cousin and for that I am grateful. You took me in when I had nowhere to go and I know I should be more compliant. The trouble is that I have been on my own so much, making my own decisions, that it does not come easy to play by society's rules, especially when they seem nonsensical.'

'I understand, more than ever since I read your manuscript, but I am sure the rules have evolved to make young ladies more secure.'

She was reminded of her adventure that afternoon. It was a case in point. If she had not defied the rules of society she would not had been in such a pickle with Mr Jessop and the Count. They had frightened her, still frightened her, and she did not think Alfred would keep his word to say nothing to the Duke. 'I will bear that in mind in future.'

'It is the future I am thinking of. Young ladies need to feel safe in their choice of a husband and abiding by protocol means that parents and guardians are able to oversee the courtship. Most marriages are made that way.'

'Are they any happier for that?'

'As happy as those made in defiance of the rules, I do not doubt.'

'Like Papa and Mama,' she murmured wistfully. 'They were happy at first and if their families had loved them enough to respect their choice and accept the marriage, Papa might not have turned to gambling and drink and we might not have had to leave the country. That made Mama miserable.'

'Is that why you are so averse to marriage?'

'It is one of the reasons.'

'And is that why you rejected Count Cariotti?'

'He was, and probably still is, a hundred times worse than Papa ever was.'

'And do you think I come from the same mould?'

'I have never seen you disguised in drink and I do not think you are a heavy gambler,' she told him thoughtfully. Then, in an effort to bring matters to a head, added, 'But no doubt you have your own ideas about why a man should marry.'

'And what do you suppose they are?'

'Why, to beget an heir.'

'Is that all?'

Sophie could see the conversation was becoming decidedly tricky and her shaking was becoming more obvious. She had to put an end to it somehow. 'Of course. What other reason would there be, unless it be to acquire a hostess acceptable to the *ton*? You could hardly install your mistress at Dersingham Park. Of course, now that she is a widow, you could marry her, but I have heard she is barren.'

'I would rather marry you.' He quelled his annoyance with an effort and spoke quietly, pulling her hands apart as he did so and taking them in his own. 'It is what I had in mind the night I kissed you and when we were out in the garden. If it had not been for the storm...' He paused. 'Did you guess? Was that why you said "No" so vehemently?'

'I did not need to guess. I overheard Harriet advising you to marry me to put an end to the gossip about you and Lady Colway.'

He tried to remember exactly what had been said, but it eluded him. His sister knew how much Sophie meant to him and he could not imagine she would say anything so cold-blooded. 'Oh, Sophie, you must have misheard. How could you believe I would use you in that fashion?'

'Easily when everyone is saying the same thing. I heard the tabbies making wagers on whether you would marry your mistress now she is free or take me for a wife because I am young and healthy and would probably breed well.'

'Good Lord! No wonder you are angry. But, gossip apart, would you mind very much? Marrying me, I mean.'

She did not know how to answer that. If only he had denied the gossips, told her he loved her, then she might have been able to reciprocate and tell him that she loved him and wanted more than anything in the world to be his wife. But he had not. 'Yes, I would, under those terms,' she told him. 'It is too humiliating to be borne. Now, if you will excuse me, I will bid you goodnight.' She rose to leave him, but he still had her hand in his and pulled her down again.

'I have not finished and I insist you hear me out. Gossip can be cruel, but I thought you had more sense than to let it influence you.' He paused and started again. 'There is no one I can ask for permission to offer for you, unless it be your uncle Langford and I cannot think he would object, so I come direct to you. Sophie—Miss Langford— will you do me the honour of consenting to marry me?'

Her heart cried out, 'Yes, yes', even while her tongue was forming the words to reject him. 'My lord, I do not think we should suit.'

'Why not?' Had he expected her to fall on his neck with gratitude, as others might have done? Had he expected her to ask for time to think about it, simply for form's sake? Or had he known all along she would turn him down and he had humiliated himself by asking?

'I do not conform to society's idea of a compliant wife; as I do not intend to change simply to satisfy the proprieties, we would do better to remain cousins and friends, guardian and ward, anything but husband and wife. I must love the man I marry and I would have him love me. There would be no room for mistresses…'

He laughed suddenly, more at his own foolishness than at her. 'That is a high ideal and most men of my acquaintance would say it was impossible…'

'Then I shall remain single, as I said all along I would,' she put in before he could elaborate. 'I am sensible of the honour you do me, my lord, but it is not enough.'

'By God, what do you want? I am wealthy beyond avarice. I have a title and estates, the envy of almost every man in England, all of which I would share with you. And you say it is not enough!'

She stood up, realising that nothing more could be said, nothing except a declaration of love he was not prepared to give, and there was no point in prolonging the interview. 'Goodnight, my lord.'

She left the room at a sedate walk, but, once in the corridor, dashed up the stairs and locked herself in her room before flinging herself on the bed and succumbing to great waves of despairing grief. He had proposed, but he had not said he loved her, had given her no assurance that he would not continue to see Lady Colway—just the opposite, in fact. Impossible, he had said. In that case, marriage to him was also impossible. Why, oh, why did she have to fall in love with him? He was heartless. She sobbed until she had no tears left.

Dry-eyed at last, she lay and stared at the canopy of the bed above her head. The last time she had wept like that was when her mother died and she had realised she was alone and her father was no help to her. All she had to rely on was her own courage and determination. It was the same now. She sat up, left the bed and undressed, then crept beneath the covers to lie for hours, thinking, planning, summoning all her courage for what she had to do, before finally falling asleep.

The following morning, she packed a small valise with the clothes and small items she had brought with her from Italy, including what was left of her money, and left the house before anyone was about.

* * *

'James, whatever did you say to Sophie last night?' Harriet asked, rushing downstairs in her dressing gown to confront her brother, who was morosely munching his way through a piece of dry toast. 'I expected to come down this morning to find you both all smiles; instead, I discover the silly girl has gone.'

'Gone?' He knew he had bungled his proposal, but then he had never proposed before and Sophie was so prickly and so ready to believe the worst. Instead of whispering sweet words of love to each other, they had become embroiled in an argument about propriety and mistresses and why she would not marry him. It had resulted in a sleepless night of self-castigation and a determination to make her see and understand the truth. He loved her, he loved her to distraction, and no amount of wilfulness on her part could alter that. He should have told her so last night. 'Gone where?'

'I do not know. You had better read this.' She handed him a sheet of paper on which he recognised Sophie's handwriting. 'Rose found it when she went to wake her.'

'Dear Harriet,' he read. 'I have decided to bring forward my plans to find somewhere else to live where I may be independent and eccentric and, if I choose, to flout the conventions, a fault his Grace finds so irksome in me. I am truly grateful for all you have done for me and am sorry that I cannot be the young lady you would like me to be. Please convey my gratitude to the Duke…'

She did not wait for him to finish reading before she interrupted. 'Really, James, whatever did you say to her?'

'Nothing to make her do this, I swear it.'

'I thought you were going to propose to her.'

'I did. She said we would not suit.'

'That's nonsense, you are made for each other. Or you

would be if you could subdue the stiff-necked pride you both seem to be encumbered with. Tell me exactly what was said.'

So he did, only to be given a roasting the like of which he had not had since he was a boy and had angered his father with some prank or other. 'You are a ninny,' his sister said. 'For someone who has the reputation of being a ladies' man, who knows exactly the right word and tone to use to have them eating out of your hands, you have made a real mull of it. You love her and she loves you…'

'How can you know that?'

'It is written in her face, the way her eyes follow you about, the sound of her voice when she speaks of you.'

'I never knew…'

'They say love is blind—in your case, they are right. You kissed her, did you not?'

'She told you that?' he asked in surprise.

'She did. Did her response not tell you anything?'

'I thought it did.'

'Then what are you going to do about it?'

'Find her, of course. Bring her back.'

'Have you any idea where to look?'

'I'll find her if I have to scour all London.'

'And while you are doing that, think about what you will say to her when you do find her. Try to refrain from ringing a peal over her and attempt a little humility. She is vulnerable, James; she has had a strange upbringing and is afraid to trust anyone. She needs reassurance, not a roasting.'

Before he could answer, the door opened to admit Collins. 'Your Grace, Lord Carstairs is here and requests a few words with you. He says it is urgent. I have taken the liberty of showing him into the book room.'

'Thank you.' He strode past the footman and entered

the library to find his friend pacing up and down. 'Carstairs, what brings you here at this ungodly hour? Have you news of our conspirators?'

'Yes and no. I am afraid it concerns your ward…'

'Sophie,' he breathed. 'Do you know where she is?'

Carstairs looked startled. 'No, I assumed she was here. Do you mean she is not?'

'No, she has gone out.' He paused, unwilling to tell the man the truth. 'Let us start again. Why have you come? To do with Sophie, you say?'

'Miss Langford, yes. James, you must do something about that chit. She is getting into very deep water and could well ruin everything.'

'I am not sure I know what you mean.' He was defensive. 'I know you have my interests at heart, but Miss Langford's conduct is surely my affair…'

'Hold on, old friend. It is not as simple as that. She was seen coming out of Count Cariotti's lodgings on Piccadilly.'

'When?' he asked sharply, unable to suppress his anxiety. Surely, surely she had not gone to the Count? Had she not said he was worse than her father? But if she thought he was the only one who would help her…

'Yesterday afternoon. If she is mixed up with the Italian, it can have dire consequences for you and for her. He is our man, I am sure of it.'

His heart sank. Sophie must have met Cariotti on the way back from the publisher, if she had ever been to the publisher in the first place. And she had denied it. Why? Why lie? If he had her in front of him now, he would shake her until her teeth rattled and make her tell him the truth. Cariotti was dangerous. But that happened yesterday, before his bungled proposal. What of today? Where was she now? 'Who told you this. Who saw her?'

'My wife and Mrs Jessop. They had been on a shopping expedition to Bond Street and were in a carriage passing along Piccadilly when they saw Miss Langford emerge from one of the houses, looking, in their words, "dishevelled and furtive". Later they met Mr Jessop and spoke of it to him. He told them he had met Miss Langford earlier in the day walking alone and done his best to persuade her to allow him to escort her home, but she would have none of it and was determined to visit the Count.'

His first reaction was to accuse Alfred of lying. Sophie would never do anything so foolish, but past experience told him she might very well do so, if it suited her purpose. But what purpose? Surely she was not involved in espionage? And if it was not anything subversive, then it must be an affair of the heart. She had denied it, but hadn't Alfred told him earlier that the pair were in love? He did not know what to believe.

'I tell you this so you may be prepared,' Carstairs went on.

'For the gossip.'

'My wife will say nothing of it. She is very fond of your sister and would do nothing to harm her, but the street was busy, so others might have seen and recognised the young lady. But, as you say, that is your affair, but national security is not, or not only yours. Did you get a look at that book?'

'Yes. It is all very innocuous, no mention of Jack Costerman, so we were worrying for nothing.'

'And Cariotti?'

'He is mentioned as a friend of her father with whom he played cards. She was often required to act the hostess at these sessions and expounds some of his political views garnered in conversation, which he would not like published, but nothing we could use…'

'Perhaps she knows more than she has written.'

'I do not think so. But I cannot do anything about it until I find her.'

'You mean she is missing?'

'From the house, yes, but I have no doubt that is only a temporary situation. You may leave Miss Langford to me.'

'Very well, but if you take my advice you will send her somewhere out of harm's way and take charge of that book.'

James made no comment to that, being more concerned with ushering the man from the house without being rude, so that he could go after Sophie before Cariotti embroiled her in his nefarious activities and her reputation was irretrievably lost. He loved her, believed it was her innocence that led her into these scrapes but the woman he made his duchess must be above reproach. Had he been mistaken in her? His pride, his concern for the family name, did battle with the urge to find Sophie, enfold her in his arms, kiss the breath out of her and tell her she was safe, would always be safe with him. But that must all be put on one side until he found her and brought her back.

He had hardly turned from the door and instructed the footman to go to the mews and order his curricle brought to the door than the sound of knocker reverberated through the hall and Collins, on his way to obey, opened it to admit Mrs Jessop.

'James, I am glad I find you at home. There is something very particular I must discuss with you…'

'Not now, Aunt, I am in haste to go out.'

'It has come to something when you deny your aunt a few minutes of your time,' she said, sailing into the withdrawing room, the black plumes in her hat fluttering as she moved.

Harriet, who had been sitting staring unseeingly into a cup of cold coffee, rose to greet her and, because her cousin's disappearance was the only thing on her mind at the moment, failed to greet her properly. 'You have news?' she asked.

'Good morning, Harriet.'

'Oh, good morning, Aunt. Please be seated. I will ring for more coffee.'

'I do not need refreshment; if you were not family, nothing on earth would persuade me to set foot over the threshold, but it is my duty to enlighten you…'

'What about?' Harriet sank back into her seat.

'That *nobody* you have taken into your home. James, you must do something about her. She has already ruined her own reputation and, if you are not careful, she will ruin yours.'

'That, surely, is my affair.' James had followed her into the room, knowing what was coming and determined to silence her if he could. 'Now, if you will excuse me, I am in haste to be about my business.'

'Goodness knows what her foolish mother taught her about how to go on. Nothing good, it seems,' she went on as if he had not spoken. 'But what can you expect when she defied everyone to marry that mountebank.'

'Aunt, please come to the point.'

'The chit was seen coming out of Count Cariotti's lodgings…'

'No,' Harriet said. 'I will not believe that of her.'

'I saw her with my own eyes. And Alfred had seen her earlier and tried to persuade her not to go, but she would not listen to him. James, you must pack her off, back to where she came from, before she does untold damage to the Dersingham name.'

'We cannot send her away,' Harriet said. 'She is kin and she needs us…'

'Oh, she needs you, there is no doubt. She is a penniless fortune hunter. Why, you have no proof that she is who she says she is. I can understand you being taken in, Harriet, having lived a sheltered life with your mama and papa and then being protected by your husband, but I am shocked that you should be so gullible, James.'

He did not want to hear it, not any of it. Hearing Collins return from his errand, he excused himself and left his aunt to elaborate on Sophie's faults and Harriet to defend her, while he hurried upstairs to change into outdoor clothes. Then he dashed from the house to where Tom stood beside the curricle. The next moment, he had jumped into it and urged the horse forward, leaving the young groom looking after him, scratching his head.

His first call was to Cariotti's lodgings, where he thundered on the door. As soon as the door was opened, he pushed past the startled housekeeper. 'Where is he?'

'If you mean Count Cariotti, I shall enquire if he is at home,' she said coldly. 'That is, if you give me your name and state your business.'

He turned towards her, intending to give her the benefit of his fury, but suddenly realised bluster would achieve nothing. And letting Cariotti know that he was in a blue funk over Sophie's disappearance would give the man a great deal of satisfaction and probably alert him to his danger. Carstairs would certainly not thank him for that. It was why he had called on him that morning, to warn him to watch his step.

He turned to the woman, once again his usual urbane, charming self. 'I beg pardon, ma'am. I spoke too sharply. Would you please ask the Count if he can spare a few minutes of his time. My name is Belfont. The Duke of Belfont.' This was accompanied by a pleasant smile and a doffing of his hat.

Her manner changed completely as she took his hat and laid it carefully on a side table before asking him to be seated while she discovered if the Count was at home. Then she climbed the stairs sedately. James watched her go, fuming with impatience. Instead of sitting, he paced the small hall. The minutes ticked by, long enough for the Count to hide any incriminating evidence, long enough to hide Sophie if she were there. He was tempted not to wait, but dash upstairs in the woman's wake and find out for himself what was going on. He had made his sixth turn of the room when she returned.

'The Count will see you, your Grace. His room is on the first floor, the second on your left. I will leave you to see yourself up. I will bring some refreshment.'

'That will not be necessary, ma'am. I do not intend to stay long.' He turned from her and forced himself to ascend the stairs in a slow and dignified manner.

Cariotti was standing by the window, looking out on to the street when James entered, but turned to smile at his visitor. 'This is an unexpected pleasure, your Grace. Please be seated. Mrs Davies will bring some refreshment.'

'I have already declined that,' he said, sitting down, though he longed to put his hands about the other man's neck and squeeze until he begged for mercy. 'Count, I believe my ward visited you yesterday.'

'She did, but why should she not? We are betrothed and soon to marry.'

'She needs my permission.'

'I do not think so. Her father was all in favour...'

'He is dead and she is now in my care.'

'Only because she chose to come to England ahead of me and needed a home.' He gave his visitor an oily smile. 'What better than to apply to her cousin, the Duke? It would give her—and me—an entry into English society. You see, my mother was English and disowned by her family for marrying my father, in much the same way as her parents were driven from these shores by family disapproval. We both have scores to settle.'

James did not want to believe it, told himself he did *not* believe it, that the man was lying, but underneath it all, there niggled a tiny doubt. Could Sophie be so mercenary? Did she bear the family a grudge? But if she wanted revenge, why had she fled his house? Surely she would have stayed to wring every last ounce of advantage out of the situation? 'If being under my roof is so convenient, then why has she left it?' he demanded. 'I should have expected someone such as you have painted her would have milked the cow to the last drop of cream before leaving.'

'Has she left?' It was spoken casually, but James caught the tiny expression of surprise in the man's voice and realised he did not know where Sophie was. His relief was profound. And that was followed quickly by the thought that if she was not here, then he had no idea where to look next.

'To be independent, she says. No doubt she thinks that now her book is to be published, she does not need me.' He gave a wry smile. 'Nor you either.'

'It is to be published?' Now the surprise was more overt. Count Cariotti was worried.

'So I understand. The publisher, I gather, is enthusiastic and expects it to be all the rage.'

'The publisher already has it?'

'No, I have it for safe keeping. Can't take any risks, don't you know.' He watched the man's face; his expression was bland, but his eyes gave him away. They were furtive. If he had not been so worried about Sophie, James would have felt a certain satisfaction in knowing that he had unsettled him. 'I will bid you good day.'

He left and hurried back to the young lad he had paid
to hold his horse's head. How long before Cariotti realised his visitor had abruptly departed without stating the
business that had brought him and from there to try to de-
cipher the meaning of his last remark? He climbed on to
the seat and urged the horse into a trot, weaving in and out
of the traffic, which had become thicker since he set out.
His attention was not entirely on his driving, but he was
a good whipster and could steer a clear course even while
his mind was elsewhere. Where now? he asked himself.
Where was Sophie? Where would she go? Whom did she
know? Whom could he trust not to spread gossip if he admitted she had left his house?

He went first to the publisher, but Mr Murray said he
had not seen her since the day before when he had made
arrangements for her to return with an amended manuscript two weeks from then. 'She assured me you knew
of her intention to publish,' he told James.

'Oh, I did. She has my full support, but you have read
it, you know what an unconventional lady she is. I am
afraid she may have gone off in search of new material and
landed herself in a bumblebath.'

'Oh, I hope you do not think I encouraged her in that.'

'Not at all. But if she comes to you, will you endeav-
our to find out where she is staying and let me know?'

'Of course, your Grace.'

He tried Mrs Jefferson, questioned Ariadne, then Dorothy, then the Buskins. Though Theodore was not at home,
his parents could not throw any light on Sophie's intentions. Peter Poundell was a bachelor and had gone out of
town to the Newmarket races, so he could not be questioned. Would Sophie have gone out of town? How could
she do that without money? He had no idea if she had any
funds or not; he had always assumed not. In spite of that,

he began asking at the coaching inns, but they were too busy to notice details of every traveller and he could not be sure she was alone. Dispiritedly he turned for home, in no hurry to face Harriet and his aunt and letting the little horse find its own way.

'Good morning, your Grace.'

He turned to see Theodore Buskin riding alongside him. 'Hallo, Buskin. You haven't seen anything of my ward, have you?'

'Miss Langford? Yes, saw her this morning boarding a coach at the White Horse in Piccadilly, thought it was a bit rum seeing she was on her own. Bit risky that and I asked her where she was off to…'

'And?' James's voice betrayed both relief and anxiety. 'Where was she going?'

'Said she was going to visit relations in the country. Only she didn't have enough for the fare. Borrowed two guineas off me.'

Langford! Why hadn't he thought of him? But would she go to her uncle, even after he had refused to receive her? The answer was yes, if she were desperate enough. And who had made her desperate? Guilt flooded through him. How could he have been so stupid? 'I'm sorry you've been troubled.' He felt in his pocket, only to discover he had left the house so hurriedly he had no money on him. 'Come home with me and I will repay the loan.'

'Ain't dunning you for it, sir. It's all the same to me if it's never repaid, but it all seems a bit queer. Why leave without an escort and with no blunt either? Was she running away?'

'No, not exactly. I think she did not want to trouble me. Now, if you are not coming home with me, I am in some haste.' Without waiting for a reply, he whipped up the horse and returned to South Audley Street at the fastest pace the pressing traffic would allow.

* * *

Harriet was waiting anxiously for his return, but his aunt had left, for which he was thankful. 'Well?' his sister demanded as soon as he was in the door, even before he could remove his hat. 'Did you find her?'

'No, but I know where she is.' He flung his hat on the table and followed her into the drawing room where he collapsed into a chair, bone weary. 'She's gone to her father's family. Buskin saw her boarding the coach and asked her where she was off to.'

'A stage? Alone? Oh, James, what have we done? Even if she arrives safely Lord Langford will never countenance her. Or if he does take her in, how will he treat her? He is known to be a cruel and violent man. You must go after her, you really must.'

'And what am I to say? Am I to drag her forcibly from the arms of her family?'

'We are her family too. And I am sure Lord Langford will not mind having a Duke for a nephew-in-law.'

James laughed harshly. 'Even if he is a Dersingham?'

'You can persuade him.'

'I would have to persuade Sophie first.'

'Then do it. Don't just sit there, James. Go. Go or I shall have to go myself.'

'I have every intention of doing so. I have told Sadler to make the travelling coach ready. The mail might be quicker, but then we would have to return the same way and I think it might be better if we had our own conveyance. Can you arrange something to eat while I go and ask Talbot to throw a few things into a valise for me? Tom can ride ahead and arrange for the horses at Stevenage and bring mine back.'

'In that case, I am coming too. You will need a chaperon.' It was a statement that set him laughing wildly. 'What is so funny?'

'Miss Langford wanders all over London on her own, visits dubious characters, takes the public stage without a companion and you worry about chaperons! She is probably this very minute starting a new book, even more scandalous than the first.'

Sophie was not beginning a new book. Her book was the last thing on her mind. She was standing with her back to the gates of Langford Manor, her bag at her feet, doing her best not to cry. She was a fool to have come. After the letter she had received from her uncle in Italy, she should have known there would be no welcome. She had not expected to be greeted with open arms, but neither has she expected to be turned from the door like some common beggar.

Her uncle had refused to see her, sent a message by the butler, a man Sophie remembered being in service to her father when they lived here, though he pretended not to recognise her. 'His lordship is not at home to callers,' he said pompously. 'Not to those without an appointment.'

'But I am his niece.'

'I acquainted his lordship with your claim, miss, and his reply was that he had no niece.'

'How can he say that? My father was his older brother, Hugh. You know that very well, Dobson.'

'His lordship's message was quite plain, miss.'

Desperation had made her bold. 'Then I shall stay here on the doorstep until he comes and delivers it himself.'

'I wouldn't, if I were you, Miss Sophie,' he said in a whisper. 'This is not a happy house. You would not like it here. Go back where you came from. It has to be better than this.' She had heard her uncle roaring inside the house, demanding to know why it was taking so long to deliver a simple message and get rid of the beggar. Niece!

She was no more his niece than the man in the moon. Angrily she had pushed her way inside, not to plead for a home, but to demand to know just what he meant.

She had found him in the drawing room. It was just as she remembered it; even the wallpaper and decorations, faded so badly the pattern was hardly discernible, were the same. The once-elegant sofas were frayed, the tiles about the hearth cracked. Her uncle had moved in the minute her father had vacated the place, supposedly to look after it, but it was in a dreadful state. He was standing with his back to the fireplace, much fatter than she remembered, his face an unhealthy puce. In a chair to one side sat his wife, grey-haired and cowed, with a nasty bruise on her cheek.

'Who let you in?' he roared. 'By heaven, I'll have Dobson's hide…'

'Dobson did not let me in. I knew my way, or had you forgot this was once my home?' She spoke calmly because she was too angry to be upset.

'Get out! I'll have no bastard in my house.'

She heard her aunt gasp, but ignored it. 'How dare you! My mother—'

'Your mother was a Dersingham whore. She made out she was carrying Hugh's child to trick him into marrying her. But I know Hugh, for all his weakness, would never willingly have begotten a Dersingham.'

'That's not true!'

'How do you know?' he sneered. 'You hadn't been born. But you came along soon enough after the nuptials. I never thought to see the day a Langford would marry a Dersingham and I never would have if the whore had not blinded Hugh with her wiles. You are a Dersingham like your mother… '

'And proud of it,' she said. 'I am sorry I troubled you.

Good day, my lord.' And with that she turned on her heel and strode away to the accompaniment of raucous laughter.

Now she stood at the gate, penniless because the money Theodore had lent her had gone on the coach fare and the hire of a trap to bring her from the Red Lion in King's Langford to Langford House. She was miles from a town where she might obtain employment. She picked up her bag and started to walk.

Her memories of the area came back as she made her way along country lanes that had once been familiar. Here was the church and the vicarage where she had been sent for lessons when she was small; here was Willow Farm, where she had often gone with her mother to see the animals and watch the harvest. How happy she had been, roaming the countryside, listening to birdsong, fishing for tiddlers in the stream with Josh Ridley, the farmer's young son. But now everything had a neglected air. The corn lay flattened in the fields, weeds grew chest high, the village cottages were lacking a coat of paint; doors hung lopsidedly. This had all happened because her father had been forced to flee his creditors and her uncle had taken over the house and estate, which was entailed and could not be sold. He knew he would inherit it one day, so why had he not kept it in good heart?

None of that concerned her now. Her problem was to find somewhere to sleep and quickly too, because it would soon be dusk. Whom did she know hereabouts who would give her a bed for the night? Not the cottagers, they were too poor, their houses too overcrowded already to admit a guest, especially one they would consider above their social standing. The nearest landowners… And then she began to laugh hysterically. The nearest landowner was James Dersingham, Duke of Belfont. His country estate,

Dersingham Park, lay six miles distant, but it was no good going there. She had burned her boats; anyway, his Grace was still in London.

In the opposite direction lay the small town of Baldock. And there she might find lodgings, but as she had no money she would have to offer to work for her keep. How stupid and short-sighted she had been! She should have stayed calm after the upset of last night, stayed where she was and found work and lodgings before she left, then she would not now be in this predicament. But how could she have faced the Duke, her tormentor, day by day, slept under his roof, eaten his food, pretended to Harriet all was well, when it was very far from well?

Of course, she could have swallowed her pride and accepted his proposal; he would have dealt fairly with her even if he did not love her. But how could she, loving him as she did, accept second best? He wanted a wife, but was not prepared to give up his mistress. Many women might accept that situation as normal, glad to have the protection of a husband and the social standing, but perhaps they did not love the men with the intensity she loved James Dersingham. It burned through her, made her fiery and illogical, made her want to laugh and cry together, would admit of no rival. She could not coolly assess the advantages and tell herself that, as long as he was discreet, she could live with it. She could not. Nor would she marry a man who did not trust her.

He had behaved badly over that book, creeping about her room in the dead of night, quizzing her about it, afraid she was going to expose his love affair with Lady Colway when everyone knew about it anyway, asking her about the Count, as if anything in the world would persuade her to marry that man, then almost in the same breath offering for her himself. It did not matter now. She had looked for the manuscript before she left, searching the drawing room and the library, but could only surmise he had locked it in his desk drawer for safekeeping. She had toyed with the idea of forcing the drawer, but decided such an action was beneath her. Later, when she was settled, she would write and ask him to return it. When she was settled.

Her feet, clad in the soft shoes she wore in town where she did little walking, were beginning to throb with fatigue; her valise, so light when she set out, was becoming heavier and heavier. She put it down to sit on a low stone wall to rest, watching without interest as a carriage bowled along the road towards her and passed her in a rattle of harness and rumble of wheels, but not before she had caught a glimpse of its occupant. It stopped suddenly a hundred yards further on, the door was opened by the coachman and Lady Myers stepped out and began walking towards her. 'Sophie, Sophie, can it possibly be you?'

She stood up, laughing with relief. 'Yes, my lady, it is.' She had forgotten her mother's lifelong friend lived within a short carriage ride of Langford Manor.

Chapter Eleven

'What are you doing here?' her ladyship asked when Sophie was ensconced in the seat beside her and they were on the move. 'And all alone too. Where is your escort and your maid?'

'I do not have either.'

'But what can his Grace be thinking of? It is beyond believing. A lady simply does not travel alone in England. Anything could happen to her.' She stopped and searched Sophie's face. 'What *has* happened?'

'It is a long story.'

'Then you had better tell it at once, for, to be sure, I shall not know how to proceed until I know the whole.'

Sophie took a deep breath and plunged in. 'I found I could not settle at Belfont House and went to visit my uncle.'

'Why could you not settle and why go to Langford? You knew he would not make you welcome.'

'I thought he might change his mind.'

'And did his Grace make no attempt to stop you?'

'I did not tell him.'

'I see. You ran away.'

'Not exactly.' She remembered telling Harriet she never

ran away from anything, and, if she decided to leave, she would tell her. She had persuaded herself that writing a scribbled note was telling her, but she still felt guilty. 'I said all along I would only stay until I had found a way of earning a living, then I would find somewhere else to live.'

'Earn a living, Sophie? What can you mean? You are surely not still pinning your hopes on writing a book.'

'I have written it and it is to be published, but it has caused such a fuss.'

'I am not surprised. A kinswoman of a duke, living under his protection, reduced to writing for a living, I can understand the Duke making a fuss.'

'Oh, it was not the Duke who made the fuss, it was everyone else. I had to leave.'

'Oh, Sophie, how could you? The Duke and his sister made you welcome. Why throw it up to go to an uncle who does not care one iota for you?'

'He was the only one I could think of.'

'You had done better to come to me in the first place.'

'I would have done, but I thought you were about to leave the country.'

Lady Myers smiled wryly. 'And you knew I would send you back.'

'Oh, no, please do not. I only want a night's lodging, then I will trouble you no more.'

'And tomorrow?'

'I will look for work.'

'Hmmph. We shall see.' They had arrived at the door of the Myers's country home on the outskirts of a small village between Royston and Baldock. It was an old Tudor manor, which had been brought up to date and made comfortable. No more was said as her ladyship instructed the groom to bring her parcels and Sophie's valise into the house and ushered her uninvited guest through the great oak door and into a vast drawing room. It was dusk and the lamps had been lit all about the room and a cheerful fire blazed in the enormous fireplace.

Lord Myers rose from his armchair by the hearth and turned to greet them. He seemed rounder and ruddier than ever. 'Why, Lady Myers, whom have we here? It cannot be little Sophie, can it?'

'Yes, my lord, it is,' Sophie answered, dipping her knee. 'Lady Myers and I met by chance on the road…'

'And she has such a tale to tell you would never believe,' Lady Myers put in. 'But we shall hear it later. Now, I will take her up to her room and see that she is comfortable, then we will have supper, and then we will talk. Come, Sophie.'

She led Sophie across the room and up a flight of stairs at the end, which led up to a gallery that ran all the way round the great hall. Several doors led from it. 'That is the dining room,' her ladyship said. 'It has a wonderful aspect over the countryside. That is Lord Myers's study and dressing room. The one next door is our bedchamber and the rest are guest rooms. On the other side of the gallery are the servants quarters.' She flung open a door where a maid was already making up a bed. 'This will be your room. There is hot water in the jug and towels on the rail. Can you manage without a maid?'

'Oh, yes, easily.'

'Then I will leave you. Come to the dining room when you hear the gong. We keep country hours so it is supper, not dinner, but I do not suppose you mind that. You look done in.' She stopped and took Sophie's hand. 'You are very welcome, child.'

'Thank you,' Sophie said, but Lady Myers was already closing the door behind her.

Sophie sank down on the bed and put her head in her hands. She was so weary, so very, very weary she did not know how she was going to sit through supper and stay awake. Not only sit through it, but make conversation and she knew what that would entail: explanations, detailed explanations that she would have to provide for courtesy's sake. And the biggest question of all would be 'Why?' And how could she answer that?

What was happening at Belfont House now? Had they accepted her disappearance or were they searching for her? Would the Duke understand why she had to do it? Would he be sorry or would he simply shrug his shoulders and console himself with his mistress? Were they laughing at her, the naïve chit of twenty-one who thought she could hold a Duke to ransom? Why did she torment herself thinking about him? Why remember a couple of kisses that had meant nothing at all, except as a prelude to a proposal that was as insincere as it was unacceptable? But, oh, how sweet those kisses had been! They had stirred her insides until she was a quivering mass of desire.

Resolutely she pushed the memories from her and began on her *toilette*, dragging off the black silk and donning her old lilac muslin, which was the only other dress she had brought with her. The lovely gowns Harriet had helped her buy had been left behind, symbols of his Grace's generosity and her dependence. She would have to buy her own clothes in future. What future? It was a blank page, nothing was written on it, nor would there be until she began to live it. She stood before the mirror and brushed her hair, tying it back with a ribbon. The gong sounded as she finished and she took a deep breath and made her way to the dining room.

As she guessed, she was made to repeat the story she had told Lady Myers while they ate and, on his lordship's gentle probing, to enlarge upon it, little by little, until they had the whole sorry saga.

'My dear, I do think you were too hasty in turning his Grace down,' Lady Myers said, helping herself to more vegetables. It might be called supper and not dinner, but the table was laden with roast beef, chicken dishes and several different vegetables. 'He is an undoubted catch and you would be the envy of every unmarried gel in the country. You could surely have come to an accommodation with him over Lady Colway.'

'I did not see why I should.'

'Lady Colway ain't important,' Lord Myers said. 'From what I heard, the affair ended over a year ago when his Grace found her with his cousin. He wouldn't go back to her.'

'Why did he not say so, then? Why let me believe…?'

'Pride, I shouldn't wonder. Pride, same as you have, coming from the same stock.'

'But even if you had turned him down, that was no reason to leave,' her ladyship put in. 'You were set up there. I felt pleased that I could leave you in good hands. And you had to run away and go to Lord Langford, of all people! He is much worse than your father, you know. Since we have been home we have seen for ourselves how bad everything is and his poor wife never let out of the house. The only time I ventured to call, she sent a message she was not at home, but I know very well she was. She was too afraid to admit me.'

'I saw her,' Sophie said, remembering her mother being in the same state on more than one occasion and hiding herself from public view. 'She had a poor bruised face; she would not want you to see it.'

'As bad as that, is it? Are you not glad now that you were turned away and met me coming home?'

'Oh, indeed I am. But I cannot understand why Lord Langford is so against me. I have done nothing—'

'Except to look like your mama and she was a Dersingham. He cannot forget that.'

'Is it true they were on opposite sides in the war between Charles the First and parliament?' she asked, the food growing cold on her plate.

'Yes.' His lordship was the one to answer her. 'The Lord Langford of the time stayed loyal to the king and his home was sequestered by the Roundheads and given to the Dersinghams as a reward for their support in the war. It was renamed Dersingham Park and Lord Langford was relegated to living in a nearby manor house, the house in which you were born. The family tried to get their property back after the Restoration, but were unsuccessful, though some of the land was returned to them...'

'Oh. I see. And when Mama met and fell in love with Papa, the hate all started up again. Why did they not see it as a way of mending old grievances and becoming friends?'

Lord Myers laughed. 'Because the present Lord Langford wanted your mama for himself. The two young men met her when she was out riding. She had taken a tumble from her horse and they stopped to help her. They did not know who she was at the time, but even when they did find out, it made no difference, probably added piquancy to their meetings. The three of them would go riding together and little by little they became close, both young men vying for her hand. When your mother chose your father, the rift between the brothers became irreparable.'

'I did not know that. Mama never said.' She was thoughtful, thinking of her mother being young and in love. Had she had any difficulty in choosing between the young men or had it always been Papa? 'But my uncle called Mama a dreadful name.'

'Pride again. He would not admit he had been hurt. Pride is all very well in the right place, but in the wrong, it can do untold damage.'

'And you think I am too proud?'

'Too hasty, perhaps. You know the Duke of Belfont has a great deal to contend with in his work for the Prince Regent and there are evil men at work. He does not need the distraction of a ward who defies him and sets off to travel the countryside unaccompanied.' He paused to smile at her. 'I say this in a spirit of friendship and concern,' he said. 'And my advice is to return to him and try to be content.'

'How can I? He will not have me back now.'

'Oh, I think he will. I will wager he is even now searching for you and becoming more and more concerned that you have fallen into the hands of those evil men I spoke of.'

'Count Cariotti and Mr Jessop,' she murmured.

'What do you know of them?' he demanded sharply.

'My father called the Count his friend, but I am sure he was responsible for Papa's death and he is afraid I have put something about it in my book. And as for Mr Jessop, he is the Duke's heir and, according to Lady Harley will do almost anything to make sure the Duke does not marry and have a son. They seem to have joined forces.'

'That is dangerous knowledge, my child, and all the more reason to return to the protection of the Duke, who knows who his enemies are and how to deal with them. I will make the arrangements, shall I? Lady Myers and I are leaving for India two days hence and must leave for Plymouth tomorrow. We cannot accompany you, but I will make sure you have a reliable escort. What do you say?'

'If I am out of the way, will it not be easier for his Grace to deal with his enemies and do the work he has to do?'

'Not if he is worrying about you, and, knowing the Duke, I know that will be the case.'

'I don't know what to say.'

'Sleep on it and tomorrow we will talk again.'

She did not think she would sleep ever again, but she was so exhausted that she fell into a deep slumber almost as soon as her head touched the pillow. And she dreamed. She dreamed of Naples and her dead parents who had loved each other so disastrously. She dreamed of the Count and the Duke, locked in combat, not over her but a sheaf of papers. She dreamed of Harriet, whom she had come to love like a sister. But most of all she dreamed again of the man who had carried her to bed and kissed her so tenderly. It seemed like he was saying goodbye for ever. She was crying softly when the maid sent by Lady Myers drew the curtains and flooded the room with light.

James stood outside the gates of Langford Manor just as Sophie had done the afternoon before, but he was not alone and not on foot as she had been. His elegant travelling coach stood on the road. His groom was on the driving seat and his sister sitting inside, waiting for him. But he had had the same reception as Sophie, the same tirade, this time accompanied by foul language and threats. Sophie was not there, the man had made that clear enough, so where was she?

Wearily he climbed in beside Harriet. 'She isn't here,' he said. 'The rotter said he hadn't seen her, but I know he was lying. He sent her away.'

'Poor Sophie. How miserable she must be, to have come all this way and be turned away. I cannot even begin to imagine how she must feel. What are we going to do now?'

'Look for her, what else?'

'Where?'

'On the road—someone must have seen her if she was on foot.'

'But that was yesterday. She would have needed lodgings for the night and would have made for the nearest town, I think.'

He ordered the coachman to drive slowly in the direction of Baldock and to stop whenever he saw a habitation where enquiries might be made, but when they reached the town late in the afternoon, they had learned nothing. No one had seen a young lady walking alone. He enquired at all the inns, but drew a blank.

'She must have been taken up by someone,' he said. 'Anything could have happened to her. Anything.' He sat in the coach and sank his head into his hands. 'Oh, Sophie, what have I done? Instead of protecting you, I drove you away. '

'It is no good blaming yourself,' Harriet said. 'And remember, Sophie is used to being out on her own. She did it all the time when she was in Italy. I do believe she can take care of herself.'

'No, she can't.' He was almost shouting. 'She is an innocent. She trusts everyone, even that no-good Italian. If he has a hand in her disappearance…'

'You said you did not think he had.'

'I don't know what to think.'

'Nor can you, while you are so tired. Let us go home.'

'Home? You think I can go home when Sophie might be in trouble—'

'I meant Dersingham. It isn't above a dozen miles away. I am fagged to death and hungry too, and I know you are. We will change and have a meal and then decide. You never know, she might have gone there.'

He brightened. 'Do you think so?'
'It is possible.'

But she was not there. They sat morosely over a meal hastily prepared by the astonished housekeeper and considered what to do. 'The Myers!' Harriet said suddenly. 'They live close. She would have known that and gone to them.'

He brightened, then sank into gloom again. 'Haven't they gone to India?'

'Oh, yes, I forgot. But I disremember the exact date, so they might not have left. And would Sophie have known it? It would do no harm to call.'

'Very well, we will go there first thing in the morning and then I am afraid we will have to return to London.'

'You are surely not giving up?'

'No, I am not. But if she is not with the Myers, I think her only recourse would be to return to London to fetch her manuscript and see Murray again. She would need money.'

'Of course! Why did we not think of that?'

'If she is still missing, there is nothing for it but to recruit assistance. It will mean her disappearance becoming public knowledge, but there is no help for that. She must be found.'

Harriet reached out and put her hand over her brother's. 'Do not despair, my dear. Sophie will be found.'

Found, yes, he supposed eventually she would be, but would she be alive or dead? He stood up and began pacing the room. 'Where is she? How is she managing? I cannot help thinking of all the dreadful things that could befall her. She could be set upon by thieves, cheated by landlords, taken for a lightskirt out for adventure, used and then—' Sophie's piquant face, colourless in death, swam before him.

'Don't, James. Don't torture yourself. Remember, Sophie has not been brought up in the restrictive atmosphere of genteel drawing rooms, she has been used to looking after herself. She is strong and brave and resourceful.'

'And that is more than half the problem. She will rush headlong into things without thinking. When I get her home…'

'When you get her home, James, you will treat her kindly. No more bullocking.'

He looked at his sister and gave her a wry grin. 'I will treat her as if she were made of fragile porcelain, even if I am tempted to wring her neck.'

'Please do not do either, if you want to keep her by your side, that is.'

'Of course I do. I love her to distraction in spite of her headstrong ways, or perhaps because of them, I do not know. All I know is that she is different from any other woman I have ever met, that she has hold of my heart and I shall not have a moment's peace until I have her in my arms again and I do not intend ever to let her go.'

She smiled. 'Tell her that, James It might make all the difference. Now, I do not know about you, but I need my bed.'

'Do you think Sophie has a bed tonight? Can I go to bed and sleep when she may be lying in a hedgerow somewhere?'

'You must try. If you do not, you will be good for nothing tomorrow.'

He conceded she was right and took himself to his room, where, in the absence of his valet, he stripped off his clothes and flung them on a chair before climbing between the sheets. What a day it had been! What a summer! Oh, Sophie, you came into my life like a whirlwind and you have stirred up my very soul. I cannot live without you, cannot sleep, eat or think without you. I should be out combing the countryside for you. Why do I think you are not far away? Why can I feel your nearness in my bones? Wherever you are, I will find you... He did not intend to sleep, did not think he could, but after two days and a night of travelling with only snatched minutes of sleep in the coach, exhaustion overcame him.

The London-bound stage left Baldock at seven in the morning and at a quarter to the hour Sophie was standing in the inn yard, saying goodbye to Lord Myers who, in spite of being extremely busy with last-minute preparations for his own journey, had insisted on accompanying her to the inn. He had paid her fare and that of Madison, the head groom who would be looking after his stables in his absence, and Annie, one of the maids who was to be part of the skeleton staff left behind to look after the house. Madison was a big, muscular man used to physical labour and Annie a well-built girl with clear blue eyes and fair hair screwed into a tight bun under her plain straw bonnet. Once they had safely delivered her to Belfont House, they would return to their usual duties. Sophie knew his lordship was thinking of her safety and reputation, as if that were not already lost beyond redemption, but she could not help feeling like a parcel.

Did she really want to be delivered in that fashion? Did she really wish to return to Belfont House at all? Lord Myers had persuaded her there was nothing else for it and she needed to retrieve that manuscript, but she did not think she could stay. She would perhaps no longer be welcome there. After all, she had behaved in a way that would have every right-thinking matron in polite society throwing up her hands in horror. Harriet, for all her tolerance, would be one of them. As for the Duke, he would have nothing more to do with her. He would never believe she had managed to travel alone in safety and would undoubtedly believe she had made an assignation. With Count Cariotti perhaps; after all, he already believed that of her. No, there was no going back.

'Now, you will be quite safe with Madison and Annie,' Lord Myers told her, as the coach rattled into the inn yard to have its horses changed and take on new passengers. 'They have been in my service for years. If you need to leave the coach at any of the stops, Annie will accompany you, otherwise stay in your seat. You are due to arrive in the capital in the early afternoon.'

The coachman was calling for the passengers to board and Sophie turned to thank him. 'I do not know how to repay you,' she said, then gave a little laugh, though laughing was something she was finding increasingly difficult. 'I once told Lady Myers I would repay her from the proceeds of my book, and that is all I can offer.'

'My dear child, I do not want repaying, except to know that you are safe. Lady Myers has given you our direction in India, hasn't she?'

'Yes, I will write, I promise.' The coachman was becoming impatient and she turned from him to climb aboard. Annie got in beside her and Madison clambered up beside the driver, and they were away. In six hours she would be back in London with nothing achieved by her escapade except more opprobrium. She had been awakened very early; as the other passengers did not seem inclined to conversation, she sat back and closed her eyes.

She was hardly aware of the stops to change horses, not as frequent as they would have been with the mail, considering the stage did not proceed at the breakneck speed of the mailcoach. Lord Myers had considered sending her on one of those, but as it left at one in the morning, he had decided against it. Sophie was agreeable—not only would it cost him less, but she was in no hurry to reach their destination. She knew she would be in for the biggest jobation of her life. If only she could creep into the house and out again with her manuscript without encountering the Duke, she would be saved the humiliation, but she did not think that was possible. There were dozens of servants, one of them was bound to see her and inform his Grace.

She was roused by Annie. 'Miss, we are coming up to Barnet. Do you wish to step down? I believe it is a longer stop for refreshment.'

'Yes, I would. I am a trifle hungry.'

All three went into the inn and, while the ladies went to relieve themselves, Madison found a table for them and ordered ham and eggs and bread rolls for all three, paying for it with money Lord Myers had given him for the purpose.

Sophie noticed the way he looked at Annie when they returned and the bold way the girl smiled at him, and concluded the two were head over heels in love. Oh, how she envied them! There would be no obstacles in their way, no strict protocol to observe; they were both mature adults and needed no one's permission to marry or to make love without the benefit of a wedding ring, if they chose.

'You will be glad to return to your posts,' she said, by way of conversation while they waited for their food to arrive.

'Oh, we ain't in no hurry, miss. The master and mistress will be gone time we get back...'

'But perhaps you would rather be elsewhere than escorting me?'

Annie looked at her lover and smiled. 'We don't mind, miss, it give us time to be t'gether.'

'Ah, I see. You are sweethearts?'

Annie giggled and Madison chuckled. 'You could say that, miss. We've bin walkin' out for years, but we don't often hev a chance to be alone. There's always someone around.'

'Then why don't you take the opportunity to spend some time together now? You do not need to come the rest of the way with me. It is only another short ride and we shall be in the capital, I can manage that very well on my own.'

'Oh, no, miss, Lord Myers said we was to deliver you—'

'I am not a parcel, Mr Madison. I am perfectly used to travelling on my own.'

'All the same, it ain't right. Lord Myers would have our hides.'

'How is he to know? He will be in India for years.'

They looked doubtfully at each other, but duty prevailed and they insisted on returning to the coach with her. But she had obviously tempted them and when they arrived at the White Horse in Piccadilly, she had no difficulty in persuading them that she could accomplish the short walk to South Audley Street on her own. They ran off, hand in hand, to see the sights and, if Sophie guessed aright, find a lodging house to be together for the night before returning to Hertfordshire. She smiled fleetingly and started to walk very slowly in the direction of Belfont House, telling herself she did not want to come face to face with the Duke. But she knew she was deceiving herself.

What she wanted most of all in the world was to see him again, to see him smile, to hear that he had forgiven her, to be held in his arms, content and safe from all harm, to be with him for the rest of her life; most of all, to be told he loved her and wanted no one else. But it was a dream, an unattainable dream. The reality was that she had to creep into the house unobserved and make her way to the library where she would have to break open the drawer of his desk to retrieve her manuscript and then she would have to leave the same way.

'Why, if it isn't Miss Langford!'

She turned to find Alfred grinning at her. Alfred of all people, the person she most wanted to avoid, apart from Count Cariotti. She was reminded of the conversation she had had with Lord Myers about evil men and suddenly she was afraid. 'Mr Jessop.' She inclined her head in polite acknowledgement, but he did not stand aside for her to pass.

'Where have you been hiding yourself?'

'I have not been hiding. Now, please let me pass.'

'Why the haste? The Duke is from home and so is Cousin Harriet, went off in their travelling coach a few days ago, I ain't sure exactly when seeing I am not privy to their comings and goings. My mother thinks they have most likely gone to Dersingham Park—it is nearly the end of the Season—washed their hands of you, left you to the tender arms of your intended.'

She did not want to believe it. Surely, surely the Duke knew her better than that? But did he? If he knew and understood her, he would not have made that cold-blooded proposal. He would not have accused her of having an assignation with the Count. He would not have believed her capable of publishing scandal about him. Had she been hoping against hope that the situation could be recovered, that they would come together because love always triumphed in the end? She felt like weeping, but Alfred was still standing, blocking her way, looking into her face for her reaction, wanting to hurt her, though she did not know why. Oh, but she did know. He had an interest in ensuring she did not marry the

Duke, and aiding and abetting the Count might achieve that end.

'Mr Jessop, I am not at all interested in what you have to say. Please step aside and allow me to pass.'

He smiled and offered her his arm. 'Then let me escort you.'

'I do not need your escort.'

'Do not be so top lofty, Sophie. My carriage is just along the street. Do you not think it would be better to ride quietly in that than attract more attention?' He waved his arm to encompass the crowds who came and went around them. 'You would not like to add to the scandal?'

'What scandal?' she asked, in spite of her determination not to rise to his bait.

'Why, that you had visited Count Cariotti in his lodgings.'

'You promised not to say anything about that; considering you tricked me into it, it was the least you could do.'

'I said nothing. You were seen.'

'By whom?' She was walking beside him towards his tilbury, which was stationed at the side of the road. It had its hood up, she noticed, and would serve to conceal her from public gaze, because he was right—she could not afford to cause any more scandal, not for her own sake but the Duke's.

'Lady Carstairs and my mother.'

'Who lost no time in conveying the fact to his Grace,' she said bitterly.

'No doubt they considered it their duty.'

They had reached his carriage and he paid off the urchin that held the horse's head and helped her into it before seating himself beside her and taking up the reins. Only then did she begin to wonder why, of all people, Alfred Jessop should be the one to see her come from the coaching inn and more importantly, if she could trust him to take her to Belfont House.

She was right to doubt him, she realised, when, instead of going down Piccadilly towards Hyde Park and South Audley Street, he turned down a side street and after one or two more turns, came out in a street that was vaguely familiar. 'Where are you taking me?' she demanded.

'Home, my dear.'

'But this is not the way to Belfont House.'

'No more it is, but then Belfont House ain't home, is it? Not any more.'

She knew where she was when he drew up outside the terrace house where Count Cariotti lodged. 'I am not going in there again.'

'Why not? It is home, the only home you'll know from now on.'

'Never!'

'But it is the only house in which you will be received. Your reputation has gone. News of your previous visit has gone the rounds and the Duke of Belfont is so humiliated at being gulled he has resigned his position at court and retired to his country estate. No doubt he will be visited there by Ellen Colway when she is out of black gloves and all the fuss has died down.'

'If that is so,' she said as calmly as she could, while her mind was casting vainly about for a way of escape, 'you do not need me, you have achieved your aim.'

'Perhaps, perhaps not, but my friend Tony has yet to achieve his.' He jumped down and reached into the carriage to pull her out. 'And don't cry out or struggle or I shall be obliged to knock you out and carry you inside.'

She could not escape or learn what they intended to do with her if she was unconscious, so she mustered her dignity and stepped down. He took her elbow firmly in his hand and ushered her up to the door, which opened as they approached. She was pushed past the housekeeper and bundled upstairs and into the Count's sitting room.

'I've got her,' Alfred said triumphantly. 'You were right. She was coming back.'

'I knew she'd have to come back for that book of hers,' the Count said, coming forward with a smile. 'It's a little gold mine, isn't it, sweetheart?' He reached out and put a lean finger under her chin to raise it.

She stood in her faded black silk and faced him defiantly. 'I shall be content if it is moderately successful and makes me a name as a writer. There is nothing in it for you.'

'Oh, but there is. There is money to be made in *not* publishing it.' He laughed. 'You look puzzled, my dear. Would you like me to explain?'

She stared at him, trying to subdue her shaking, but did not dignify his question with an answer.

'There is scandal in it, lots of scandal, names are named and people will pay not to have their dirty linen washed in public.'

'That's blackmail! And there is no scandal in my book.'

'Not even about me, my dear?'

'Definitely not about you. You are not interesting or important enough for people to want to read about you.'

He took a step towards her and raised his hand as if to strike her. She flinched and he laughed. 'No, we do not want to mark that beautiful face, not yet. And it does not matter in the least what is in the book, considering it will never be seen in print. It is enough that you have hinted of its contents and worried those with secrets to hide, those who spent the war years abroad and now expect to come home to a welcome and sympathy for their suffering. They would not like their real activities to be made public—'

'Such as you.'

He ignored that and went on. 'All we have to do is approach people who are vulnerable—'

'We! Do not expect me to collude in this. Besides, I do not have the manuscript.'

'Oh, I know that. His Grace, the Duke of Belfont, has it, but he will hand it over.'

'Why should he?'

'Because you will ask him to. Now sit down, while I think how it is to be done.'

She made no move, but Alfred pushed her into a chair. She was suddenly glad of its support for she did not think her legs would hold her upright much longer.

'Now,' he said, fetching out pen and ink and a sheet of paper from a desk in the corner and placing it on the table beside her. 'Write this.' He put the pen in her hand. '"Your Grace, I am being held against my will."'

'Why tell him that?' Alfred demanded.

'Shut up and listen.' Then to Sophie, 'Go on, put it down. You have no quarrel with the truth of that, have you?'

'None at all.' She dipped the pen in the ink, but her hand was shaking so much her writing was a scrawl. Perhaps James would not recognise it.

'Good,' he said. 'Carry on. "I shall be released in exchange for my manuscript…"'

'You are never going to let her go,' Alfred put in again. 'She will shop us.'

'I told you to shut up.' He spoke in rapid French. 'I am using her as bait. He will come to her rescue and then we will have him. It's what you want, is it not? The dukedom will be yours, lock, stock and barrel. And I shall be free.'

Sophie, who had understood perfectly, gave no sign that she had done so, but sat with pen poised, waiting for him to continue dictation. Somehow she had to convey that it was a trap. The Duke's life was in terrible danger. But what did he mean he would be free?

Alfred asked the question for her. 'Free? Ain't you free now?'

'No. She knows too much. She knows where I was during the war and when. And why. Her father told her, told her what to write in that book so that I would be exposed. It's no ordinary book, it's code for something and Dersingham knows it. I can't risk him rumbling me. The Emperor is still the Emperor, when all is said and done, and his plans for a return are well advanced. I have to stay under cover and report the plans being made to meet the threat.'

'There are none because no one here believes in it.'

'Except Belfont.'

So that was it! Sophie would have laughed if the threat to her and the Duke was not so dire. Her father had never told her anything, there was no code in her book, nothing that might expose the country's enemies. The Duke knew that, so he would not mind in the least handing the book over. But would he be walking to his death?

'How did Langford know so much? Careless, were you?' Alfred said in very bad French.

'Yes, a mite careless. I thought he'd act as my contact in England, seeing he owed me thousands, but the muck-straw suddenly became virtuous. He knew too much. I had to silence him. I didn't reckon on the old fellow being sober enough to cover his back.'

'I see. But why are you so sure it's all in the book?'

It was something Sophie wanted to know and she waited silently for the answer. 'I had worked out a code for when he had to send me information and we had talked about it, so I have to get my hands on that book.'

'You could have stolen it.'

'Then you would not be rid of the Duke and neither would I.' He turned back to Sophie and resumed speaking English. 'I know you speak fluent Italian, but did you understand any of that?'

She shook her head.

'We were discussing ways and means of meeting the Duke,' he lied. 'It cannot be here. It would be the first place he would think of and we cannot have him rushing to the rescue before we are ready.'

'What makes you think he will rush to the rescue?' she asked. 'Mr Jessop told me he had washed his hands of me and retired to the country.'

'Then we shall have to lure him back.' He turned to Sophie. 'Write this. "If you value my life, bring the manuscript of my book and five thousand guineas to the Stanhope Gate of Hyde Park on Saturday at seven o'clock of the evening. You will be met and brought to me. Come alone and on foot and bring nothing but the money and all copies of the manuscript." That's three days away and should give him time enough to return to London.'

'Why Stanhope Gate?' Alfred asked, while Sophie finished writing. 'It's but a stone's throw from Belfont House.'

'Good. We will be able to watch him leave the house and make sure there is no one following him.'

'I'm not doing any watching. He'll tumble me straight away.'

'I haven't asked you to. Get Simpson and Flowers.'

'How do you know James didn't get a look at them the day we made the attempt on Wellington? Or that O'Grady didn't talk? They've still got him in custody.'

'He didn't talk. It's more than his life's worth. And if he had, the militia would have been swarming round here long before now.' He dismissed the danger and turned back to Sophie. 'Now sign it.'

'What with?'

'Your name, of course. Get on with it. The sooner it's on its way, the better.'

'Perhaps he will not come,' she said as she wrote her name in a flourishing scrawl, nothing like her usual signature, and ending it with a cross and an exclamation mark. Whether the Duke would understand that it was meant as a warning, she did not know. 'You have made it plain to him that you intend to marry me, though why you should want to I do not know. We have no love for each other.'

'No, but it occurred to me that a wife cannot give evidence against her husband.'

'Evidence of what?' she asked, remembering just in time that she was not supposed to have understood his conversation with Alfred.

He paused, then gave a bark of a laugh that sent a chill through her bones. 'Whatever I decide needs to be done.'

'You cannot make me marry you.'

'We shall see.' He went to a drawer in the desk; when he turned back to her, he held her lost fan in his hand. She gasped. 'Where did you get that?'

'Why, my friend, Alfred, found it. I was not sure at the time how I could use it, but I think now I will return it to its original owner. He might be very pleased to see it again.'

She made a grab for it, but he easily held it away from her, speaking to Alfred as he did so. 'Go and fetch Simpson and Flowers and hire a closed town chariot. The sooner we have her out of here and in a safe place, the better…'

Chapter Twelve

The Belfont coach had no sooner drawn up at Belfont House than James was out of it and sprinting towards the door, leaving Harriet to make her way more slowly. He could not wait to see Sophie, to know she was safe, to enfold her in his arms and declare his love for her, that nothing would ever again come between them, to ask her again to marry him before they could begin any argument about why she had run away, why he had bungled his first proposal, before either of them had a chance to fly into the boughs. First things first.

'Collins, where is Miss Langford?' he asked the footman.

'Your Grace?' He looked puzzled.

'Miss Langford. Is she in her room? Send Rose up to ask her to come down. No, never mind, I will go myself.' And he bounded up the stairs and threw open the door of Sophie's room.

It looked exactly as it had done the last time he had seen it. The bed was tidily made, the dressing table devoid of brushes, combs and hair pins. The towels on the stand were unused. He strode over to the wardrobe and pulled open the doors. All her beautiful clothes were hanging just as he had seen them last, the day he had searched her room for a clue as to where she might have gone. He turned to find Rose standing behind him. 'She ain't come back, your Grace.'

He sank on to the bed and put his head in his hands. After seeing and talking to Myers, he had been so sure she would be here, waiting for him. 'I could not take her myself,' he had said, sweeping his arm to encompass the huge room, which was piled up with boxes, chests and bags and servants scurrying to and fro loading them on to a wagon. 'As you see, I am about to leave. But I sent two reliable servants with her, with instructions to see that she is safely delivered to Belfont House. No doubt she will be waiting there for you.'

But she wasn't. Where had she gone? What was the silly chit up to now? He really could not endure much more of her antics; it was playing havoc with his nerves. Harriet came into the room and he looked up at her, stricken. 'She did not come back. She only pretended to agree to it to placate Lord Myers.' He got up and ran his hands through his hair. It needed the attention of his valet, but he did not have time for that. 'I had better go to the coach stop and see if she even arrived back in London.'

He went on foot; it was quicker than sending to the mews for his horse or a carriage, and it was all he could do not to break into an undignified run. At the White Horse—which according to Myers had been the destination of the coach he had put Sophie on—he discovered, on giving their descriptions, that the three people had completed the journey. At least that meant Sophie was back in London. He turned to go, stepping out of the way of an incoming coach as it clattered into the yard to disgorge its passengers. One of them was Captain Richard Summers.

'How did you know I would be coming off this coach?' he asked, catching the valise flung down to him from the boot by one of the inn's servants, and falling into step beside James.

'I didn't, but I am certainly glad to see you. I need help.'

'At your service, just as soon as I've been home, changed my linen and had something to eat. I've been on a wild-goose chase. That fellow we have in custody gave me the name of one of his accomplices, told me where to find him, but the bird had flown.'

'They seem to be one step ahead of us all the time, but I don't think my problems have anything to do with that. At least, I sincerely hope not. It is a personal matter…'

'Fire away while we walk, then.'

By the time they reached the captain's quarters at Kensington Barracks, James had told him everything.

'I heard you had left the Smoke for Dersingham,' Richard said. 'Word was you'd taken the knocker off the door. Thought it a mite queer when we hadn't finished our business. Not like you to go off half-cock…'

It occurred to him then that Sophie might have thought that was what had happened. She would think he had washed his hands of her, thought so little of her he could not even be concerned for her welfare, could not even bother to leave a message for her. 'I've been combing the countryside for her. That's why I need your help. I have to find her…'

'Are you sure she's not involved with Cariotti?'

'Of course I am. If you are suggesting—'

Richard held up his hand. 'Hold your horses. No need to fly into the boughs. It was only an idea. Of course, if he still believes she knows his secret, wouldn't he want her where he could keep an eye on her?'

'You mean he might have abducted her?'

'It is a possibility.'

'Then let us go and find out.' He set off at such speed that Richard, hampered by his hand luggage, could hardly keep up with him.

'Hang on, old man, let me get rid of this and then we'll take a cab.'

James slowed down. They left Richard's valise in the hall of his lodgings and hailed a cab, but when they arrived at Cariotti's lodgings, the housekeeper told them that the Count had moved out. 'Found more spacious lodgings, he said, seeing he has a wife to accommodate now,' she said, with a sniff.

'Wife!' James yelled.

'There's no need to shout, sir,' she protested. 'That's what he said, but I don't reckon they were married, not yet anyway, 'cos I heard him send for witnesses to the ceremony.'

'Where did they go?'

She shrugged. 'They didn't tell me.'

James forced himself to stay calm, but he was raging. She couldn't marry that snake, she couldn't. She wouldn't. She did not even like him. Or so she said, but there was a little niggle in his brain that would not go away. It was the echo of the Count's words only three days before: …she chose to come to England ahead of me and needed a home. What better than to apply to her cousin, the Duke? It would give her— and me—an entry into English society… We both have scores to settle.

'May I look round his room? He might have left a clue to his direction.'

'Go and look if you like, but I can tell you he left nothing behind.'

James bounded up the stairs, followed by Richard.

The room was tidy, just as Sophie's had been tidy. There were no clothes, no personal possessions. Richard went over to the desk, expecting it to be locked, but it slid open easily. 'Nothing here,' he said. 'Completely empty, except for this.' He turned towards James, holding up a fan, a fan James recognised, a fan that had been lost and now was found. Left for him to find, he knew. He could just imagine them laughing as they put it there, knowing he would look for her.

'Come on,' he said, through gritted teeth. 'I've seen enough.'

They returned to the cab in silence, brushing past Mrs Davies who stood in the hall. Richard threw her a guinea when it became obvious that James was oblivious to her, oblivious to everything except his own anger and misery.

'James…' Out on the pavement, Richard put a hand on his friend's arm, but it was shrugged off.

'Leave me. Take the cab. I'll walk.'

'Where are you going?'

'For a walk. I need to clear my head.'

He walked for hours; when he returned home in the grey light of dawn, he had no recollection of where he had been. He had stopped in some ale house somewhere and slaked his raging thirst, but that was all. The paving stones, the streets, the muddy walk alongside the river, the Palace of Westminster, London Bridge, the Tower, all passed in a blur. His vision was clouded by anger and then tears. He had not cried since he was in leading strings, not even when he had lost good comrades in battle, not even when his mother had died. He had been brought up to face adversity and sorrow with stoicism, but how could he be stoic in the face of this treachery? They had made a fool of him, those two, and he wanted his revenge. The need for it burned inside him until he felt as if he were on fire. But that was on the surface; deep down in the very core of him, he was hurting.

He went into the breakfast parlour where one of the maids was setting the table. 'Mercy me, you startled me, your Grace,' she said, bending her knee. 'I'll have your breakfast in here in a tick.'

'There's no hurry,' he said wearily. 'I'm not going anywhere.'

She gave another bob and went off to tell Janet to tell her mistress the master had just come in, looking in a fearful state. And then she went back to the kitchen to tell Cook to look lively, for his Grace was waiting for his breakfast.

But when, half an hour later, she took the dishes of ham and eggs and pork chops to the breakfast parlour, it was to find his Grace sitting in the chair at the head of the table, with his head on his folded arms. She put the dishes on the sideboard and crept out again.

'James!' He felt someone take his shoulder and shake it. 'James, bestir yourself. You cannot sleep down here.'

He looked up, bleary-eyed, to see his sister standing over him in an undress robe of flowing blue-green silk. 'They tricked us, Harri, they tricked us,' he said.

'Who did? And where have you been? Did you find Sophie?'

'She's gone with that muckworm, Cariotti. They left a calling card.' He drew from his pocket the mangled remains of the fan. He had been turning it over and over in his hand as he walked and ruined it. 'It was left behind at his lodgings. A message to me, a message of triumph.'

'Fustian! I do not believe it. He's playing games with you.'

'You think so? Why would she go to him a second time? Why deny she had ever seen him the first time? It was all a plot to gull me. Dersinghams and Langfords! Will it never end?'

'Go to bed, James. You need rest. You cannot think clearly while you are so tired.'

'I am thinking clearly. I am thinking clearly for the first time for weeks…'

'No, you are not.' She pulled on his arm until he was on his feet. 'James, please go to your room and lie down. When you have rested, we will talk about it because I refuse to believe Sophie could be so cruel and you won't believe it either when you think about it coolly.'

It was easier to comply than argue. He was dead on his feet. He went up to his room, waved Talbot away and flung himself on his bed fully dressed. He was asleep in seconds.

He woke several hours later, feeling marginally better, rang for Talbot, who clucked disapprovingly as the state of his garments, washed and allowed himself to be shaved and clad respectably in biscuit pantaloons, yellow waistcoat and a brown superfine frock coat with a velvet collar. Feeling more civilised, he pulled on his Hessians and went downstairs to find his sister.

'Better?' she queried, putting down the book she had been reading.

'There's a little man using a hammer inside my head,' he said. 'But, yes, I am feeling more the thing.'

'Then sit down and tell me everything that happened from the time you left here until you came back this morning looking like a scarecrow.'

He told her, trying not to let his fury bubble up again. 'What a fool I feel,' he added when he had finished.

'Yes, you are,' she said. 'Is that the strength of your love? Is it love at all if it can fluctuate so wildly? If you truly loved Sophie, you would never believe ill of her. You would know deep down that she could never deceive you in that fashion.' She paused. 'Think back, James, think of the times when you were together and not brangling. Remember the things she said to you, especially about that mountebank, Cariotti. Remember how she grovelled in the mud, looking for that fan. She was distraught at losing it, was ill for days afterwards. Was that all play acting?'

He did not answer, still too distraught to agree she was right, but he was beginning to wonder...

'Had it not occurred to you that someone else might have picked up that fan, someone who saw a use for it?'

'Cariotti was not at the Myers's ball.'

'No, but someone else was, someone who would hate to see you happily married.'

'Alfred!' He slapped his forehead with his open palm, which did little to help his headache. 'Sophie told Myers that she thought they were in league.'

'There you are, then.'

'I'm off to see what that muckworm of a cousin has to say for himself.' He grabbed a sugar plum from the dish at her side, stuffed it in his mouth and hurried from the room. 'If either of them have harmed a hair of her head...' His last words were lost as he left the room and disappeared down the hall, shouting for Collins to go and tell Sadler to bring Hotspur round to the front of the house By that time he had changed into riding coat and boots, his horse was waiting for him. He bounded into the saddle and cantered off, weaving skilfully in and out of the traffic.

Alfred was away from home, his aunt told him frostily when he burst into the drawing room where she was entertaining her cronies.

'Where has he gone?'

'I am sure I do not know.'

'Have you seen S— Miss Langford?'

'No, and glad of it. She is beyond redemption. Try the Count.' And she looked meaningfully at her companions, who smirked behind their gloved hands. They had all heard of Sophie's indiscretion, it seemed, and she was not to be forgiven.

'I am sorry I troubled you,' he said.

His next call was on Richard, where he told him he thought he might have been right and Sophie had been abducted. But where was Cariotti hiding? And what did he want?

'Are you sure she hasn't gone off on her own?'

'No, not this time.' He had to have faith; that was what Harri had been trying to tell him, wasn't it?

'Go home and wait,' Richard advised. 'If he has got her you will hear soon enough. He won't harm her until he has what he wants.'

'Have another go at that prisoner, Dick, will you? I daren't trust myself to do it. I'd throttle him before he could open his mouth. Find out where the rogues hide out. If we are prepared, we might stand a chance of foiling his plot before Sophie suffers too much.'

But if she was being held, then she was already suffering. He did not know how he was going to find the patience to wait. Surely, there was something he could be doing?

He went back to Harriet and relayed his abortive conversation with their aunt and his subsequent meeting with Captain Summers. 'Sophie was right,' he said. 'They are in league. That's why Alfred has gone to ground.'

'Alfred is a jackstraw, but I cannot believe he would become embroiled in something truly evil. He doesn't have the courage for it.'

'I hope you are right. I'm going to send Sadler to Baldock.'

'Baldock?'

'Yes, to question those two servants who brought Sophie to London and find out exactly where they left her and if she was seen talking to anyone. I'd go myself, except I dare not leave in case a message comes for me. He can ride Hotspur. With luck he'll be there before midnight. He can put up at Dersingham and go to Baldock the following morning and be back again by tomorrow night.'

'Hotspur will never make it.'

'Yes, he will, ridden sensibly. He carried me many a mile when we were campaigning.' He hurried off to give his orders and then settled down to wait, something which he found inordinately difficult. He was a man of action and doing nothing irked him. He cleaned and primed his pistols in readiness, then paced up and down until Harriet lost all patience with him 'Sit down, James. Find something to read. Do your accounts.'

He retired to the library to take her advice, but he could not make the figures in his ledgers add up and none of the books he took from the shelves held his interest. He paced about, then fetched Sophie's manuscript from his desk drawer and sat down to read it again.

It made him feel very close to her. He could hear her voice as he read her words. They were softly reassuring. He leaned back and closed his eyes and then he could see her. She was wearing that shimmering blue-green gown; her hair was piled on her head, thick dark coils, sparkling in lamplight; her shoulders were bare and there was a pearl necklace about her throat. She seemed to be reaching out to him and her eyes implored him. 'Sophie,' he murmured. 'Where are you?'

* * *

Sophie did not know where she was. Cariotti and Alfred had draped a large burnous over her and pulled the cowl down over her head so that she could see nothing but her feet, then bundled her into a closed carriage that had taken them to the river; there they had transferred to a rowing boat. Two men already in the boat had picked up the oars and began rowing steadily. She thought they had rowed downstream, judging by the salty tang in the air. It had made her think they must have a rendezvous with a ship and that had terrified her.

No one would ever find her if she left England. She would never see James again, never again hear his voice berating her, teasing her, laughing with her. Oh, how she wished she had not been so forthright, so independent, so foolish. If she had not boasted about that book! But if that was what the Count intended, why bother to send the Duke a letter demanding the manuscript and money? Surely he would not leave until he had both.

It was not a ship she was being taken to, she had realised when they turned up a small creek, and a few minutes later, the rowers had shipped their oars, tied a mooring rope to a post and hauled her unceremoniously out on to soggy grass. The Count and Alfred followed with the fourth man bringing up the rear. She was guided up a narrow track and pushed roughly through a door, heard them strike a flint and saw, through the thickness of the hood, a faint glow. The cowl had been pushed back from her face, making her blink as she tried to focus her eyes.

They were in a rough hut. It was furnished with a table, a couple of chairs and a rough truckle bed. 'I am afraid I must leave you here,' Cariotti had said. 'I am expected at the opera tonight and it would not do to be absent. Everything must appear normal. And I do believe Mr Jessop is taking a lady to Lady Holland's soirée. My men will look after you.' He had nodded towards two ruffians, one dark as night, wearing filthy black clothes, the other bald as an egg with a deep scar from the corner of his eye to his chin. 'Do not give them any trouble because they are not gentlemen and will not hesitate to use violence, though I have forbidden them to kill you. At the moment you are more valuable alive. I am sure you understand me.'

Unable to find her voice, she nodded.

'Good.'

Alfred was looking scared, as if he could not wait to be gone, though Cariotti seemed icily calm. He had killed before and the prospect did not frighten him. He stopped to give last-minute instructions to the ruffians and to warn them that if they allowed the prisoner to escape, their heads would roll, then he followed Alfred from the hut, leaving Sophie facing the two men.

Her prison could not be that far from the capital, she surmised, if the two men had time to return and fulfil evening engagements. But that was little help when she did not know how James could possibly know where she had been brought. He would never find her. They wanted to kill him, but they would not do it before he had handed over her manuscript. He would realise that, wouldn't he? He would hold them off as long as he dared. But supposing he did not care what happened to her? She had quarrelled with him, defied him, run away—why would he put himself in danger for her? She needed all her strength and will power because, if he did not come, there was no one to save her but herself.

'How much has the Count promised you?' she asked.

'Enough,' the bald man said.

'Is that why you are doing this, simply for money, or is there more to it than that? Count Cariotti has no love for the English. He is a cold-blooded killer and he's very good at shifting the blame; he has done it before. Why do you think he went off and left you here? So that if there is trouble, he will be miles away doing something else. Do you want to hang for him?'

'No one's going to hang.' He looked the more nervous of the two.

'Stop yer chawin',' the dark one said. 'We ain't supposed to talk to 'er.'

'I was only trying to find out what made you collude in kidnapping,' Sophie said. 'I have powerful friends—'

'Where are they, then?' he cackled.

She fell silent. Did she have any friends at all, let alone powerful ones? Did anyone care what had become of her. She was a hoyden, had flouted convention, had boasted about a book that was nothing but a travelogue, and had made enemies. But friends? Lady Myers had gone to India with her husband. Harriet might be fond of her, but she would never defy her brother. As for the young people whose acquaintance she had made since coming to London, people like Ariadne and Dorothy, they could not possibly understand or care about the coil she was in. And James Dersingham, what of him? Had he received the letter she had been forced to write? Had he done anything about it?

James was sitting opposite Harriet in the small dining room, toying with the food on his plate. A day had passed, a whole day and nothing had happened: no demand from Cariotti who, according to Harriet, had been seen at the opera the evening before; no word from Richard that he had discovered anything from the prisoner; no news from Baldock that could throw any light on Sophie's disappearance. He was in despair. His hair was wild because he had raked his fingers through it so many times, his eyes were glazed with fatigue, his face pale as parchment. If he did not hear something soon, he would go mad.

'I begin to think Cariotti does not have her,' he said. 'We would have heard long before now if he had.'

Collins came in, bearing a dish containing a heavy plum pudding. James groaned. More food was the last thing he wanted. 'Your Grace, Sadler is back.'

'Back? Then send him in here. At once.'

'Your Grace, he is dusty from travel.'

'Send him in, I said. Do I have to give all my orders twice?'

'James!' Harriet remonstrated quietly, as the man scuttled away.

'Sorry. This waiting and doing nothing is like waiting for a battle to commence. The troops are ready, the guns are primed, swords are sharpened, and still we wait for the order to advance…'

Sadler, begrimed with travel, took a step into the elegant drawing room and stood, his hat under his arm, reluctant to venture further. 'Your Grace.'

'What have you to report, man?'

'The two you asked me to question knew nothing, your Grace, though I promised they would not be punished for telling me. They said Miss Langford dismissed them in Piccadilly, told them she could find her own way from there. They didn't see her speak to anyone.'

'Damn!' James swore, forgetting the presence of his sister.

'I stayed at Dersingham Park as you instructed, your Grace,' the servant went on. 'The housekeeper gave me this letter. Said it had only just arrived and she was going to post it on.' He took a step forward to meet James, who had come to his feet and was striding towards him.

'Thank you, Sadler, you may go,' he said, ripping open

the seal. He scanned the missive quickly. 'This is it,' he said, feeling relief surge through him, followed almost immediately by anxiety. 'She's being held to ransom…'

'Then pay it. How much are they asking?'

'Her manuscript and five thousand guineas. I have to take it to the Stanhope Gate at seven…' He glanced up at the clock on the mantel. 'It's nearly that now. There isn't time to warn Captain Summers. He was going to follow me… Collins,' he shouted, and when the footman returned, 'Tell Sadler to come back. I have an errand for him.'

The order for battle had been given. He was full of purpose and energy, though how he was going to outwit his enemies he did not know. He had been counting on Richard's help. He sent the exhausted Sadler out to find Captain Summers after dragging him away from his dinner in the kitchen, and then went upstairs to change into a plain suit of Bath cloth, fling a black cloak about his shoulders and put a small pistol in his belt, resisting the urge to hurry. Whoever had been instructed to meet him would wait a while; they would not give up before they were certain he was not coming and the longer he kept them waiting the more time he would give Richard to arrive. He picked up his hat and returned downstairs.

Harriet was waiting in the hall. She followed him into the library, where he unlocked the safe and took out a bag of coins. 'Count out two thousand,' he said, 'while I make up a parcel.' He grabbed several old newspapers and folded them to the same size as Sophie's manuscript and wrapped it neatly in plain paper, trying it with tape.

'Aren't you going to take the manuscript? she asked.

'No. Sophie put too much work into that for me to hand it over.'

'But surely, if they realise there is nothing to fear in

what she has written, no secrets, I mean, they will let her go and give it back? If you try and gull them, they will be sure to think there is something to hide…'

'Possibly,' he said laconically. 'But they might destroy it out of anger and I cannot let that happen.'

'I hope you know what you are doing.'

'So do I.' He dropped a kiss on her forehead, picked up the parcel and the bag of money she had counted out, crammed his hat on to his head and made for the door. 'If Richard comes, tell him what has happened.'

It was only a few hundred yards to the Stanhope Gate. He walked slowly. In spite of the feeling of urgency, the need to be at Sophie's side as quickly as possible, he was calm. He went over everything in his head, his instructions, written in Sophie's hand, though he could tell that she was trembling by the uneven writing and the strange wobble at the end of her signature; the arrangements he had made with Richard; the possibility that it was a trap and that neither he nor Sophie were meant to come out of it alive. That last thought was enough to quicken his step, but he deliberately slowed down again.

'The Duke of Belfont?'

He turned to face the speaker. He was of middle height, thin as a rake and bald as an egg. He had an ugly scar on his face that James recognised as a battle scar. An old soldier, then. And poorly dressed.

'Yes.'

'Do you have the goods?'

'I do, but if you think I—'

'No, sir, no. I am sent to fetch you, nothing more.' He was obviously nervous, not only about what he was about to do, but because as a soldier he had learned to respect and obey those who were put in command of him and he recognised an officer when he saw one, even if he was in civilian clothing.

'Then lead on.' He scanned the jostling crowds, looking for Richard or any of his men, but there was no sign of them, but then there would not be; they were meant to be invisible.

The man led him to a carriage, with a man already on the box, waiting to move off. If he got into that and it carried him away, how was Richard to know his direction? He hesitated. 'Sir,' the scarred man said. 'I must ask you to get in the vehicle.'

'Where are you taking me?'

'Why, to the young lady, sir.'

There was nothing for it. He had to go. There was already a man in the coach, a wiry little man with grey hair and an equally grey complexion, who ran his hands over James as he seated himself beside him. Finding the small pistol, he took it from him and sat holding it, grinning to himself. The bald man sat opposite.

They journeyed in silence for some time, until they left the capital behind and were on the open road. 'How far do we travel?' James asked.

'Not far.'

'A soldier, are you?'

'I were.'

'What do you do now? When you are not kidnapping young ladies, I mean.'

'Didn't do no kidnapping. The mort were already with—' He stopped suddenly.

'The Italian Count?'

'Ain't sayin'.'

'Why d'you do it?'

'Got a wife and six childer and no work, that's why.'

'You know it's treason? There's a particularly brutal punishment for that. What would your wife and children do then?'

'Treason? It ain't treason, sir. It's an affair of the 'eart, so he told me.'

'He lied. He's a spy for Napoleon, the man you spent years fighting. Do you want to see the tyrant come again?'

The man made a noise that was half-laugh, half-grunt. 'It'd put me back in work, wouldn' it?'

'I think you will be back in uniform before you know it, my friend, but in the meantime, I can give you work.'

'An' if you think you can bribe me to turn my coat, think again, sir. It won't serve.'

'Why not?'

''Cos he's took me wife, ag'in me not obeying orders…'

'Then we are in the same boat, my friend. He has my woman…'

'Can't 'elp you, sir.' He was uncomfortable and nervous and James knew he had rattled him.

'How much are you being paid?'

He laughed. ''Tis in that bag you got in yer pocket.'

The other man scowled and muttered something in French.

'Who's your friend? James inclined his head towards the man sitting next to him.

'Ain't my friend. Never saw 'im afore today. He's the Eye-talian's valet, so I ha' bin told. He don' speak no English.'

James forced a smile. 'Then he's been set to watch you, watching me.'

'No doubt of it.'

James fell silent. There was nothing he could do, nothing he wanted to do, until they reached their destination.

In the close confines of the coach he did not think that it would be wise to attempt to overcome them, not with the valet playing with that pistol. Finding Sophie was his first priority, then he could think about freeing them both from the Italian's clutches, though how it was to be done, he had, as yet, no idea.

It was dark now but it was not difficult to detect where they were; the stench of the river was strong in his nostrils. The coach turned down an alley and stopped at some river steps. It was then he realised they were going to continue their journey by boat. Like Sophie before him, he wondered if he was being taken out to an anchored ship. If that were the case, it was going to be doubly difficult for him to effect a rescue and bring her safely back to dry land. But there was nothing for it but to go along with them. The coach driver remained behind while the other two did the rowing.

After they had been making their way steadily downstream on the ebbing tide for some time, he recognised the bend in the river. He was in Limehouse Reach with the Isle of Dogs on his left; but though there was some moored ships waiting their turn to go into one of docks, the rowers did not seem to be making for them. Instead they turned up one of the dozens of small creeks that crisscrossed the Isle, and a few minutes later pulled in to a dilapidated landing stage. James's senses were alert as they left the rowing boat and squelched across marshy land towards an isolated hut, surrounded by a few overgrown bushes that half-concealed it.

He had fought in a war, endured gunfire and explosions, crept about behind enemy lines, pretending to be one of them, knowing if he were discovered he could expect no mercy, and his feelings were the same then as now. Fear gripped his belly, while his mind remained sharply aware of everything around him. The land was flat, much of it below the high-water mark, kept from flooding by embankments. There were a few stunted bushes dotted here and there, but for the most part it was pasture where cattle grazed. Some way off he could see buildings, which he supposed to be dockside warehouses. Once away from the hut, there was little or no cover for anyone escaping on foot, unless they were prepared to submerge themselves in the dykes.

He turned his attention to the building. It was crudely made, but stout enough, probably a hiding place for smugglers or criminals fleeing the country, somewhere where they could wait for a suitable ship. Was that what Cariotti intended? Was the man there, with Sophie, only feet from him? His heart began to race.

The bald man walked ahead of him, the older valet behind, carrying James's pistol, which he prodded into his back now and again to keep him moving. It was now or never. He whipped round and seized the man's wrist, twisted the pistol out of his grasp and felled him with one of Gentleman Jackson's favourite punches to the side of the head, though on this occasion he had the advantage of the pistol in his hand to lend weight to the blow. It was done so speedily, the man did nothing but grunt and crumple to the ground. The man ahead, hearing him go down, turned to find himself looking down the barrel of the pistol.

'It's either a bullet somewhere where it will hurt, but not kill,' he said, 'or you can take this and conveniently disappear.' He tapped his pocket. 'Which is it to be?'

'How much longer are you going to keep me here?' Sophie asked. 'I am tired and thirsty.'

Cariotti smiled. 'Do you think he will not come? Do you think your entreaties have fallen on deaf ears?'

'What would you do if they had?' They were alone, had been for several hours, waiting for his two accomplices to bring the Duke. Sophie had been in fear of her virtue, if not her life, when the Count had returned and sent the other two on their errand, but apart from tying her to one of the chairs he had not touched her. She had been trying to engage him in conversation, if only to mask the fact that her mind was on ways of escape and she was busily trying to rub her bonds against the back of the chair, though it was having little effect.

'I would have no choice but to kill you.'

'As you killed my father when he would not cooperate. Everyone thought he had died in a drunken brawl, but he didn't, did he? He was a patriot and in spite of your threats would not turn spy. I am proud of him.'

The door was suddenly flung open and James stepped into the room, carrying the package. He took in the scene at a glance. The table and Sophie sitting beside it with her hands tied; Cariotti, who had been lounging on the bed, scrambling to his feet, the fire and the pan in the hearth. The fact that there was only one door and only a foot-square opening that served as a window and a lookout on to the river.

'James!' she breathed, relief flooding through her. He had come! But how was he going to get them away? In the hours she had been incarcerated, before Cariotti had come and tied her up, she had peeped through the window and seen the desolate landscape. Anyone running across that could be seen against the skyline for miles, even if they did manage to avoid the dykes.

'Glad to see you,' Cariotti said, smiling his oily smile. 'Please be seated next to your paramour while I peruse what you have brought.'

'I am afraid it is not as simple as that,' James said, going swiftly to Sophie. 'Are you all right?'

'Yes. Oh, I am so glad to see you.'

'And I, you, sweetheart.' The endearment brought tears to her eyes. She never thought to hear it from the Duke's lips.

'Enough of that,' Cariotti interrupted. 'Where's the book? And the money?'

'First things first. Release Miss Langford.'

'Do you take me for a gull? Flowers, Simpson, get yourselves in here…'

'I am afraid they will not be coming. Other things to do, don't you know.' He spoke languidly, but he was watching the Italian so closely he could see the twitch in his cheek and the gleam of malice in his eyes. Angrily the man rushed to try and wrest the manuscript from James, which he had been holding in front of his pistol to conceal it. The parcel fell to the floor and Cariotti found himself facing a gun. He backed away.

'Now release Miss Langford.'

Cariotti did as he was told, taking his time. 'What have you done with my men?'

'Oh, I have not put an end to their miserable existence, though it might be better for you if I had. I am keeping them hale and hearty to give evidence against you.'

Sophie, who had been marvelling at the coolness of the Duke, suddenly found herself pulled to her feet and held in front of Cariotti. She struggled ineffectually as he hauled her to the door, keeping her between him and the menacing gun. James cursed aloud. Cariotti had his back to the door, slowly inching his way out to freedom, when there was a shout from outside. To Sophie that meant the other conspirators were returning. A shot sounded so close and so loud, she screamed with terror, thinking James had risked a shot and had hit her.

James bounded across the room in time to catch her as she fell out of the unconscious Cariotti's arms. Richard appeared in the doorway, grinning. James, kneeling on the floor cradling Sophie in his arms, looked up. 'You damned fool! You could have killed her.'

'And is that all the thanks I get for riding *ventre à terre* to the rescue? You were at an impasse, my friend.'

'I had the situation under control.'

Sophie stirred to find herself lying in James's arms; he was looking down at her with an expression of such tenderness her heart turned over. She smiled weakly. 'You came.'

'Of course. Did you think for one moment that I would not?'

She thought about this for a moment. 'I wasn't sure…'

'Then be sure of this.' He pulled her close against his chest, tipping her head up to his with his finger. 'I am never, ever, going to let you out of my sight again, if I live to be a hundred.' He lowered his head and kissed her lips and the wild stirrings she had felt when he kissed her before came back a thousandfold until she was breathless. 'I love you, Miss Langford, and I will not rest until you become the Duchess of Belfont.'

She did not hear or see what was going on around her, that Captain Summers was issuing orders to half a dozen uniformed men, that the Count had recovered consciousness and was being hustled, along with the valet, into a large rowing boat, crewed by more uniformed men. She knew only that James loved her.

'Is that a proposal, your Grace?'

'It is. And my name is James. Let me hear you say it. Say, "I love you, James."'

'Oh, I do. I love you, James.'

'Are you two going to lie there on the floor until the

tide comes in and drowns you both?' Richard's teasing voice brought them back to a sense of where they were.

'No, of course not.' James scrambled to his feet and held out his hand to help Sophie up. She was still very shaky and could hardly stand, though whether that was the result of her ordeal or the proposal she had just had, she did not know. She only knew she was light-headed with happiness. He picked her up in his arms to carry her to the door. Halfway there she caught sight of the package he had brought with him, lying on the floor.

'No. We can't go without my book.'

'Yes, we can. It doesn't matter.'

'Oh, yes, it does. Put me down.' She struggled in his arms, but he held her tight, laughing. 'Put me down, James Dersingham. If you think I am going to abandon six months' work, you are sadly mistaken. Put me down at once.' She was fighting in earnest now and the tears were rolling down her face, tears of frustration and disappointment. Nothing had changed; he still did not understand.

'My, what a virago,' Richard said, grinning. 'You've got your hands full there, my friend.'

James set Sophie on her feet and watched as she retrieved the parcel. The outer covering was torn and, as she stooped to pick it up, she saw newsprint. With dawning understanding she tore the cover off. It contained newspaper, nothing but newspaper. She turned towards him. 'You devil! You let me think…'

He laughed and took it from her, tossing it on the table. 'Did you think I would risk losing it? You would never have forgiven me. Now, will you please come home? I want to find somewhere private where I can kiss you without being interrupted.' And he glared at Richard, who grinned back and led the way along the path to a road that went round the coastline of the Isle of Dogs. Here, to Sophie's immense relief, stood a carriage that she recognised as the Duke's. Sadler was sitting on the box, whip in hand, ready to convey them back to Belfont House.

James turned to Richard. 'How did you manage to follow me?'

'I didn't. O'Grady was persuaded to talk. He told us about the hut and I felt sure that was where Cariotti would bring Miss Langford. I am sorry if I startled you, miss, but I had to get my shot in before he turned round and saw us. He would have had no compunction about using you as a shield.'

'Then I thank you with all my heart.'

'Did he tell you anything else?' James asked.

'All he knew, enough to convict Cariotti of conspiracy to murder the Duke of Wellington.'

'And Alfred? How involved was he?'

'Not really involved, except as a dogsbody. He simply wanted to prevent you marrying Miss Langford. He thought if Cariotti compromised her, you would not have her.'

'That was flawed thinking. I could have married someone else...' He grinned at Sophie to reassure her. 'Theoretically.'

'Perhaps he was more perspicacious that you give him credit for and knew no one else would do.'

'Is it that obvious?'

'To everyone but the two of you, it seems. Anyway, I do not think we need trouble Mr Jessop, we have evidence enough without him.'

'Good. I would not like to see a kinsman of mine in the dock on a treason charge.' He ushered Sophie into the coach and climbed in beside her. Richard shut the door. 'Have a safe journey, my friend. I will come to you tomorrow...' He looked up at the eastern sky, where a pink dawn tinged the horizon. 'No, later today...'

'Much later,' James said, laughing and taking Sophie's hand. 'I shall be busy for some time.'

The horses were whipped up and they were on their way. James put his arm about Sophie and drew her head on to his shoulder, where it nestled comfortably. 'Such an adventure,' she murmured. 'It is all a fairy tale, like a book…'

'Don't you dare! Write what you like, I will not mind, except the story of our adventures and how they came about. They are private. For one thing, I would not like it noised abroad that the Duke of Belfont was so besotted by a self-willed hoyden, he turned into a quivering mass of fear that he might have lost her…'

She tipped her head up to his. 'You, fearful? I do not believe it. You were as cool as ice in that hut.'

'I was shaking with fear.'

'It did not show.'

'I am still shaking. He held up his hand and made it tremble. 'See. That is what you do to me.'

She seized his hand and put the palm to her lips. 'Is that better?'

'Yes. Do it again.'

She obliged. He laughed and pulled her on to his lap and kissed her soundly, making her ache with desire, a desire she had tried to stifle but had never succeeded in doing. If they were not in a coach, travelling at some speed, she might have given it free rein. But she could wait; she could savour it in the anticipation, as well as in the act when the time came. She was not afraid because she trusted him. She put her arms about his neck and pulled his head down so that she could kiss him back.

When he finally came up for air he was laughing. 'Richard was right. I certainly have my hands full, but I was never so thankful or grateful. You did say you would marry me, didn't you?'

'I do not remember saying it.'

'What? But you said you loved me…'

'So I did. So I do. It is not the same.'

'You mean you won't?'

'I did not say that either. I am waiting for you to ask me.'

'I did. Days ago.'

'I mean again. Properly.'

'Oh, Sophie.' He dropped to his knees on the dusty floor of the coach and took her hand. 'Miss Langford, will you take pity on this poor wretch who loves you so very, very much, and agree to marry him?'

'Oh, how could I ignore a plea like that, it would be heartless…'

'And you are not heartless, are you?'

'Only in as much as I have given it to you.'

'Does that mean yes?'

'Of course it does, silly.'

In the middle of hugging, they were interrupted by a discreet cough from the box and realised that the coach had come to a standstill. 'Home,' he said, opening the door and jumping down before turning to open his arms for her. She sprang into them. He held her a moment, then gently set her down. 'Let's go and have breakfast and tell Harriet our news.'

* * * * *

MILLS & BOON®

Live the emotion

Look out for next month's
Super Historical Romance

THE NINEFOLD KEY

by Rebecca Brandewyne

A Dream... Ariana Lévesque has been haunted for years by a recurring dream about a handsome young man and a dark, forbidding castle. But when her nightmare begins to come true, Ariana is caught up in a dangerous intrigue that began over two hundred years before she was born.

A Quest... Malcolm Blackfriars barely escaped with his life after his father was murdered and his home burned to the ground. He must discover what lies behind these devastating events – even if it places his own life in jeopardy!

A Ninefold Key Ariana and Malcolm are fated to meet and to fall passionately in love. But will their search for the ninefold key unlock the deadly secrets of their past – or utterly destroy them both?

"...a lush novel brimming with rich historical details and written in the grand tradition of the Victorian gothic"
—*Romantic Times*

On sale 3rd February 2006

Available at WHSmith, Tesco, ASDA, Borders, Eason, Sainsbury's and most bookshops

www.millsandboon.co.uk

2 FREE

BOOKS AND A SURPRISE GIFT!

We would like to take this opportunity to thank you for reading this Mills & Boon® book by offering you the chance to take TWO more specially selected titles from the Historical Romance™ series absolutely FREE! We're also making this offer to introduce you to the benefits of the Reader Service™—

- ★ **FREE home delivery**
- ★ **FREE gifts and competitions**
- ★ **FREE monthly Newsletter**
- ★ **Exclusive Reader Service offers**
- ★ **Books available before they're in the shops**

Accepting these FREE books and gift places you under no obligation to buy, you may cancel at any time, even after receiving your free shipment. Simply complete your details below and return the entire page to the address below. You don't even need a stamp!

YES! Please send me 2 free Historical Romance books and a surprise gift. I understand that unless you hear from me, I will receive 4 superb new titles every month for just £3.65 each, postage and packing free. I am under no obligation to purchase any books and may cancel my subscription at any time. The free books and gift will be mine to keep in any case.

H6ZED

Ms/Mrs/Miss/Mr ....Initials ....
BLOCK CAPITALS PLEASE

Surname ....

Address ....

....

....Postcode..................

Send this whole page to:
UK: FREEPOST CN81, Croydon, CR9 3WZ